Acclaim for Nicole Seitz

"I look forward to a new book by Nicole Seitz because I know I'll be treated to a well-written, thought-provoking read. *Beyond Molasses Creek* does not disappoint. Nicole is a writer I can count on to consistently tell a story containing deep characters and original plots."

> — **Marybeth Whalen, author of *She Makes**
> **It Look Easy* and *The Mailbox***

"[*The Inheritance of Beauty*] gives us pause as we consider the road ahead, and it also makes us thankful for the world we have today. Any story that causes that much reflection is one to be appreciated."

> — ***The Huffington Post***

"Seitz grabs the reader by the heart at the beginning of the book and doesn't let go until the end."

> — **ChristianBookPreviews.com,**
> **regarding *The Inheritance of Beauty***

"[*The Inheritance of Beauty* is a] tender tale of childhood secrets and lifelong ties, from a skilled writer who understands the beauty of enduring love. George and Maggie will make you want to learn your own family stories!"

> — **Lisa Wingate, national best-selling author of**
> ***Larkspur Cove* and *The Summer Kitchen***

"In *The Inheritance of Beauty*, Seitz has skillfully brought life, depth, and beauty to an often forgotten part of society, reminding readers of the power in strong bonds of love and friendship, the weight of memory and childhood, and the significance of reckoning with the past. Through the voices of an intimate group of individuals brought together in an elderly center, a haunting story unfolds with striking fluidity and the underlying presence of spirituality. Seitz has weaved into the lines of this moving page-turner a mysterious tale of healing, wrought with a sweet touch of southern warmness that truly speaks to the soul."

> — **Noni Carter, author of *Good Fortune***

"Nicole Seitz joins a long line of distinguished novelists who celebrate the rich culture of the Lowcountry of South Carolina . . . She joins Josephine Humphries, Anne Rivers Siddons, Sue Monk Kidd, and Dorothea Benton Frank in her fascination with the Gullah culture. Her character, Essie Mae Laveau Jenkins, is worth the price of admission to *The Spirit of Sweetgrass*."

> — Pat Conroy, best-selling author of *The Prince of Tides* and *South of Broad*

"This beautifully written, imaginative story of love and redemption is the must-read book of the year. The ending is so surprising and powerful that it will linger long after the last page is turned."

> — Cassandra King, best-selling author of *The Same Sweet Girls*, regarding *A Hundred Years of Happiness*

"An unforgettable novel about sisterhood, salvation, and miracles."

> — Karin Gillespie, author of *Dollar Daze*, regarding *Trouble the Water*

"Seitz has a gift for creating wonderful characters . . . marvelously memorable."

> — *Publishers Weekly* review of *Saving Cicadas*

"Nicole Seitz takes the loose threads of her characters' lives and ties them together in a vibrant pattern of love, forgiveness and truth. In words that resonate with emotion, Seitz writes of things that are only understood with the heart."

> — Patti Callahan Henry, best-selling author of *Driftwood Summer*

" . . . A surprisingly creative tale that will leave readers guessing until the end."

> — River Jordan, author of *Saints in Limbo*, regarding *Saving Cicadas*

"Her words are magic. Pure magic."

> — Tim Callahan, author of *Kentucky Summers: The Cave, the Cabin, and the Tattoo Man*

Beyond Molasses Creek

Books by Nicole Seitz

The Spirit of Sweetgrass

Trouble the Water

A Hundred Years of Happiness

Saving Cicadas

The Inheritance of Beauty

Beyond Molasses Creek

a novel

Nicole Seitz

THOMAS NELSON
Since 1798

NASHVILLE   DALLAS   MEXICO CITY   RIO DE JANEIRO

Published in Nashville, Tennessee, by Thomas Nelson. Thomas Nelson is a registered trademark of Thomas Nelson, Inc.

Interior sketches created by Nicole Seitz.

Thomas Nelson, Inc., titles may be purchased in bulk for educational, business, fund-raising, or sales promotional use. For information, please e-mail SpecialMarkets@ThomasNelson.com.

Library of Congress Cataloging-in-Publication Data

Seitz, Nicole A.
 Beyond Molasses Creek : a novel / Nicole Seitz.
   p. cm.
 ISBN 978-1-59554-505-3 (trade paper)
 1. Fathers and daughters—Fiction. 2. Self-realization in women—Fiction. 3. Kidnapping—Fiction. 4. Female friendship—Fiction. I. Title.
 PS3619.E426B49 2012b
 813'.6—dc23   2011041984

Printed in the United States of America

12 13 14 15 16 17 QG 6 5 4 3 2 1

To those who long to be free.

I saw the angel in the marble and carved until I set him free.

—MICHELANGELO

Prologue

Ally

WHEN I WAS A GIRL, I WOULD LIE ON THE BANKS OF Molasses Creek with soft green grass beneath my back and look up into the sky, dreaming of being there. In my upside-down world, the clouds were pieces of land that I would hop to and the vast blue sky was the river, the ocean that would beckon to transport me far, far away. That vast blue sky has taken me to all sorts of foreign lands since then. Sometimes the most foreign place is home.

I'll be flying in just a few minutes, cloud-hopping back to a city I never thought I'd see again.

I close my eyes and imagine myself feeling weightless again, my body traveling at five hundred miles an hour yet perfectly still. Someone clears a throat. I open my eyes and see a woman before me in uniform, standing at a podium. She's holding out her hand. "Oh yes," I say. I reach in my bag and pull out my wallet. Through the airport window, a jet leaves the wet runway and rises into thick gray rain.

I hand the uniformed woman my driver's license, and she looks at me to see if there's a match. "My hair's a little different now," I explain. "And . . . I'm a little older." So much about me is different now. I wonder if she can read it in my face—the years, the tragedy, the love, the moments of hope. I smile at her, but she doesn't return it. They've gotten a lot stricter with flying these days, and that's not such a bad thing. I don't mind waiting a few minutes longer to take my shoes off and have them search my belongings. There's a poor old lady up ahead of me, hunched over. They have her to the side and are patting her down. Really? Her? Never in a million years. After flying as many times as I have, you get an eye for these things.

The woman hands me my license back and the young lady behind me reaches to hand her a passport. "Charleston is very nice place," she says in a foreign accent. You can tell she's worked hard on her English. That warms my heart. I take a deep breath and move to the conveyor belt. I set my shoes in a gray bin along with a lightweight jacket and carry-on bag. The top of the bag is open and when I set it on its side, a large, tattered book peeks out. My heart flutters and my mind spills over with images, sketches of my life, as if I'm having one of those near-death experiences and life is flashing before my eyes.

I blink and move forward. Did I remember my pencils? Yes, I did.

I shuffle along with everyone else, barefooted, until I pass through the metal detector. Oh, the things I've seen people get caught with over the years—guns, drug paraphernalia, tiny switchblades in unusual parts of the body. Some people are flat-out crazy and criminal.

2

Criminal. Crime. Why would anyone ever return to the scene of the crime? For closure? To find that part of them that was lost there? To make things right? I'm going back for all of these reasons. I can't believe it. I never thought I'd see the day.

The airport is fairly empty this time of the morning, but our wait isn't long. A cup of coffee and a *People* magazine later, we've entered the plane. It's a Boeing 737. I look into the cockpit to see who's flying us. I'm looking to see if a certain old lover is there, but that would be too much of a coincidence, even for me. I nod at the pilot, a fiftyish gentleman I have never seen before, and carefully eye the flight attendant. She's about thirty-five, a little heavy in the hips, blond hair, nice looking. Back in my day she never would have gotten a job here. Back then, getting and keeping a stewardess job was as hard as making the cut on *American Idol*. But not today. Times have changed. Part of me wants to relieve this lady and do her job for her. I could take care of this entire plane, all these passengers, all their needs, without blinking an eye. I'm not too old, no matter what they suggested. So what, my back went out and I dropped a cup of coffee on a passenger. It happens. My heart just wasn't in it anymore, and when your passion leaves you, well, it might just be time to move on to something else.

To be honest, flying turned painful emotionally as the years went on. I was always torn between wanting to fly to the other side of the world and keep searching—or going back to see him. A woman is lucky in life if she finds true love. Twice as lucky if she holds on to it. Three times the luck if she loses it and it comes back to her even stronger than before.

I've got to go back. I can't believe I'm going back. I left in the first place because of him, and now, I can feel this strong pull within me—*he's* pulling me. He's leading me, telling me I must return to the scene of the crime, where my whole life changed in an instant. It's now or never. No more wasted time.

I close my eyes as the plane rumbles to takeoff. I've never been much of a praying woman, but this time, I hear the faint mumbling of the young lady beside me. I turn to look at her, a pretty girl, obviously nervous about flying today too. Her eyes are closed and fists clenched. We all have our fears, don't we? Our own stories. And our reasons to go back to the place that changed us. She catches my eye. I take a deep breath and give a reassuring look. I squeeze her hand like I've done a thousand times with passengers, then turn to the window as the plane lifts off the runway. My heart lifts along with my stomach, and I say a little prayer to the clouds for the both of us. *Great white bird, take us over the river. Make us brave and remove our fears.*

I think of his rugged face, those dark eyes, those sweet lips smiling for me. *I know what I promised you, but you know me, Vesey. You always have.*

Sometimes stepping back in time is the only way for a girl to move forward.

Part One

In rivers, the water that you touch is the last of what has passed and the first of that which comes; so with present time.

—LEONARDO DA VINCI

ONE

The Stone Garden

Mount Pleasant, South Carolina
Ally

THERE'S A BEND IN THE CREEK WHERE MARSH GRASS waves, calling egrets and ospreys from their high places. It's as familiar to me as the bend in my elbow, yet now, years later, it almost seems exotic. Standing here, I can't look at the creek and not see them all—the Ganges, the Seine, the Baghmati—all the beautiful rivers that have carved valleys into my soul.

I'm home now, Huck on the Mississippi, winding my way, finding my way home.

Why did someone have to die for me to come back? I wonder. Isn't it just as glorious and miraculous a waterway as any other?

I am sitting Indian-style in my stone garden, at least it will be after I'm done with it. Right now, it's just a patch of grass in Daddy's yard. It's overgrown, wild and empty at the same time. Much like my heart. I close my eyes. I can see them all around me, the statues I've collected over the years. I'll put them all over this yard and create my own Garden of Dreams. It was the last place I was truly happy. A faraway garden. Stone statues. True love. Daddy would understand. If I'm going to stay here for any time at all, I'll have to do things my way, and right now, I feel destitute. I need someone to carve a god of peace for me, something I can touch and hold, something to take away this awful, gnawing grief.

I am too old to be sitting on the ground in the middle of the yard. The neighbors will think I've gone batty. I push to standing and wipe off my ample rear. I head to the dock and breathe in the salty marsh air. I see a rope hanging off the edge and disappearing into the water. Daddy's crab trap. I breathe in deep and exhale. Tears spring to my eyes and I fight them off.

Crabs. I'm hungry. Is it possible I'm hungry after eating a whole rotisserie chicken with coleslaw on the side? I look down at my ripply thighs. The sunlight this time of day does a number on me, pulls out every little bulge and pocket, every wrinkle. I will miss my father, I will, but I do not miss shorts weather in Mount Pleasant, South Carolina. Some people are not made to wear shorts. I struggled through it in Bali and on the shores of Hawaii, but only because I did not know a soul there. Here? Here, there's a slew of people who've never even left this place and know the old me from long ago. Can you imagine? Can you even imagine never wanting to see the world, to partake in it all? To find your place in it?

I pull up the trap to see if anything is in there. Of course, there's not.

"Give it time."

A voice like butter rolls down my back.

I drop the trap with a splash and nearly fall into the water.

Clutching the pole, I turn around and realize the sun is beaming off my flabby arms. And there he is. *There he is.* Just look at him. Is it possible black people don't age the way we do?

"Dad-gum, Vesey. Scared me half to death!"

"Sorry, Miss Ally. Here, lemme help you up."

He reaches for me, a long, strong, sinewy arm with forearm muscles rippling. I feel faint. *This is Vesey, Ally Green. The boy you played with when you were little, the one who was off limits because you are white and he is not. Vesey Washington. This is the South and always will be. Remember that.*

"Thank you, I'm . . . I'm fine," I say. "Just been a long day. What with the . . . well, coming home and all."

His face breaks out into a grin, not a sly one, but a genuine, heartfelt smile with teeth so white, I'm feeling dizzy again. Reminds me of the white sands in Fiji, so pure.

"You are a sight for sore eyes, Mr. Washington. You still climbing trees or something?"

"Or somethin'. Look here, just come over to see if there was anythin' you needed from me. I been checkin' on him, Doc Green, every day for a good while. Hard to break the habit." He looks down at the cracks in the pier, then off into the sunset behind me. "I'm real sorry . . . a good man, he was. Good man."

"Thank you. Yes, he was." I turn around and face the sunset too. In a minute it will be gone, just a memory, like Daddy. The red meets the greens of the trees, and the yellows and oranges fan out to pinks and purples, and yes, this is one of the most spectacular sunsets in the world. In fact, wherever the sun sets is where I want to be. So tonight I want to be right here, on this dock, with Daddy's house behind me and Vesey just feet away. We watch the sky silently for about thirty seconds, and then the sun dips behind the trees and it's gone for another day.

I am suddenly aware of the hideousness of the backs of my legs and turn around quickly. Is it possible he's standing closer? I swear I can feel his heat. He's close to sixty now, my age, and I'm hoping that means his eyes aren't as good as they used to be. Perhaps he can't see me well, and all my ripples and wrinkles smooth out nicely. Yes, I'm sure that's it.

"You look tired, Miss Ally. You feelin' all right?"

"Vesey Washington, never, ever tell a woman she looks tired. You hear me?"

"I didn't mean no—"

"I am tired. Very tired. My daddy just died. I just came halfway across the world for his funeral and to clean out his old house on the creek, and at the moment, yes, I am exhausted. There's much to do. Did you see the inside of that place? It's like a museum. Looks like he's never moved a thing in the twenty years Mama's been gone."

Vesey looks in my eyes and I can tell I've frightened him from saying anything at all.

I smile and move closer to him. I lean up on my tiptoes and put my hands on his firm shoulders. I press myself to his stiff chest and breathe in the smell. How long has it been? This man could be Molasses Creek itself, the salt, the pluff mud, the snails on tall grass, the fish jumping in hot sun. With my eyes closed, my mind erases the years and takes me to a cool evening on this very creek. I can hear music playing and see moonlight dancing on his face. I imagine his tender lips on mine . . . then I pull myself together and away from him. I smooth my hair.

"It's good to see you, Vesey. Thank you for being here . . . for Daddy."

Vesey grabs his hat and backs away. "I'll be just over there, 'cross the water, if you need me. All you got to do is holler."

All I have to do is holler.

I nod and he walks away from me, a slow, limber pace that's carried him surely for six decades. He doesn't wear shorts. Never has. I do not know how he handles this Lowcountry heat in long pants. There are some things so different about us. The color of our skin. The desires of our souls. I could never have stayed in the same place my whole life and been content with it, yet he is. Or so he seems to be.

I watch as he steps gingerly into his fishing boat. It creaks and rolls with his weight, but he steadies it. Always steady, that's Vesey. He nods my way and I wave a tiny, pathetic wave as the water parts for him to cross over like Moses, back to his side of the creek. He looks so natural in that old boat. I feel like a fish out of water here. There are so many walls and layers of difference between us, like honey-drenched Greek baklava. We may have known each other as children, but now, what do we really know of one another? We're as opposite as night and day.

But maybe now we'll have the time to learn each other all over again. I push the thought away and shake my head. *Ally Green, what to do with you? You're not here for Vesey. You're here because your daddy is dead.*

I walk back into Daddy's musty house and throw open all the windows as fast as I can. I've got to air this place out. I've got to let Daddy's spirit free, let the memories of me when I was a child loose to run around in this place. I am such a different person from who I once was. I think it's good. No, I can't think about it at all. I'm tired. Tomorrow will be a new day and I'll be able to clean this place out and start to make it mine. Daddy wanted me to have this lazy spot on the river . . . why? He knows I don't like to stay put. *Knew* it, anyway. But I'll honor him. I loved him. I still do. I'll pretend I've inherited some exotic place on the Nile and I've got to make my way, learn to eat the native food, learn to talk like them, to fit in. Deep down, I know in three months I'll be done with Charleston, itching to leave again, but for now, I will do this for him. For Daddy.

The rain comes on with thunder and lightning, and a storm suits me fine right now. I think about Daddy, how he lay on this very bed. I can smell him here in this house, on these sheets. I turn out the lights. Strangely, it's not my father I'm thinking of, but Vesey on the other side of the water, how much distance there is between us. I think of the lines in his face, how I'd love to draw them again. But I can't. How I wish someone would bring chisel to stone and carve him for my garden so I could look at him and touch him anytime I want. I close my eyes. I am sketching again in my mind, and as my head hits the pillow to sleep in a place I once called home, it's Vesey's face I see before me. Vesey. Molasses Creek. My destiny.

TWO

Destiny

Kathmandu, Nepal
Sunila

THERE ARE STORIES OF MY BIRTH IN WHICH A LARGE
white bird swooped down close enough to the earth to drop me
in a betel nut tree. Sometimes I picture long wings flowing, flapping, and me, carefully wrapped in gold cloth, a descendant of the
heavens. Perhaps it was a great egret or eagle with sharp talons.
Perhaps the aim was to leave me at a royal palace, but the winged
beast was attacked in midair and did only what it could do—it
dropped me here.

Amaa tells me my skin was once the color of the tops of the
mountains of Nepal. She says I was born of snow and carried in a
bird's beak until swallowed and passed out through the creature,
flung into the filth of the streets of Kathmandu.

Buba thinks I'm a curse. He blames me for the squalor we live
in, for the stones we must carry and break, but he was born into
this life a Dalit. He was cursed at his first breath. He is jealous

because I was a master carver of stone at twelve years old and could sit under my umbrella to do my work, while he and the others baked in the hot sun.

My skin is now the color of terra-cotta. I spent days blistered and oozing, the dust of gravel filling my sores. Later I was given an umbrella to work under, chisel in hand. They used to show me what I was to depict in my stones. I am remembering a fat child with wings that come off her back. She was called *angel*.

There was a book once with pictures of gods and mythical creatures, beings that come from the heavens. I studied the pictures and could not turn away, could barely blink. I drank in the pages with my eyes as if dying of thirst and buried them deep in a well inside me.

My eyes are blue, the color of the sky. To me it is a sign that I am surely from the gods that I carve. Perhaps I, too, am made of stone and the lines I cut, the facial features, the arms and legs of goddesses and angels—perhaps I will cut just the right stone and when I look, I will see myself there—it will be myself I have set free with my chisel.

For the past twenty-five years, I have longed to see the Book of the Gods again. I know where it is kept—in the big office of the cruel man. I have seen him leave a child to suffer the pain of a broken foot from dropping a heavy stone. I have seen him turn away when another has coughed up blood from years of dust. The book may as well have been tossed in the seas, lost forever. In the quarry, they would let me learn as much as they wanted me to know and nothing more. Yet I would dream.

Someday, I would reach this book. I would steal it and study it. I would open the pages and the gods would open my eyes and make me understand the letters and markings that I could not read before. With my eyes wide open I would understand how to return to my true home, to fly on the great white wings again, up into the blue sky and out of the quarry. Out of this life and into the better next.

It is happening to me now.

The man before me is no longer breathing. His face is covered in dust from the gravel and stone that have been tracked into his office year after year. I am glad he is dead. This feeling should scare me, but there is little fear left anymore, only a dream coming true.

How many nights have I lain on the hard ground just outside these walls and dreamed of the day when I would be in this office, not for his cruelty, but to search for the Book of the Gods? I lift my feet and walk around the body. I must work quickly. I lean down and reach for the keys around his waist and fear grips me. What if this is all a trick? What if he isn't dead at all? He will kill me.

No. He is gone. Look. See how still he is? My hand trembles as I touch the keys. I keep my eyes on his face and then look to the door to be sure no one is coming. I can hear the children yelling outside and hear the pounding of chisels and hammers on rock. The keys are in hand. I stand, straightening my sari, and move to the cabinet. I try each key, one after the other after the other, my heart racing, and finally, the lock turns. The cabinet opens. My heart spills over and in a flood I see them all—the birds, the gods, the water, the reeds, the man, the woman, my own fate.

I grab the Book of the Gods and stuff it in my *cholo*. I clutch it to my chest and hurry away from the dead man. He can be cruel no more. He can hold me here no longer. He cannot keep me from my destiny. I rush out of the office and the sky opens up. Rain drenches the back of my head as I struggle to keep the book dry at my chest. It is my only hope, this book.

I push my calloused hands through the tarp and lean into our ragged tent. My mother is there. She is trying to wash a metal cup with the fresh water from the sky.

"Amaa," I say. She turns to me, years of misery drawn across her face. "He is dead, Amaa. He is finally dead."

"Your father? Buba?" Her eyes glisten.

"No," I say. I kneel down on the ground before her and move my face close to hers. "The cruel man, Amaa. The cruel man is dead. We are free. Look." I pull out the Book of the Gods, and Amaa drops her metal cup in the dust. I dare to smile. "The Book of the Gods," I whisper. "I have it now. I have dreamed of this day."

"Yes," says Amaa. "It has come. I have always known this day would come." Her face turns still as stone, and I watch her chest to be sure she is still breathing.

THREE

The Elephant
and the Great White Bird

Mount Pleasant
Ally

I WAKE UP GASPING FOR AIR. WHERE AM I?

I once woke up in Ghana beneath a mosquito net, looked down by my feet, and found myself face-to-face with the sobering eyes of a king cobra. I didn't breathe for a full sixty seconds until it slithered away from the cot and some natives chopped its head off outside my door. I startle at the memory, not sure where I am. It's a hazard of traveling so much. You're never quite sure where you've laid your head.

I open my eyes in the dim light and smell the dampness of Daddy's house, the mustiness of his carpet. I remember now. He's gone. I look to the foot of the bed and see yellow eyes staring back at me. My heart lurches, but it's only Katmandu, or Kat, as I call him, Daddy's beloved Maine Coon. I've never seen anyone so babied in all my life. Daddy would have done well to have a grand-child to hold and to raise up, but life stole that joy away from us, didn't it? I've got to breathe. *Breathe, Ally.*

I've had that dream again.

For thirtysomething years I've had the same dream—of an elephant and a great white bird. Now, I know there are no ele-phants in the Lowcountry of South Carolina, but I have seen them in my travels. And in this dream, there's this big gray elephant on a riverbank, wanting to cross over. The water is not wide or deep but the fella just stands there, unable to, something holding it back.

Another elephant comes on the other side and tries to pull the first one over by wrapping trunks. But as much as the one pulls, the other one pulls harder, and a great tug-of-war com-mences. Back and forth it goes, on and on and on. A war of wills. It saddens me to watch it, the two of them getting nowhere.

And then there is this great white bird that flies down and lands on the back of the first elephant. With this bird on his back, somehow the elephant is different. He doesn't feel the need to pull back anymore. Against his nature, he allows himself to be pulled for the first time and, lo and behold, crosses over that river.

The strangest thing is how that white bird sits so calmly on the elephant's back, not flapping its wings or pecking or pestering it at all. Instead, it is majestic in its great white stillness, and just by being there somehow soothes the animal, coaxes it silently to the other side.

I wonder what that means. *Probably means you've lost it, Al.*

What time is it, anyway? Kat hops up on the bed and walks across my legs, purring. He's excited or agitated, fuzzy tail flick-ing. He comes all the way up to my face and, standing on my chest, sniffs me. His eyes are huge with a squiggly green line going all the way around his pupils. One should never be this close to a cat this large.

"Okay," I say, sitting up. "You hungry? That it?" He jumps down off the bed and prances toward the kitchen. Spoiled cat. But he misses his daddy. "I miss him too, you know. I miss him too."

Morning comes in on the breeze through the window screens, and the dingy yellow curtains my mother hung thirty years ago blow and flutter. How strange to be back in this house without them here. I can still feel my parents everywhere, in the curtains, in the old tin can that holds coffee grounds, in the vinyl covering the kitchen floor.

I make my coffee and drink it black from an old mug I brought my parents from Istanbul when I was twentysomething. It was my father's favorite, and it's covered with a web of brown lines after nearly forty years of use, no doubt harboring all sorts of bacteria. I hold it to my nose and breathe in the deep rich coffee. When one travels, one gets used to not using cream or sugar because these are luxuries hard to come by. Plus, I like my coffee dark, strong, and potent . . . like my men.

I can feel my father's hand where mine is now. With my eyes closed, I pretend to be him for a moment, or maybe I do become him, I'm not sure. I open my eyes and head out for the dock where the water is clear and calm like glass. I imagine Daddy did this very thing.

There are white birds flying toward the sun, over my head and behind the gray wood-sided house. The sun highlights the green tips of trees across the waterway, the green tips of marsh grass, the green tip of Vesey's tin roof. I sit Indian-style at the end of the dock and sip my coffee while the breeze carries my hair around my shoulders and the warm sun heats my back.

Is Vesey awake? Maybe he's already had his coffee. Or maybe he doesn't need any coffee. Needs nothing but the promise of a new day to get him up out of bed, probably before sunrise. He's something else. Natural. I try to be like that. I try to sit here and be one with nature, one with the universe, but truth be told, I still feel like an outsider. I always have. I set my coffee to the side and stretch my legs, stretch the stiffness of sleeping in Daddy's old lumpy bed out of my joints. I work myself through some yoga poses, and by the time I hit downward dog, I feel self-conscious, the exact opposite of what yoga is supposed to be doing for me. Suppose Vesey is watching from his window.

I remember sitting on this very dock when I was a little girl, hanging my bare feet over the edge into the cool water. I would look to the right and see the creek winding through marsh grass. It would call me, the water would. It would tell me there was adventure to be found if I would just follow it around the bend. Vesey would come over to my side of the river in his fishing boat, and the two of us would head out in the morning air and catch fish for our mothers to fry. Vesey would clean the fish for me, and I would wait patiently on my dock for him to come back and deliver it. He was an expert at cleaning fish. Actually, he was an expert at anything he tried to do, as if he was born already having some foreknowledge. We were good friends as children go, but to be honest, his parents and mine never encouraged us to play, certainly not at each other's houses. Back then, in the late 1950s and '60s, we were still taboo, the two of us together—a black boy and a white girl. We didn't know it, or if we did, we didn't care.

We must have sensed something though, because we carried on mostly in secret.

I pick up my mug from Istanbul and hold it up to Vesey's house. Then I make my way back indoors to shower. I have a big day ahead of me. Today the movers come. It's out with the old and in with the new. If I'm going to be here for a while, the least I can do is make it feel more like my turf and less like Daddy's. I don't think Daddy would mind my removing his clutter. He always said, "You can't take it with you," and he was right. It's all stacked up in boxes and drawers and nowhere close to where Daddy is now.

By lunchtime, I have made it through his closet and Mama's. They had separate rooms for as long as I can remember. Daddy snored and Mama liked her beauty rest, and it just seemed normal to me that married people would sleep in different rooms. Could be one of the reasons my marriage to Ronnie didn't work out. We had different ideas of what normal was. And anyway, we never should have been married. We were much better friends. We still are. Being friends with your ex-husband? Well, I guess it goes right along with the normalcy of separate bedrooms.

Ronnie calls me every day of his life, though we've been divorced for sixteen years. How one person has that much to say, I do not know. How he finds me all over the world, I do not know either. It's like he has some tracking device on me. Oh, his wife, Marlene? She loves me too. In fact, she calls me almost as much as he does. Go figure. I think she loves the fact that there's someone out there who knows him as well as she does and will listen to whatever stupid thing he's done lately. Like putting a down payment on a new tractor with his bingo prize money. They could have used that money for almost anything, savings, groceries, but no, he's wanted a stupid tractor as long as I've known him. Always wanted to plant roots and grow something, as if he could ever grow anything in that Georgia red clay. Ridiculous.

The phone rings, and I stumble over stacks of old *Time* magazines and *National Geographics* in the hallway to find it, yellowed, by Daddy's favorite La-Z-Boy chair. The old chair is the color of moss and faded on the side closest to the window.

"Hello? Oh, hey, Ronnie. Yeah, it's going all right. I've got the movers coming this afternoon. Yeah. No, I'm not getting emotional, I'm just cleaning up. I'm approaching this like any levelheaded person would do. I don't have time to get sentimental; they'll be here in two hours." I sit down on the arm of Daddy's chair. "Because I planned it that way, Ronnie. If I gave myself more time, I might get all weepy and I don't want to do that, all right? Yes. I promise I'm fine. How's your tractor, anyway? No, I'm not being smarty, I'm just asking." I wrap the telephone cord around my finger and stare out the window at the creek. "Hmm. That long, huh? You do realize Marlene could've gotten that new sewing machine she wanted. She would have been a lot happier right now and you might have some curtains in your dining room. Okay, I'll lay off, but . . . yep. All right, honey. Uh-huh. Listen, Ronnie, they'll be here before I know it and I have so much to do . . . Okay? All right. Talk later."

I press the phone down into the cradle and darn if I don't have to press back tears. See what he did to me? Too much to do to stop and think and talk about how I'm feeling! I bend down and pick up a box of magazines in the hallway, and when I lift it back up, a pain shoots down the right side of my rear end like hot lead. It tingles in my knee and lingers and smarts when I move. Dad-gum! I curse under my breath. This can't be happening. I have too much to do!

"Kat? Kat!" I do not know why I am calling a cat. What in the world can he do for me? Sure enough, he comes, tail quivering, eyes bright. He rubs his back along my leg, then turns and rubs the other side. "I can't move," I tell him. Carefully, I walk into Mama's bedroom and let the box fall several inches onto the mattress. The pain is radiating down into my right leg. Stupid pinched nerve. This happens to me occasionally when I'm stressed. It's as if the universe knows I'm stressed and wants to make it just a little harder for me. I scowl up into the ceiling at whoever's in charge here. I've got to get to my purse but it's in Daddy's bedroom, a whole fifteen feet away. Might as well be Mars.

"Kat, can you fetch? Go get my bag. Please? Fetch, boy." Nothing. He looks at me all cute-like and lifts a paw to lick it.

After an excruciating five minutes or so, I make it stiff-legged and gritting my teeth to my purse and take two muscle relaxers with no water. They scratch down my throat and stick there, dry lumps. I hold my breath, waiting for them to kick in. *Please kick in.* I just need a few minutes. I grimace as I plop down on Daddy's foam pillows that still smell like him—as if he's still here—moaning and deep-breathing for a good long while until sleep, blessed sleep masks all the pain.

Bang, bang, bang, bang!
What the—

Bang, bang! "H'lo! Anybody in there?"

Kat jumps off the bed and hides under it. I jerk up, fully awake now, and feel the pain in my hip. My mouth is filled with cotton. "Hold oo-on!" I roll over onto my stomach and slip one leg off, reaching with my toes to the floor. *Ow, ow, ow.* "Just a minute!" The movers are here? I'm not ready! Look at this place!

It takes me a good long while to shuffle past the boxes of books and knickknacks on the floor—Daddy's western rodeo lamp, a stack of his wool sweaters. I open the front door, never checking what I look like, though I must look like I woke from the dead. "Sorry, I—is it really time? I hurt my back." The movers are two men, one burlier than the other, midthirties, I'd say. They look at my mess unsympathetically and confer with one another. "S'posed to be packed up. You need us to pack for you? We ain't planned for that. Gone be extra three hundred dollar."

I turn and look at the house from their point of view.

"We got a truck full of stuff we got to unload first. Lemme call the boss."

I feel helpless and tears spring to my eyes. Dad-gum hip. Dad-gum sexy Juan Carlos. I was riding a moped through the streets of Bermuda with him when a man hit me from behind at a stop sign in 1978. I've had issues with my tailbone, sitting on silly round pillows for half my life because of it. Usually it's no problem, but the stress, I tell you, it does a number.

"Miss Ally?" The deep, sultry voice of an angel comes through the kitchen.

"Vesey, that you?"

"You all right? I heard banging this way. Come to check on you."

"Thank God you're here. Can you come round and help me with these movers?"

Vesey lumbers around the house to the front porch and the two men sum him up as he climbs the steps. He's twice their age and nearly as strong. I see respect in their faces at the sight of his black suspenders. "It's my back, Vesey. It went out and I haven't done a thing. Not one thing in here." I pull the hair on the sides of my head and squeeze.

"No worries. You go on and unload the truck," he tells the men with a motion of his hand. "I'll be ready for you by the time you get it all out."

"Vesey, nobody can do that."

"Just leave it to me. You wanna lie down?"

"Think you could just help me over to that chair?" Vesey takes my arm and I limp to the living room. He is a gentleman escort and I am a crippled slug, nowhere close to being ready for the ball. He smells of motor oil and fresh-cut grass. He lowers me down slow and steady into the chair, even pulls the reclining lever down so the back flattens out.

"I don't know how to thank you," I say. I'm a beached whale, legs straight out, head swimming.

"I had two daughters go off on their own, and a son . . . well, I know moving. If there's one thing I know, it's that."

"You mean, just another thing you know." He studies my face to see if I'm upset or freaking out, but I smile at him reassuringly and lay my head back. I'm getting sleepy again. But Vesey's here. Good ol' . . . He'll take care of everything. Everything's gonna be just . . .

FOUR

Monsoon Season

Kathmandu, Nepal
Sunila

IT IS DONE. I CANNOT CHANGE THINGS NOW. I CANNOT go back home. I am so far away from home.

I have the handle of a rainbow-colored umbrella in my hands, slippery and wet. It is hard to hold on. It is monsoon season in Kathmandu and the umbrella that once covered my head from the sun now shelters me from the rain. It's been raining for six days and already a river flows around my feet. I step into the road and struggle to keep standing. I slowly make my way across, looking to see an old woman in the window of a crumbling building, a chicken there in her windowsill.

At the sight of it, my stomach rumbles. I haven't eaten since yesterday, since I set out on this journey.

I am thirty-seven or thirty-eight now, I am not sure. Amaa and Buba never talked about my birthday, for they didn't know when it was. They found me, abandoned near the quarry on a rock before monsoon season. But every year, my father would complain that with me in his presence, disaster had befallen them. In our little one-room hovel, Amaa would tell him that I was the only reason we were not all dead. Yet. She would say it as the tarp on our tent blew in the wind and the white dust of stone covered her dark hands and feet and swirled up into the air like an angry spirit. "We are alive because of her," she would tell him. Then she'd touch my arm, my untouchable arm, and beg me to get back to work. "The rains will come soon," she would say, "and then there is no work for any of us."

A gust of wind blows the rain under my umbrella and plasters my *cholo* to my body. I touch beneath my arm and make sure it's still there, my treasure, my way to a better life. The book is still there, unharmed and dry. I think of the man, the look on his face as he lay there, no longer able to harm me or anyone else. No more threats, no more debts, no more violence.

I am a Dalit. I am an outcaste in Nepal. Dalit people are discriminated against and often treated badly. A Dalit woman is lower than a Dalit man. Amaa is too shy to look someone in the eye. She is not worthy, she says, so she does not speak up. Yet I am bolder. I learned to beg when I was a child and learned that I would not eat unless I opened my mouth to speak.

Once, many years ago, when I was begging food from a café, a man sat watching me. He said I would not have to beg if I went with him across the border to India. He told me that he could promise a marriage to a very prominent man and I would never have to work another day of my life.

I was very close to saying yes, I would go with him. What young girl would not want a better life? I had worked with stone since before I could remember. *And my mother and father?* I asked him. What would become of them?

"Look at your eyes," the man had said to me, his own eyes dancing. "I see much light in there. Your eyes, your blue eyes . . . The lord Buddha had blue eyes. You must be descended from the heavens," he whispered. "You should not be here, having to beg for food. Come with me. You'll see. You will be rich and send home money for your parents to live. You will save them from this life. They will never have to work another day. Trust me. I know this man. He is good and handsome. I promise, I will take you to him."

Although I was thirteen, I was an untouchable. Upper-caste people would sprinkle purified water on themselves if I touched them. I would get screamed at if my shadow fell across a high-caste person. Many Dalit women were raped and stripped in public. Some murdered. Some burned. I had seen these things with my own eyes. I had not escaped all of them. I could not read or write, so the promise of marriage to a wealthy man was beyond my dreams. My heart stirred as the man in the café reached out and handed me eight hundred rupees. It was more than I had ever seen. My hand shook. "Wouldn't you like to be able to buy food whenever you want it? Are you hungry now? Hmmm?"

There was another man in the café that day who had been watching the conversation between me and the well-dressed man. He beckoned for me and, reluctantly, I went to his side. I was begging, after all, and thought perhaps he had something for me.

"Do you know that man?" he asked me, pointing with his chin.

I lied and said he was my cousin. It was easy to lie. My dreams were bigger than the truth.

"I know this man," he said. "He takes young Nepali girls from their families, promising them work and marriage in India. It is what he promised you, no?"

My heart grew still.

"And then he takes them across the border where they are sold into brothels. They become sex slaves and never get out. They are there until they die miserable deaths."

I took a step back, looking behind me for the man, but he was gone.

"If you follow a man like this one, you will be sold into a terrible life. You will have no money. You will have no future. Is this what you want?"

I wanted to tell him that I had no money. That I had no future. That I would never be able to leave the life I was living in the stone quarry, but my throat had no moisture. I swallowed hard. The man offered to get me a drink, and I tried to refuse, but he told the waiter I would be joining him. I found my voice and said, "I would rather die than sit with you."

I was stunned. Nothing like this had ever been uttered from my lips, but this man had stolen my dreams from me. I had watched them grow up before my eyes like green sprouts beneath granite, and in an instant, he had trampled upon them, turning them into dust.

"You don't know what you're talking about." I scowled at him.

"I do," he said. Then he pushed a small piece of paper toward me on the tabletop. It had letters on it, and I tried to look away, but I couldn't help myself. I picked it up.

I studied it for a while, feeling the weight of it in my calloused hands. "My name is Davidson Monroe," he said. "Mr. Monroe. I'm an American. I work at the US Embassy. That's what it says there on that card. It has my address at the embassy and my telephone number." His voice grew softer. "You are very pretty . . . What is your name?" No one ever called me by my name except Amaa. I didn't want to tell him my name, but I longed to hear someone tell me I was pretty again. I had never heard these words.

"Sunila," I muttered.

"Sunila," the man repeated. "You must watch out for men like the one you met today. They are looking at you and seeing money in their eyes. You must trust me in this. I have seen what happens to pretty poor girls like you in Nepal."

I looked at the card and then back at Mr. Monroe.

"Namaste," he said to me.

"Namaste," I replied, which means *I honor the light I see within you*. Then I walked away, shaking from hunger, shaking from anger. I never saw Mr. Monroe again, though I did have several more offers of work and marriage from men like the one I'd met in the café that day. Surely I would have gone had I not had Mr. Monroe's warning still in my head. I never knew things could be worse than they are in the stone quarry, where children pound stone for gravel, breathe dust, and get sick, and mothers and fathers must work sixteen hours every day, and no one has the chance to learn to read or write, no chance to get out of debt. Out of the quarry, I always thought things must be better somewhere else, perhaps just beyond the border, over the Himalayas, but Mr. Monroe created in me that day a fear of the lies that men will tell. It has kept me working in this place for more than thirty years. It has held me captive. Or safe. I am not sure which.

But now, now, I am traveling under cover of rain and umbrella to make my way to the US Embassy. I am going to find that Mr.

Monroe. I am going to tell him what I believe I have in my possession. That I have found a book that holds the key to my freedom.

After all this time I'm not quite sure what this means, freedom.

I pass the temple but do not dare go in to pray. I am untouchable and therefore unclean. I would be thrown out or worse, even under this new government. Things have not changed for me. For people like me.

May he still be alive. May Mr. Monroe still work at the US Embassy. May he be able to read the words that I cannot read but that I know hold secrets to my past and to my future. I say my prayers silently as I trudge on by the temple in the river around my ankles that was once a street of Kathmandu.

FIVE

Make Yourself at Home

Mount Pleasant
Ally

SOMETHING WONDERFUL FLOWS AROUND ME, A RICH, roasted, savory smell that rouses me from a deep sleep. I wonder if I'm in Africa, or maybe New Orleans again. Smells like spices, tomatoes . . . gumbo? I open my eyes and rub them to be sure I'm really awake and not dreaming. I am still lying in Daddy's moss-green La-Z-Boy, but the chair seems to have been planted in some other living room, like maybe a tornado plucked my recliner, spun me around, and landed me in Oz. I see Kat, sitting in the windowsill. He looks just as confused as I am.

Daddy is gone. Every bit of him, the old TV with bunny ears, the bureau beneath the windows with pictures of me when I was a girl, the boxes of books and magazines, the faded rug my mother made with her own two hands. It's all gone. Instead I see pieces of me, my travels, my world. The television is a flat-screen type, not yet up on the wall, but leaning against it. The coffee table is a round brass one with intricate carvings of Ganesha, the Indian elephant god. A colorful rug I brought back from Guatemala covers the brown carpet and a large Greek lamp shaped like Nike stands beside me, her wings pointed toward the kitchen. I feel as if I stepped into some foreign bazaar. I can almost smell the spices of Kandahar. But no, I really do think it's gumbo.

"Vesey?" I call to him, but only hear the breeze coming in the windows, the far-off call of a crow. I cannot believe that he did all this for me while I slept like an invalid. Vesey did this. How did he pay the men? Where did he send Daddy's things? Did I tell him I wanted it all sent back to the warehouse in Georgia till I can handle it later? My mind is foggy. My hip still aches, but the pain is a little further away now. Just a few days probably and I'll be back to new.

I grab the lever and grit my teeth as the seat pulls me back up to sitting. A piece of paper ripped from Daddy's old prescription tablet falls to my lap. My hand trembles as I turn it to the fading light in the window. I'd know that scribble anywhere, right there below the Rx and the symbol of a mortar and pestle. I can hardly believe it but I'm reading a note from my dearly departed father. For a moment I imagine it's him in the kitchen, cooking up a storm like old times. This dying thing has all been a cruel joke. He'll pop out and yell something like *Surprise!* Some play to get me home.

Make yourself at home, it reads.

I press the paper to my chest and hold my breath. The pain inside could rip me apart, but I won't let it. I breathe in through my nose and out through my mouth slowly until it subsides. Did Daddy leave this for me? No, it's impossible. I don't ever remember him writing me anything. I've sent him postcards from the Orient Express, from Bali, from Australia, but never a word back. For a second I wonder if Vesey wrote this note. Would he do that? My head feels groggy, and I have to get up. I'll get through this pain; I just need to clear my head.

I open my mouth and mean to call for Vesey again, but what comes out is, "Daddy?"

It sounds so ridiculous, a grown woman calling out for her dead father. The fan whirs above me; a flock of geese flies, honking, toward the sunset outside my window. Part of me expects him to answer me back. The other part of me knows it will never happen. I swallow and head to the kitchen on tender feet for a glass of water. When I get there, my hand involuntarily crumples the note and my knees go weak.

There he is, wrapped in white steam. My father is standing at the old stove, one hand holding the lid of the blue crab pot, the other stirring something with a long wooden spoon.

"Daddy?" I hold myself up on the edge of the door frame and he turns around as if in slow motion. "Da—"

"Miss Ally, you all right? Don't look good." As soon as he sets the spoon down and comes toward me, I know it's Vesey. I know it, but I swear, my father was there. He *was*. I guess I need to lay off the muscle relaxers. I feel like I'm losing it.

"Can you sit down?"

"I don't want to sit." It sounds childish and I shouldn't snap. I feel so out of control. "I'm sorry, I just . . ." I look around the room. Daddy's crab pot is there, but the old Krups coffeemaker is gone. It's been replaced by my fire-red Cuisinart. The old wooden table and chairs have been changed into a carved set of mahogany I picked up in England, an antique from an old castle. The table has claw feet. It barely fits in the room.

"You got rid of all his stuff," I say. "It's all . . ." I look at Vesey and notice he's graying around his temples. Funny, I didn't notice it before. He looks tired.

"Sorry if I didn't do it right. Hope you don't mind I set it all out. I can change it 'round anyway you like."

"No, it's fine. Everything. I just can't believe—"

"And your daddy's things, I packed 'em up myself. They said you told 'em to take it all back to some storehouse in Georgia—"

"Yes, with Ronnie. It's ours. At least it was. He and Marlene still let me use it. I'd travel and have things shipped back there over the years. I can't believe I have amassed all of this. Not sure it really goes together." He seems unsure of what to say, so I laugh, then he laughs right along with me, shaking his head.

"No, ain't never seen the likings of these before. You been all over creation, ain't you?"

"Yes, I have." I sniff the air. "And what are you cooking? You didn't have to do all that, Vesey. Truly. The moving and now this? How am I ever going to repay you?"

"Don't owe me a thing. Just being neighbors."

"Neighbors, my behind. People don't do what you just did. What in the world is that heavenly smell?"

A wide smile comes over his face and his eyes sparkle. "Gumbo. Lots of crab. That's a good trap you got. Had near sixteen big'uns. Here, lemme get you a bowl."

"I can get it." But before I can move, he's already at the stove, ladling a big bowl of steaming rice and red gumbo. My mouth waters before the food hits the table. "I didn't know you can cook. Doesn't surprise me though."

"Oh, been livin' 'lone a long time now. Man's got to survive."

I lower slowly into one of my antique chairs, gritting my teeth, and he serves me. I can see diced celery and tomatoes, lumps of fresh crabmeat on top. His hands are strong and lean, the backs of them dark and weathered, the undersides of his long fingers, two shades lighter. He stands there, waiting, so I take a bite, and I tell you, it's like falling in love. I moan. "Oh, how did you . . . You have got to give me this recipe, or teach me, or something." He rubs his hands on a dish towel.

"Glad you like it. It was Beulah's. She sure could cook." My heart pricks at the sound of her name. He looks out the window over the sink. Beulah was his wife of twenty-two years. She died giving birth to his youngest daughter. It was tragic. A hideous tragedy. "It's right near dark now," he says. "I best be going."

"You're not going to stay and eat with me?"

"No, ma'am, but I'll check on you tomorrow evening if that's all right."

"Goodness. 'Course it is. And don't *ma'am* me, neither. How about you take some of this gumbo back home. It's enough to feed Texas."

"Cuttin' back." Vesey rubs his fit midsection, then pulls out an old grayed fishing cap from his pocket and fits it on his head. He reaches for the screened door that leads to the side yard, then stops. "You ain't gonna try to lift nothin', are you? Don't mess with them stones or statues out here without me. I'll be back to spread 'em out where you want 'em."

I hold my hand up, scout's honor, and smile.

Vesey walks out into the night and I am left, a guest in my new-old house. I stare at my things, at my daddy's walls, and at the most amazing food made by a very old friend. I pick up the spoon again and remember Daddy's note. I meant to ask Vesey about it. I set it to the side of my bowl and spread it out, tracing his words with my left hand. When did he write this? Right before he died? I picture him, lying in bed, knowing I'd be home soon. Did he know I wouldn't make it in time to see him alive again? That a note was all we would have between us?

Tears spring to my eyes as I stuff another steaming bite into my mouth. The sweet crabmeat melts on my tongue, the steam finally dissipates, and I find that I am alone here. An orphan at sixty. All alone.

SIX

Faith and Postcards

Ally

IT COULD BE WORSE. HAS BEEN WORSE. ONE TIME I couldn't get out of bed for three weeks. I've been careful with my back since hurting it this morning, so it's much more comfortable, just a dull ache that bristles when I bend the wrong way.

My father had a bad back too. It's one of the frailties of our genes, I suppose. When Daddy's back would go out, he'd be laid up for days in the bed with Mama and me waiting on him hand and foot. I never minded. In fact, secretly, I relished those days when Daddy couldn't go to work, couldn't go check on someone else's family but was captive to my stories and I to his focused attention. He had one particularly bad spell when I was around, oh, seven or so. Daddy usually didn't talk about his patients around us at home, but he'd had a tough case, and a little boy had died after contracting a parasite from standing water. It had happened so fast. Daddy was torn up pretty bad. I heard him behind closed doors crying to my mother about it.

"There, there," she was saying. "You did all you could do, Reid. You did all you could do."

I'd never heard my father cry before and it scared me. It made me think that death was real, that it could actually happen. To me. To Mama or Daddy.

With his back out, I took advantage of the situation. I would sit there next to Daddy, reciting to him Grimms' fairy tales, Rapunzel and Rumpelstiltskin. He in turn would tell me Uncle Remus stories of Brer Bear and Brer Rabbit. He did it in a low, gruff voice too, and I would cackle and roll to the floor. "That rabbit is smarter than Brer Bear and Brer Fox," I'd say. "If they throw him into the briar patch, he won't die, will he?"

"No, he won't die. The briar patch is where he was born, sugar. He's trickin' 'em, see?"

"But . . . someday he'll die, won't he? Brer Rabbit, I mean. Everybody has to die, right?"

My father knew we weren't talking about the fairy tales anymore, and his eyes moistened as he lay there helpless on his back. He reached for me and winced with pain. I fell into his arms and lay there on the bed next to him, feeling his warmth and listening to his heartbeat. "You know, dying isn't all that bad. Considerin'."

I didn't dare speak.

"What I mean is . . . Well, there's heaven, you know. Heaven is a wonderful place. My mother and father are there right now, matter of fact."

I turned to look at him, inches from his whiskery chin. "How do you know?" I whispered.

"Well, faith, for one."

Faith in some invisible, intangible place, to me, was as elusive as touching a rainbow. It was far, far out of my reach. Beyond my understanding. It hurt me to think about such things and I began to tear up, to breathe faster. Daddy knew it.

"Well, faith, and also . . . they sent me notes."

"From heaven?"

"Yep."

"Like postcards?"

"Sort of."

"Well, where are they? What did they say?"

Daddy breathed in deep. "I don't have them anymore. They . . . they washed out into the river, accidentally, you see."

"What'd they say? Grandma and Grandpa?"

"They said that they had made it safely to heaven. And that it was a beautiful place. Even better than they had imagined."

I inhaled, picturing them, Grandma and Grandpa with suitcases at their sides, smiling and waving and dropping postcards into heaven's mailbox. It was the closest I'd ever been to having faith and I clung to it, trying not to let the image go.

"Daddy?"

"Yeah, baby?"

"Who do you think will die first? You or me?"

"What kind of a thing to ask is that?" Daddy ruffled, shifted, and felt the pain in his back, then he said, "I suspect it will be me to go first. At the rate I'm going . . ."

"Will you write to me?"

"Write to you?"

"If you get to heaven first. Will you send me a postcard and let me know you made it? Tell me what it's like? If I go first, I'll send you one, all right?"

My father was quiet for nearly a full minute. Then he squeezed me tight and pulled my face to his lips. He kissed me, sandpaper on my forehead, and whispered, "Yes, Ally. I promise. I'll write to you if I get there first."

Night has come. With a new bed in Daddy's room, I'm looking forward to sleeping so I can shake this day from me. Imagine, skirting my duties and letting Vesey and two strange men move all of Daddy's belongings out of his house. I hold his note to my chest: *Make yourself at home.*

Apparently I have, Daddy. I'm feeling a little ashamed now. Maybe this wasn't such a good idea. I stare out the window toward the river, at indigo shifting up through the water and glassy chards of white on top. I watch as the birds all skitter to their nests and a chill runs through my body. For half a second I almost believe Daddy sent me this note from heaven, but I know it must have been from some other time, perhaps when I came back from Bali and he was out at the grocery store. That's it; he left me this note long ago—it's probably eight years old by now—and I simply don't remember it. It must have gotten stirred up while Vesey and the movers were changing things around in here. That's it.

I smile to myself and head to the bedroom slowly, tenderly for my hip.

I turn on the light. I scream, a far-off sort of scream that sounds as if someone else is doing it.

On my new red futon and littering the floor are little square pieces of paper from Daddy's old prescription pad, at least a dozen or so. I lift one up, shaking, and see these words:

> Made it to heaven safely, Ally.
> Better than I expected.
>
> Dad

SEVEN

Sunshine All the Time

Ally

KAT JUMPS OFF THE BED AND SCURRIES UNDER IT. Someone's at the door, but I can't move. I haven't slept a wink, and I'm still hugging my knees, staring down at the papers on the bed. The sunlight is peeking in through the slats of my bamboo shades, drawing long lines across the floor. It may have been one of the longest nights of my life.

I hear the knock again, and this time, it breaks through my fog. I wince as I set my feet on the floor and pad to the bathroom to check my face. Oh, my face. I splash some cold water on my puffy eyes and pat them dry with a white towel. It's too scratchy. Too new. I need to do a load of wash.

Please be Vesey at the door. I could use a friend right now. I need someone to see these notes from Daddy so I know I'm not losing my mind.

I hope I'm not losing my mind.

I walk through the golden dancing dust in the living room

and run my hand along Daddy's green chair. There's a sliver of Vesey showing through the transom window, and my heart stirs at the sight of him.

I turn the lock and welcome in the warm morning air. Birds are chirping. His face is so kind, so familiar, it almost reminds me of my father. "Mornin'." He nods and takes off his hat, holding it to his chest. He has a brown paper bag of fruit and pushes it to me. "Thought you might like some."

"Thank you, I'm . . . I'm sorry I look this way." I run my hand through my hair and wish I could go make up my face. "I didn't sleep."

"It's overrated. Sleepin'." He smiles and likes to melt my heart. "Can I come in?"

"Yes, sorry, please. Come in." I take the fruit into the kitchen and check the stove clock. It says 8:32.

"These look wonderful." I unload peaches, apples, and plums and lay them out upside down on some paper towels. "Let me just make some coffee so I can think straight."

Before I know it, we are sitting at the kitchen table, this massive wood thing, and I am ruing getting rid of Daddy's small dinette. It went much better with the linoleum floor.

I have so much to tell Vesey. I don't know where to begin.

"Feelin' better?" he asks as I sip, eyes closed.

"Getting there."

"I thought I'd help you with the outside today. Got all them statues and such."

"Oh, gosh, I'd forgotten all about that. They're so heavy, you shouldn't be lifting—"

"I'm a man, Miss Ally. I'm fine."

"I know you are." Something sharp flits between us, a spark, some current. I set my cup down and say, "Vesey, I have something to tell you, and I don't want you thinking I'm crazy, all right?"

He nods, brown eyes focused on mine.

"I, well, I was up all night, thinking about Daddy. It's harder than I thought it would be. Somehow when I lost Mama, it was softened by his still being here. I think I took solace in that, but now . . ." Vesey pushes up from the table and grabs a paper towel for my eyes. He folds it carefully and hands it to me. His gesture only makes me want to cry more. I blot my eyes and take a deep breath. "My father and I once had a conversation about dying. I was a little girl. He was laid out because of his back and . . . well, he was trying to make me feel better, so he lied. A pretty big lie."

"About what?"

I smile, remembering. "He said that when he got to heaven one day, he'd write me letters and tell me all about it. Can you imagine? That Grandma and Grandpa had done the same for him."

"And did it help . . . when you were little?"

"Yes, actually, it did."

"Don't see the harm in it then. He was just looking after—"

"There's more, Vesey." I stare him down. "I'm almost afraid to tell you this, afraid that when I go back there, you won't see anything and they'll have to call the paddy wagon and haul me off for good. I'm overdue, you know."

He's concerned now. He rubs the knuckles on his left hand.

"Come here," I say.

I stand slowly, and Vesey grabs my arm, helping me up.

"Back any better?"

"A little. I just don't want to take any more pills that knock me out. Give me a good bottle of wine, but I don't like those pills. It'll be fine in a few days, I'm sure."

We walk arm in arm to Daddy's old bedroom, mine now, and I stop at the doorway. Kat runs ahead of us and jumps on the bead, turning and biting at a flea on his leg. I point to the unmade bed and watch Vesey's face. He looks at me, then walks forward and picks up a piece of paper by my pillow. He does see it. He straightens his glasses, reads it, and turns it over. His eyes search for the others and he bends and picks up each and every one as if picking delicate flowers in a field.

I close my eyes and see them in my mind.

Weather's real nice. Sunshine all the time.

Thinking of you.

Dad

Mama says hello. She's young and beautiful!
She loves you with all her heart. Me too.

Dad

Did I tell you we have a mansion by a glittering river?
More beautiful than I imagined.

Dad

Ally, sweetness, I've seen her. She's here.
Time for you to rest now.

Dad

EIGHT

Uncertainty

Kathmandu, Nepal
Sunila

I'VE GOT TO REST. I CANNOT KEEP GOING. I HAVE NO food. I am wet. Why did I ever leave? I belong in the quarry with Amaa. I am destined for nothing but misery and bad luck here. I duck in from out of the rain and find an alleyway between stores. I don't know which street I am on. They all look the same now. I wedge myself behind piles of rubbish and pull my knees up. I am sore from my shoulders to the bottoms of my feet. My shoes are barely there anymore.

Why did I set out on this journey? I am not this brave. I am stupid, just as they have always told me. I feel the hard edges of the Book of the Gods in the tops of my thighs and I allow my mind to go to the images. I have carved them many times. I feel calmer now. I breathe in deeply. *You have come because you must. Because there was no other way.*

I hear a noise and lift my head. I wish to be invisible, to blend in with the garbage. There is a man coming toward me. I wrap my hand around my chisel. I will use it if I must. He comes closer and bends down. My arm tenses. He reaches his hand into the garbage and pulls things this way and that, and suddenly he is staring right at me and my hand with the chisel is pointed back at him. He is a Dalit like me. Who of us is more afraid?

He lifts his hands and says in a coarse voice, "I mean you no harm. I am hungry."

I look at him and feel pity. No more fear. "I am hungry as well," I say. Then I put my head down and listen as his heavy footsteps slosh away.

NINE

Letters from Heaven

Mount Pleasant
Ally

"Miss Ally?" Vesey touches my shoulder. I'm lean-ing against the door frame of my father's bedroom and feel like I might have dozed for half a second. "What is all this?"

I smile, sadly. There are pieces of paper all over the bed, the floor. "So you see them too?"

"'Course I do," he says.

"It's his handwriting, Vesey. I'd know it anywhere."

"Where'd they come from?"

"I don't know," I tell him. "One minute they're not here, the next, they're all over the bed and the floor. I found one yester-day too"—I fish it out of my pocket—"and I meant to ask you about it. It suddenly appeared on my stomach after I'd been lying in Daddy's chair out there. I assumed you'd found it and put it there."

Vesey grunts and furrows his brow. He looks through the

papers, then around the room. "So, what, you think he's sendin' you notes from heaven?"

"Isn't that what it looks like? I just can't believe it. I don't even believe in all that mess."

"In what mess?"

"You know, heaven, God. I don't know, maybe I do."

"Y'either do or don't. No in-between."

"Well, maybe there is an in-between. Maybe I'm in it."

I turn and leave him standing in the bedroom. I can feel the coffee kicking in, heart pounding.

"I didn't mean to offend—"

"Oh, come on, Vesey, you didn't. I'm just tired. I just . . . don't understand . . ."

Vesey is staring at the ceiling now. He sets his hat down on the bed and squints up, adjusting his glasses.

"Don't tell me you can see it from here," I say. "Heaven."

"No . . ." Vesey looks around the room and grabs a chair at a little dresser I bought in Italy. He moves it to the center of the room, right next to the bed, and starts climbing on it.

"What are you doing? You'll break your neck!" I move toward him and hold on to the backs of his legs. It's a strange position and I feel slightly light-headed, feeling his strong, warm calves through his pants. He's reaching up, here, there, then he comes back down.

"What is it?"

"I reckon it's . . . putty." Vesey is holding white blobs of stuff and rolling it around in his fingers.

"Putty?" I repeat. Vesey looks crestfallen. Then he smiles. "I guess maybe I solved your mystery. Looks like Doc Green stuck these up there on the ceiling before he died. Ain't he had that big ol' poster bed? All I can figure . . ."

"Why would he do a thing like that?" I try to picture Daddy, old and frail, standing wobbly and reaching up, sticking these notes up there. "Oh." Tears spring to my face again and I sit down on the edge of the bed.

Vesey stands next to me, not sure what to do. He puts a hand on my shoulder and lets it rest there, warm heat. "Seems he wanted 'em to stay there long enough . . . just till after he was gone maybe . . ."

"Then they'd fall down 'from heaven' and I'd think he was really up there. Think it really exists."

"It does exist."

"How do *you* know?" I turn to him and realize it came out much harsher than I intended. I was really only thinking aloud, emotions all amuck. Vesey removes his hand from my shoulder. He puts his hat back on.

"Maybe I'll leave you 'lone right now," he says. "I can do the outside later."

"No, Vesey, I'm sorry, I'm just . . ."

Vesey leaves me sitting there, a swollen shred of a woman, and turns his head sideways to say, "I know heaven's there, Miss Ally, 'cause I believe it. I got to. I got family waitin' on the other side."

Then he's gone and I am lying back on the bed, staring at white dots on the ceiling like a great constellation. How could I not see it before?

Why'd you go to all that trouble, Daddy? Why'd you have to lie? I'm a grown woman now. I should never have gotten out of bed this morning. I roll to my side, curl my legs up embryo-style, and, despite the coffee, when Kat settles into the backs of my knees, I melt into a deep sleep and dream of elephants and white birds.

TEN

At First Sight

Ally

THE FIRST TIME I LAID EYES ON VESEY WASHINGTON, A white bird had skimmed the top of my head with its wing and my eyes followed it as it glided over to the other side of the creek. There was a boy standing there that summer of 1957—just a dark speck on the other side of the river, almost like looking out and seeing my own shadow.

"Mama," I hollered, "I see somebody over there. Somebody waving at *me!*" I ran down on the dock and stood on the edge of it, nearly falling off. I waved back as big and furious as I could, putting my whole body into it. I could see the small shape of a boy on the other side, a mess of cattails next to him and a fishing pole in his hand. He would throw it back over his shoulder and exaggerate, slowly casting his bait, then pull it in, making sure I was watching. I was, let me tell you. I ran back to the house. My mother was outside hanging clothes on the line. I tugged at her apron. "Can I go fishing?"

"Your daddy will be back after a while."

"I can't wait that long!"

"Why ever not? What's got into you? Look like you're about to wet your britches. Go on in, honey, before you have an accident."

"I don't have to!"

"Alicia . . ."

"But, Mama, there's a boy on the other side of the river, and he's fishing and I want to fish with him!"

A look came over Mama's face like she smelled something not right with the laundry. She looked toward the river and her eyebrows rose. "A boy on the other side of the river?"

"Yeah, come look!" I pulled her by her wrist and dragged her to the dock. The little boy on the other side was still there, sitting on the bank with his knees up, rod out in the water. He saw us and stood up quick, but he didn't wave. I did, though.

"You see? I told you! Can I go fishing?"

"Honey, that's the colored side of the river. We can't be—"

"But, Mama! Please!" I was about to cry, something I did quite well. My mother looked at me, softened a bit, and said, almost whispering, "I have an idea. How about if I let you get your fishing pole and sit here on our dock? That way you can fish and he can fish—"

"But why can't we fish together?"

Mama made a funny sort of laughing, scoffing sound, but she also sounded baffled to me, like she did when she didn't have a good answer for something. "It's just . . . not done, honey. This is the best you're gonna get. Take it or leave it."

She was firm now, and about to get back to her business, so I told her I'd take it. We set me out on the end of the dock with my bamboo pole. I'd only caught a couple things on it before, a tiny bream and a small, ugly catfish, and honestly, Daddy was the one to put my worms and crickets on my hook, so I just sat there, baitless, line and feet in the water, with the dark boy on the other side. We fished that way a good couple hours, occasionally waving, occasionally pulling our poles out and dramatically casting them again, then, just as animated, reeling in pretend fish.

I felt a special connection with the boy on the other side. I could sense he was the same kind of lonely as me. And the distance between us only made me want to know him all the more.

By third grade I knew how to read and write in cursive and could recite whole sections of the Declaration of Independence. Daddy thought I was old enough to start learning some other things about the world. He didn't say it in so many words; he just put me in the car and said he wanted me to ride along with him . . . to keep him company. Being a doctor in Charleston in 1958, Daddy made house calls. He didn't work at a hospital or doctor's office—that all came later. He spent his days entering people's sanctuaries, their homes, their lives, at their most vulnerable moments.

The day he took me out to make his rounds was the last day of my sheltered life on Molasses Creek.

The first house we went to belonged to an old lady with a goiter on the side of her neck. I'd never seen anything like it, but when I could look her way, I noticed how her blue eyes sparkled at Daddy. The way he squeezed her hand and said she was looking "mighty purdy." I suppose I knew my father to be a liar in those very moments, but in a way, I'd never admired him more. They both knew he was lying. It was his gentle way, his care, his laugh, that was true medicine.

The next house we visited was dark and smelled like old. I wanted so badly to pull the curtains back and let in some air, but after Daddy introduced me to an old man, he left me in the living room and followed the man to the back of the house. I looked on the walls and saw dingy photographs of children and family, some boat pictures, one of a man holding a large fish and smiling with crooked teeth. I imagined at one time there had been light in that house, but now only darkness fell. How did that happen? It made me want to run, to shake the darkness off of me, to run into the sunshine and just keep on running so that darkness and the smell of old could never settle on me.

Daddy came out, wiping his hands on a rag and looking the man in the eyes. He put his hand on his shoulder and spoke so softly I couldn't hear him. The man stood still, old and slumped. Then we left. "Who was in there?" I asked him when we were safely in the car.

"His wife," was all he told me. I sensed I needn't ask more, that Daddy had told me all he could or wanted to. Maybe I didn't want to know. Maybe I didn't want to put words to the fact that darkness had just shrouded the last light in that poor man's life.

I hoped we were done for the day. Surely Daddy didn't have to see more people, to go into anyone else's house. I certainly didn't want to and secretly planned to tell him I'd rather wait in the car at the next place. We traveled for a while along dirt roads, past fan palms and wild, natural Lowcountry drives, until I saw water glistening to the right of me. I watched as the sun danced on the river and it felt so familiar, although any waterway in the Lowcountry can feel like home for someone born here, even to those who weren't. But no. There was more. Through the trees, I saw the back of the Cummingses' house, our neighbors down the street. I knew it well—the playground that backed up almost to the dock, that three-swing swing set. And then, through a sliver of light as our car moved by, I recognized the back of our own house.

I looked at Daddy. We were on the other side of Molasses Creek. My heart pounded. It was as if I'd somehow dreamed it into existence. How many nights had I lain in bed, dreaming of the other side, the boy with his fishing boat, the clothes hanging on the line in the wind? How many times had I sat there on our dock, wondering what the lives of the people in that little house were like? And now we were here. Really here.

Chickens ran to the side of the car when we bumped along dirt in front of the house. It was simple, much smaller than our own, and painted mustard yellow with a rusted green tin roof. There were flowerpots to the sides of the crooked front steps made of oyster bins, round, with holes where roots and vines crawled through. A black woman in a handkerchief with a little boy on her hip came to the door and peeked out. Her face was dark and shone in the light when she stepped out. She smiled when she saw Daddy, then froze up when she noticed me.

"Althea, this is my daughter, Ally. She's helping me make my rounds today." The woman looked at me and, with stiff arms, welcomed us into her home. She looked behind her and yelled something to the people inside. There was shuffling, then quiet. A dog greeted us at the doorway, a smelly golden retriever who seemed to smile. Not having any pets, I tried to put my hand down to him, but the woman shooed him off and down the steps he ran. The door was left open.

Upon entering, my eyes tried to adjust to the light. It was dim, a single lamp glowing on a table next to the sofa. Two windows flanked either side of it, and I ducked and squinted to see if I could spy our house. I could. It seemed like a castle from here, off in the distance, white shards of sunlight making it sparkle. I longed to be there right that minute. The woman said something to my father that I couldn't understand. It was as if she was speaking another language, foreign, but he understood. My blood stirred. My father moved toward the little kitchen and told me to stay put. I melted down into a wood chair up against the wall, staring at my house through the window, wishing the dog was still indoors so I wouldn't be alone. Then I heard a voice, a young voice, say, "You de gal from d'otha side?"

I stared hard to where the voice was coming from. It was the sofa. With the bright light outdoors, the sofa was masked in darkness, and there, not one, but two children were sitting still like snakes, staring at me. I hadn't seen them before.

"Oh, hey, I . . . Yes, I live over there. See that house?" I pointed and the children got up. A little girl stood and came closer to me. She must have been about four years old. She was wearing a dress with no shoes and had her hair in these braids that stuck up all over creation. She smiled and reached forward, touching my blond hair.

"Stop it, Marcie!" the boy chided. He looked out the window for the longest time, then he turned back around. "Yo' daddy the doctor?"

I nodded.

"I gone be a doc too someday. Gonna have me a big bag to fix folk up."

I didn't know what to say, so I said nothing and the boy went on.

"My daddy catch oyster. Fish all the time. Smell like fish, but I don't mind. I like the smell of 'em. You like fish?"

"Yes," I managed. "I like fish."

"I like to catch 'em. Catched this big ol' sucker"—and he put his arms out wide to show me just how big it was—"jes' last week. You ain't never seen none bigger. We fry that thang up and mmm, mmm, it good. Best fish I ever eat."

He was animated now, and I was feeling dizzy, as if I was far away from home, in a dream somehow, and needed to pinch myself to get back. At the same time, I felt like I could listen to this boy forever.

"My name's Ally," I said finally. "What's yours?"

"Vesey my name," he said. "Vesey, name after my daddy. He Vesey too. Name after Denmark Vesey, ol' slave hero. I name after him too."

"Nice to meet you, Vesey," I said, trying to remember all those times my mother had taught me to be polite. If ever there was a time to use my manners, it seemed it was now. The moment felt important, eternal. I'd never met anyone named after a hero before.

My father came back through the kitchen with the woman, and the baby on her hip was crying now—not a screaming cry, more a whimper. Vesey said, "Rufus sick. He got da fevah. Rash."

"Hush now," said the woman and Vesey sat back like a statue, still on that sofa. Never uttered another word.

"Lots of liquids," said Daddy, and he handed the woman something from his bag. "Two times every day, all right?"

The woman thanked him and I envied Daddy at the moment for having that woman's respect. For some strange reason I longed to have that same respect from her. I understood Vesey in a deep way, I thought, right then. No wonder he wanted to be a doctor when he grew up. It was the way to his mama's heart.

We went to two more houses on that same road across the river that day, but to be honest, my mind was stuck at Vesey's house. I thought through every word he'd said to me. I remembered his cadence. I remembered the glow around his head and how I could hardly make out his features. I remembered the little girl's hand as she touched my hair, as if I were the unusual one.

I kept waiting for Daddy to ask me what I'd learned that day as he took me on his rounds, but he never did. Somehow, we both knew I'd learned too much to ever put into words.

ELEVEN

Pot Roast Says I'm Sorry

Mount Pleasant
Ally

"Ronnie?" I roll over in the darkness and press the receiver against my cheek.

"Hey, Al. You okay?"

"Not really."

"You gonna make it?"

"I guess. I hate this. I don't even have the energy . . . Let's just say I chased off my only friend."

"I thought I was your friend."

"Yeah, but I could never chase you off. I even divorced you. You don't leave."

"That's true. But how could I ever leave you?"

"I think I screwed up pretty big."

"Saying sorry always works."

"You know I'm not one for sorrys, Ronnie."

"Yeah, I do know it. But don't worry. He knows you're upset

about your daddy right now. You're not legally obligated to anything that comes out of your mouth. At least for a while. I think that's a rule of grieving somewhere."

"Maybe you're right."

"I know I'm right. Listen, Al. Get out of bed. Make some coffee. Get out of the house. All right? You got to . . . you got to just go. Can't wallow there in bed all day. That's not you."

I lie there with the silence and miles between us. I imagine the Lowcountry sunshine outside. The darkness and old in here have already started to settle on me in my grief and stiffen my bones. "Good advice," I tell him. "I knew you were good for something, Ronnie."

"I thought you said I was good for nothing?"

"Well, that too. Love you, though."

"Love you too, Al. We both do."

"Tell Marlene I'll call y'all later, all right? Coffeepot's a-calling."

My hip is slowly getting back to normal. Thank goodness for small things. I make my way to the kitchen, but just barely, as Kat weaves in and out of my legs. "Watch out now! You want me to trip? Hold on." Carefully, I bend over and pour him some food by the back door. I watch him hunch down and commence to munching. Acts as if he hasn't eaten in a week. His striped fur glows white in the bright light reflecting off the creek and through the window. I rub my eyes, stretch, and wish I knew the name of a good masseuse in town. I make a mental note to locate a day spa today. Number one on my to-do list. Time to get this hip back into shape.

The coffee percolates and sputters and the aroma stirs me,

soothes my soul. I reach for Daddy's coffee mug and set it down before me with reverence. Daddy's mug. Daddy's not here, but his mug is. It's hard to wrap my mind around. I walk past Kat and open the back door. I take my coffee down to the dock and feel the coolness of the morning air tinged with humidity. The grass is wet beneath my feet. I can tell it will be a pretty hot afternoon. Might as well get out now while the gettin's good.

Vesey's house. There it is, staring at me. If I squint, I see two shirts hanging on his clothesline with some smaller pieces I'm guessing are socks or drawers. I can't see that far anymore. Age is lovely. The only good thing is I can't see my own wrinkles very well. The closer I get to the mirror, the more out of focus I get. I'll never invest in one of those high-powered magnifying mirrors, I guarantee it. More like torture devices if you ask me.

Vesey. My mind won't leave him. What kind of a man still has a clothesline in this day and age?

I ought to do something nice for Vesey. I mean, he handled the furniture men and then moved it all himself. He's been a true, loyal friend all these years, and me, I open my big mouth and offend him. So careless, not even considering his own loss . . .

It's settled. I'll go to the store, maybe that new Whole Foods, today and get something good and fresh. Maybe I can show him I'm sorry without having to say it. I do so hate to say I'm sorry.

What says sorry better . . . pot roast and macaroni or tandoori chicken with naan and jasmine rice? Knowing Vesey, I'd say the pot roast. He's Lowcountry through and through. He wouldn't know his *tandoori* from his *naan*. I chuckle to myself and after three sips of coffee, am beginning to feel human.

Since I've come home, Daddy's overgrown yard has become littered with stone statues of gods and goddesses. His Lowcountry retreat now resembles a graveyard. I've got to get Vesey to come back over and set these out better. It should feel like an artsy garden for contemplation and meditation, not a home for the dead. I pass a font with the head of the Greek god of wine on it, Dionysius. His mouth is wide open where the water—or wine—should flow. His eyes are still, stone cold, yet watching me. I back up and nearly trip over a statue of Atlas holding the world on his shoulders.

How in the world did I acquire all these statues? Well, to be honest, they were cheap. For instance, in Greece, I bought a slew of stone gods for just a few dollars from a stone peddler. It's how I fooled myself into paying the gargantuan shipping fees. I might as well have bought them at home. I'm sure I could have found similar . . . but the fact that they're Greek gods and I found them in Greece, well, I like them . . . just not all jumbled the way they are now. It's a bit creepy, if you ask me, white specters lurking about as if in a city of the dead. Creepy is not at all what I was going for. International, yes.

Before I get in the car, my fairly new Chrysler LeBaron that I bought specifically because of its comfortable seats, I notice something perched against the side of the house. What is that? I move over and see it—something I'd completely forgotten I owned.

When I was in Bali a few years ago, I wore nothing but these silk batik saris with the bright colors and designs. I fell in love with them, the way they covered my legs, the way they felt on my body, and the way my spirit felt when I was in them. There was a woman selling her wares in a little shop. She had the most intricate designs, and I purchased about a dozen pieces of fabric to wrap around my hips. Well, she had her batik-making equipment right there in the store, which was nothing more than a couple sawhorses, some stick pins to hold the silk in place, a slew of embossed metal patterns, and a wax melter/pen combination thingy. "Is this how you make them?" I marveled. Her eyes lit up and she showed me how to do it. It looked simple enough. You have the hot wax that you draw onto the silk or press on with your template, then later you use dyes to color it all. The wax resists the dyes, so you get these wonderful, intricate designs. I was so excited that I bought it all from her right there on the spot, imagining myself in some French château, perhaps, walking to the market for bread and fruit and wine, and then spending my afternoons making exotic batiks. Living the posh life of an artist abroad . . .

Anyway, there it is—the sawhorses, the pins, the box containing the wax melter/pen apparatus, the jars of dyes, the patterns. Could I really do something like that? Make batiks? By hand? Be an artist? It's been so long since I've drawn anything. Well, this is no French château, but the water does inspire me. I look back toward the creek and remember Vesey. I must keep going. Maybe he can help me find a nice spot for my batik studio when he helps me with these statues. If he ever forgives my rudeness.

When I settle into the car seat, my rear end burns where my nerve is still pinched. I back down the old familiar drive and head out under a canopy of live oaks and Spanish moss into the town that I once called home.

There is a new bridge that replaced the old Cooper River Bridge into Charleston now. I must say, it's enormous. It could rival the Golden Gate Bridge in San Francisco or the Brooklyn Bridge in New York. It almost makes little old Mount Pleasant feel more cosmopolitan, but what I admire most is the walkway on one side for walkers and bikers. Whoever thought of that was genius. Can you imagine being able to walk the bridge all the way over to Charleston? How long would that take, anyway? I remember back in the fifties and sixties, the blacks having to wait on the side of the road for the bus to go into downtown Charleston and make a living. Imagine what this bridge accomplishes. For those with no motor vehicles, they are no longer dependent on public transportation. Sakes, they could walk to the other side on their very own now, not having to wait or depend on anyone. Freedom. My, how things change over time.

I drive slowly through the intersection and watch the walkers and joggers. I need to be on that bridge with them. I need to conquer that bridge. I need to feel alive and get some exercise. I'm feeling older and flabbier every minute.

Daddy once told me he tried to walk the bridge when it first went up in summer 2005, but he only got up to the first diamond tower. Seeing that tall white inverted V, I picture my aged father up there, struggling up that hill all by himself. Where was I? Europe? A pain shoots through my tear ducts and I turn away from the bridge and into the parking lot of the new organic grocer. Before I get out of the car, I let the engine run a minute while I shake the thoughts of Daddy on that bridge. I picture him in the sky on a cloud, writing letters to me and dropping them down like rain.

Oh, Daddy.

Daddy never did like this Whole Foods store. He didn't know what to do with spelt or veggie sausages, not to mention the freshly made sushi and cheese section to die for with everything from five-year-old Gouda to Spanish Manchego. I love it though.

I nibble on all the goodies they have set out, fresh cherries and bits of aged cheddar. By the time I've made it to the wine section, I've had a nice snack and can make more rational purchasing decisions, not ones based on raw hunger.

In my cart, I've got a nice rump roast and fresh carrots to go along with the homemade macaroni I'll be making. My secret is the cheese. I use four kinds. My mouth is watering just thinking about it coming out of the oven all bubbly. It used to be Ronnie's favorite, and Marlene tries to make it, but she never quite will. You see, I gladly gave her the recipe, but with only *two* of the cheeses. Poor things. I love them both—I'm totally over Ronnie and so thankful that Marlene can stand to live with the man—but she's already a better wife in any of a dozen ways than I ever was. My macaroni and cheese is all I have left. I can't possibly allow her to show me up in that department too. I pick out a nice Spanish tempranillo-cabernet blend and beam, thinking, *Now this is how you say you're sorry, Ally. Vesey will forgive you one hundred percent before the gravy has a chance to settle on his plate.*

'Course with a meal this good, he might just fall in love in the meantime.

Banish the thought, Ally! Get ahold of yourself. You are not trying to seduce that man; you are simply putting forth an olive branch to an old friend whom you wronged.

I really should see a doctor about these hormones. I declare, sometimes I feel more like a teenager than a sixty-year-old woman.

I adore these smaller shopping carts. Now this is progress. As a single woman, who wants to push around an enormous cart so that everyone will see how alone you are? My cart would be empty, barren, if I were pushing around the big one, but no, this one is overflowing. Someone looking at me might think I'm shopping for myself and a lover, and that would be all right with me . . . except for the fact that I haven't had a lover since the last presidential election, and only then it was because I was in Italy and feeling a wee bit homesick. I met an American in Rome in Trevi Square. We both enjoyed watching artists paint the fountain *en plein air* . . .

I unload my little cart and then, feeling I've done my responsible duty by directing the cart to the designated area, I settle into the car and head for home—well, Daddy's home, not mine, but not really his anymore, come to think of it.

I turn right and head back toward the intersection. Instead of staring at the new bridge, I watch a rainbow-colored umbrella with a black man selling newspapers and magazines up ahead. How quaint. I can't imagine standing in this heat, but he's making a living. Everyone needs to do that, right? Somebody two cars ahead of me stops and hands him money out the passenger window. Do I need a paper? Perhaps I do. I guess if I'm here for a while I really should see what's happening in the *Post and Courier*. Give this man an honest dollar. I reach into my purse and move up a little closer. I roll down my window, ready to stop, but instead, my heart stops.

It's him! Could it be? No, Vesey doesn't sell newspapers and magazines on the side of the road! Vesey is a, well, a farmer, a fisherman, a self-contained man. He fishes and grows his own food, for goodness' sake! He, he . . . I dart my eyes away in case it *is* him and press my foot to the gas pedal. When I speed through the intersection, my car hits a bump in the road and I nearly go airborne.

It can't be Vesey, can it? Maybe some look-alike? Why would he need money? At his age, why in the world would he struggle like that working on the side of the road?

My mind is scrambled. *'Course, there's nothing wrong with making a living, Ally. 'Course, there's nothing wrong with working on the side of the road. Don't be such a snob. The sweetgrass basket makers do it every day, and there's nothing wrong with hard work and selling your wares, is there?*

I look in the rearview mirror and see the man, perhaps Vesey, perhaps not, standing in what looks like army fatigues, in this heat, fishing hat pulled down over his head.

Fishing hat. Vesey's fishing hat.

And his son was in Afghanistan. He didn't come home.

My goodness, Vesey is working on the side of the road, peddling fifty-cent newspapers in his son's army uniform. I didn't see this coming. I thought he was fairly well off living on Molasses Creek, dealing well with, well, everything better than this. *Oh, why didn't you ever leave this place for good, Vesey? You could have come with me. You could have. Should have.*

I'm not sure what's up or down right now because guilt like quicksand's pulling me down. Is it possible I don't know this man at all anymore? Or is it possible he needs me even more than I imagined?

I look in the mirror again but I can't see him, only the rainbow-colored umbrella protecting him from the Lowcountry sun.

TWELVE

The Book of the Gods

Kathmandu, Nepal
Sunila

I AM USING MY UMBRELLA AS A SHIELD AGAINST THE sheets of rain, but I am losing this battle. The spokes of metal twist and bend around me. The rainbow colors are faded, gray, and ripping in two places now. I am feeling faint and losing strength. How long have I been walking? How many days? Am I going in circles? All too likely I will not make it to my destination. My escape was desperate and not well planned. I will suffer at my own hands. I will die on the streets of Kathmandu and be swept up in the morning by downtrodden Dalit women with all the other garbage lining these streets.

I think of Amaa's face. I know she loves me. In her own way. I imagine her fears now, of me out here in the monsoon, drowning, weak. She will not want me to die here. She will want me to keep moving. I hold tight to my umbrella and lean against a building. I cannot stop now; I have come too far. I must reach the US

Embassy, if not for me, for Amaa and for the person who once owned this book. My body hurts and my mind is racing. I open my mouth to scream in fear and triumph, but nothing will come out.

I have nothing, but at least I still have this book.

THIRTEEN

The Sketchbook

Ally

WHEN I WAS ABOUT FOUR YEARS OLD I WAS GIVEN A notebook by my grandmother to chronicle the beauty of the world around me. It was my comfort, my oogie blanket. I carried it with me everywhere. Pages and pages of sketches, scribbled by a child's hand, then progressing into more confident, more accomplished lines—Charleston gates and iron scrolls, palmetto trees and seashells etched in sand, statues of gods and angels adorning walkways and gardens. Nothing ever belonged to me, really. I just drew what I saw, copied the beauty others had created before me. I was not original with my art. A fake, if you want to view it that way. Yet they did have a certain quality . . .

"Your drawings are coming along, Ally," my mother would say as she wiped her hands on her apron. "If you keep that up, you might be downtown in a gallery someday. Can you imagine?"

"Or she might illustrate one of my medical books," Daddy would tell me.

"Swell. So I can either peddle my work to tourists or watch boring operations and draw blood and gore and little metal instruments. Thanks, but no thanks."

My parents weren't sure what to do with me by the time I hit puberty. It hit me hard and without much warning. My body began to grow and change and my heart would race, my blood itching to *do* something. Anytime Chubby Checker was on the radio, I'd twist and gyrate. When Pat Boone came on, I'd swoon and doodle his name. Mama and Daddy would look at each other and wring their hands. "Shame to let a talent like your drawing go to waste. After all, you have it in your blood."

Parents like to live their unrealized dreams through their children. My grandmother was an artist of sorts. She'd do some small oil paintings of stills: porcelain bowls and fruits and tablecloths. My father had always felt he'd let his mother down in that way. He had terrible handwriting and could hardly draw a stick figure. I did know it made him proud to see my drawings, my interpretations of the world. And no matter that I pretended not to care, I drew because I wanted to please him. To please them. Children so desire to make their parents happy. That's why it's devastating when the opposite happens, when the child brings shame and ruin to her family.

By the time I turned twelve years old, I'd sit for long hours on the dock, drawing the birds as they preened in the sun, arms out wide in the marsh grass, soaking up rays and the vibrations of the water. I would lose myself in the top of my pencil or chalk or charcoal. I would lose myself—and only then would I feel at peace.

I began to think about Vesey more and more. I began to think about the way his muscles were forming, his skin growing darker, his smile brighter. I began to draw his little house from my side of the river. When we'd steal away for short boat rides while Mama was at the store in town, I would take my sketchbook along with me. I began drawing Vesey as he stared off into the marsh. He'd giggle occasionally and I'd tell him to be quiet, to be still. He'd grow serious and my charcoal would capture the light as it hit his brow, the round of his cheeks, the depth of his eyes.

I began hiding my sketches and lying to my parents when they'd ask to see what I'd drawn lately. I told them I'd misplaced it or some other excuse. I didn't want them to see my drawings of Vesey. I thought they'd reprimand me, threaten me to stay away from him. Tell me how unbecoming it was for a young girl to be off with a boy of his age and of his color. *What would the neighbors think?* they might say. I didn't want to hear any of it. I knew they would see in the care of my lines how important he'd become to me. He was the beauty I saw around me now, like the water and the trees and the wildlife, worthy to be drawn.

But my friend Margaret saw my notebook. She was over at my house when we were in the seventh grade. She peeked under my bed and before I knew it, she was flipping through, looking at my drawings of buildings and gates and rivers and Vesey. She stopped flipping, and I grabbed the book away from her.

"That's mine," I said.

She reached to get it back. "But I can see it. I'm your friend."

"It's private."

"Why, Ally Green, I didn't know we had secrets from each other. I thought that's what friends are."

I bit my lip and held on to the book, tight. Then her eyes glittered.

"I saw a black boy in there. Since when do you know a black boy?"

I couldn't speak.

"Since when do you know a black boy well enough to have him sit still and draw him? I want to meet him," she said.

I shook my head. "I can't. He—let's just go out and play. I want to go take a walk or—"

"I'll find out who he is, Ally. You'll tell me. Or I'll tell the whole school you're sweet on a black boy. You think that would go over well? You'd be—"

"I'm not sweet on him! He's a friend. A neighbor. He lives there, across the creek. And you have to promise me you'll never tell a soul about him. Please. It . . . it would get him in a heap of trouble."

"Not to mention you. So I can meet him?" Margaret pushed. I hated her in that moment.

"Yeah. I guess. Sometime."

"Soon," she said. Then she smiled like the Cheshire cat, and my stomach sank to the floor.

Part Two

But pain insists upon being attended to. God whispers to us in our pleasures, speaks in our conscience, but shouts in our pains: it is His megaphone to rouse a deaf world.

—C. S. LEWIS

FOURTEEN

Pinky Promises

Ally

1959. I WAS NINE YEARS OLD. IT WAS THE SUMMER OF wailing. Howls and deep-throated cries could be heard all hours of the night coming from the other side of the river. I'd lie in bed and wake from a dream, having incorporated the screams right into it. I'd be panting, heart racing, and walk out into the halls, into the living room, and peer through the darkness toward Vesey's house where a light would be on. I would imagine her face, contorted. I'd send up a silent prayer, for there was nothing else I could do to comfort her. I was never convinced my prayers did anything at all because the wailing persevered.

The wake and funeral had already taken place, but it seemed family members would still come over day after day, bringing food maybe or sitting with Vesey's mother and father, helping to ease the pain by their presence. I could still remember when it first had happened and I couldn't get the images to leave me—the boats, the men, the way her mouth opened but nothing came out. It was all fresh paint in my mind washing over and over again.

Vesey's little brother, Rufus, was the one who died. The same child who'd been sick in his mother's arms when we'd gone to their house the summer before. But he hadn't died from the sickness. He drowned in that river, the beautiful one that melted beneath my feet as I dangled them into the water, the one that glistened where fish jumped and birds dove down, beaks open to scoop up supper, the one that meant life to me. For Vesey's family, Molasses Creek now meant death too.

The child had not been able to swim; it was as simple as that. It was nobody's fault. He'd simply gotten up early one morning before anyone was awake. They found him on the bank in some cattails with a fishing rod, Vesey's fishing rod, near him.

I'd sit on our dock against my mother's admonitions and watch as the police brought their boats in and searched for evidence, of which there was none. I watched Vesey on the other side, sitting on the bank, arms covering his head between his knees as he rocked and rocked the pain away.

I cried for Vesey. For some reason, the wails I heard from his mother didn't shake my bones nearly as much as seeing Vesey, head down, rocking.

Later, when things had quieted a little and sadness and helplessness had calmed the cries from the other side, I saw him there, getting into his father's johnboat. And he saw me too, Vesey did. We'd not spoken yet, not even waved to one another that summer. But it was time.

Vesey looked directly into my eyes. He didn't smile. He'd

gotten older, taller, his face more defined. Something around his lips had changed, perhaps from not smiling anymore. I itched to make him smile again and almost felt it as a great divine purpose. I would make him smile again.

"Where you goin'?" I hollered over.

He made a quick motion with his hand toward the main waterway. "Out there," he said.

"Can I come?"

It was brazen, and I knew the second it came out of my lips that my mother and father would not approve, finding some vague excuse why I should not go out fishing with this boy. I could almost see the look on Vesey's mother's face if she were to know a white girl was in the same boat as her son. I knew the dangers. I said it again a different way. "Want me to come with you?"

I'd put the ball in his court.

"My folks won't like it," he said truthfully.

I was only nine, mind you, but becoming bolder by the moment. "But do you want me to come, was my question. I won't be any trouble. I'd like to see the waterway."

Vesey didn't look like he had any fight left in him when it came to me and my questions, so without a word, he brought the boat closer, humming alongside my dock. He looked over his shoulder and up to my house. "Yo' folks gone be mad?" It was more of a statement. We both knew the answer.

"Maybe," I said. A look passed between us as I reached my hand out for him to help me into the boat. We were crossing a line that day, all sorts of lines. I'm not sure we understood the depth of it at nine years old, but strangely, it felt good and right to cross those lines. Defiance seemed a natural progression for me, for a good girl with no siblings, living home alone with her parents, always working hard to do whatever they said. I can't speak for Vesey, but I imagine he was ready to defy all the natural laws that existed as well. His brother had died and in anybody's natural world, it wasn't fair, and what could make sense after that?

The wind was in my face as we wound around the creek bends, careful not to make a wake and disturb nature. We looked back at our houses to be sure no one had seen us go. They hadn't. We were free.

I watched the houses that dotted the river, the marsh grass that waved as we passed by. The smells were even better out here with the ocean air mixing with pluff mud, salty spray hitting my hand as it clutched the edge of the boat.

Vesey looked straight ahead as he steered behind me at the motor. When I'd turn around to look at him, he'd stare off to the sides of me, out into the marsh, avoiding my gaze. We drove in silence until we came to the mouth of the waterway. Vesey cut the engine and pointed to a large cluster of oysters that covered an entire bank. It reminded me of a sea in wartime we'd studied in school, with mines dotting the water, waiting for some battleship to pass by and blow it to smithereens.

"My daddy find good oyster up in here." He pointed and swept his hand out over this oyster kingdom of his. "All dat. I help him sometime. Got cut up pretty good . . ." He lifted his forearm out to show me a jagged scar near his elbow and then his legs, a network of tiny, dark, jagged scars. "But he say oyster gettin' ain' for no sissy. I reckon I ain' no sissy."

I stared at his dark legs, taking in the rich color, and then off into the oyster beds. A flock of birds overhead prompted me to say what I'd been feeling all summer. "I'm real sorry 'bout your brother."

The sound of water lapping along the sides of the boat, and Vesey's silence, sent shivers up my back.

I watched his face. Something around his eyes changed, as if he was no longer looking at the oysters and marsh but had drifted to some other place entirely. He never looked at me, just down into the water. I detected a slight nod in his reflection, an acknowledgment of my condolence. It was the one and only time we ever mentioned Vesey's brother dying. Soon after, we vowed to continue our secret trysts with a pinky promise and a spit on the dock. As Vesey put it, being with me was "better than bein' all 'lone." To me, it was more than that.

Secretly, I looked forward to our boat rides with their quiet adventures and our conversations. And I hoped to save Vesey from the grief he had at home by getting out beyond Molasses Creek. I held the belief that in simply getting away, he could leave his troubles behind and start anew. Looking back, I recognize it for what it was. I saw leaving home as some sort of salvation for Vesey—or possibly for myself.

Yes, definitely for myself.

FIFTEEN

Delivering the News

Ally

THERE ARE SOME THINGS ONE CAN ONLY DO IN THE COMpany of others—telling bad news, for instance. Very bad news. News, as in, *Ronnie, I want a divorce.* Those words were delivered in 1995 at a Chinese restaurant in Atlanta just after the pu pu platter but right before the pineapple desert. There were throngs of people around us on a Friday night, sitting at red-cloth-covered tables, happily eating away, chopsticks clumsily hashing around. Even Ronnie wouldn't want to make a scene there, but I made sure to remove his chopsticks first, lest he get any strange ideas. And we didn't have a scene at all. It was very civilized, in fact— until we got back home and Ronnie had had time to digest his pu pu platter, and my news. I don't hold it against him.

There are other things one can only discuss while in a moving vehicle, with something else to look at and distract you from the meat of what is being served to you. My father used to speak to me while driving in the car. Staring straight ahead, not having to look in my eyes at all, he would deliver soliloquies on sticky subjects—the birds and the bees, the proper way to treat people who are different from us, and later, the reasons why a reputable Charleston doctor cannot continue gathering his daughter from the county jail after being collected from a naked love-in protest.

So this evening, not only am I having company over to discuss matters of peddling newspapers on the side of the road with Vesey, we're also planning a little boat trip to the harbor . . . just to keep our eyes busy and take the pressure off. Of me.

My friend Margaret called. How she knew I was in town, I don't know, but she's coming over tonight. I decided I might as well have her here when I talk to Vesey. She can be a sort of buffer between us. Plus, she's outspoken and Vesey and she go way back. I'll look like an angel next to Margaret and maybe he won't take my questioning so hard.

My macaroni is crispy with oozing cheese on the top, bubbling around the sides. I pull it from the oven, carefully so as not to inflame my hip, and set it on top of the stove next to a pan of butter-sautéed green beans with slivers of almonds nestled in. The roast in the Crock-Pot should be simmering in its own juices, ready to fall apart with the slightest provocation. I stir my gravy, smile, and wipe my hands on a little embroidered apron I bought in India decked out in gold thread and turquoise—ah. The doorbell rings. So she's here. After all this time. My stomach does a little flip.

There is no peek of her through the sidelight window, so I imagine her there as she used to be, tall and long-haired, wearing bell-bottomed jeans and a paisley-print top. Oh, that was too long ago. I imagine her face when she sees me now. How do I look at sixty? Am I still the young girl I was? Are my blue eyes just as sparkly and devious? Well, no. They're not. In fact, the only sparkly thing on me is this apron, tied around my waist strategically to cover any bulges below that line. As for devious, well, I might have mellowed just a bit over the years, but don't count me out.

"My stars, if it isn't—" The door opens and my eyebrows rise a bit. This isn't Margaret Finke at all. This is a young girl, a teenager, even, pretty blond curly hair, acne on her chin, possibly fifteen or sixteen. She wears blue jeans and flip-flops with a color-ful knit top. She smiles at me expectantly and holds out her hand. I shake it, looking behind her for Margaret, and say, "Well, hello. How do you do?"

"I'm Graison," says the girl. "Mimi's coming. She's parking the car."

"M-Mimi? Is Margaret your . . ."

"Grandmother."

"Yes! Oh yes, I can see the resemblance now, that beautiful face, strong cheekbones."

"Yeah, Mimi says I'm the one who takes after her. Poor me."

"Poor you, indeed," I say, winking. I'm definitely taking a lik-ing to this child.

"Yeah, she pretty much told me all about you and her going to jail and all. I think it's cool."

"Jail time is not cool," says a steely no-nonsense voice, accompanied by the click-clack of heels along the walkway. Margaret Finke Peabody is dressed to the nines with a big showy pink hat, complete with fresh flowers tucked in, and a formfitting matching pink dress that shows she's kept that figure and then some. Those bosoms got us into a lot of trouble once upon a time. "Though standing up for what you believe in, that's always all right in my book."

"Margaret, my dear." I reach forward and hug her tight. "You look amazing. Simply amazing."

She must have had some work done. She stops and looks in my face. A genuine smile breaks out, pearly white. "So do you, Ally. You really do. Look just the same."

"Well, a little older. But hopefully I'm in a holding pattern."

"Always did love flying. The mile-high club, I believe it was?"

"Margaret. Behave."

"I see you've met my granddaughter, Graison. I knew you wouldn't mind if I brought her along. She's staying with me—well, for the time being. Did you say hello, Graison? Did you use your manners?"

"Of course she did! She's a delightful child. And I've got enough food to feed the Citadel tonight."

"What I wouldn't do to be forty years younger and have a Citadel knob on my arm."

"Oh, Margaret, not in front of Graison."

"I don't mind, Mrs. . . . ."

"Miz. But you can call me Ally."

"Miz Ally, I'm used to my grandmother's mouth. That's how come they sent me to her. Mine gets me in trouble all the time. My parents thought we could relate, I guess."

"Well, amen to that. Relating and such. Listen. Come on in and let's get you a drink. Graison, you like ginger ale? Margaret, I know what you like."

87

"Sorry, Al. Not anymore. Ginger ale's fine for me too. My liver will thank you later."

"Oh, I see." I think of my nice bottle of tempranillo in the kitchen and wonder about the etiquette of opening a bottle of wine when you're the only one drinking it. I know Vesey won't have a sip. Never has had a taste for alcohol or any other mind-altering substances.

"Ginger ale all around, then. It'll go great with my pot roast."

"I'm a vegetarian," says Graison.

"You are? Why, that's wonderful, so much healthier, don't you think? One of these days I'll quit eating meat too. I've got some macaroni for you, dear. You do eat cheese?"

"I'm sort of on a diet."

"Well . . ."

"Don't go to any trouble, Ally. She barely eats a thing. I promise you. Thinks she's heavy. Which you are not, young lady. Men like curves, and don't forget it."

"I hope so."

"I have lots and lots of fresh green beans," I say. "Okay? Now listen, Margaret. You know who else is coming tonight, right?"

A look comes over her face as if she's far away and here at the same time. "I do. Mr. Vesey Washington. Long, long time since I've seen him. Last I knew he was laying that wife of his to rest. Poor, poor man."

"I know it. It's awful. Now, he'll be here any minute and I want you to be nice."

"I'm always nice."

"What I mean is . . . don't mention anything about . . . well, you know." For a moment my stomach drops and I'm wondering if this wasn't a grave mistake. Maybe I shouldn't have invited Margaret over after all. Maybe I should have had a nice quiet talk with Vesey alone instead.

"What?" says Graison. "What can't we mention?"

"Never you mind," says Margaret, wrapping her arm around her granddaughter's shoulders. She pushes her toward the screen door.

"Why don't you all go out and enjoy the fresh air on the dock," I tell them. "I'll join you in just a minute. Got to stir my gravy."

I hold the screen door open, the breeze gracing my face like a cool spirit while I watch the two maneuvering arm in arm across the lawn. Margaret is awkward in her high-heeled shoes on grass. She turns back to me. "Speak of the devil. Here he is now, arriving in style on the water," she says. "Just like a savior might."

"I said be nice."

"Relax, Al," says Margaret. "We're Southern, and we all go way back. Back to another time when all that was expected of us was to be proper and nice. If I know anything, it's how to be proper. And nice. Just ask Graison."

"She could charm a snake," says her granddaughter. "She's giving me lessons."

"That's my girl. Now move on over. I want Mr. Washington to get a nice. Long. Look at me after all these years."

SIXTEEN

Poodle Skirts and Aprons

Ally

IMAGINE, MARGARET FINKE IN MY HOUSE AFTER ALL these years. I met her at her ten-year-old birthday party in 1960. Goodness, has it been fifty years already? I remember her hair was pulled up in a white ribbon and she had neat bobby socks and a poodle skirt bigger than Texas. She had just moved to Charleston from Memphis, and not knowing a soul, her mama had invited every girl in the fourth grade, which is why I hadn't actually met her until I got to her house. And what a house it was.

The Finkes had money. It was clear by the servants they had offering us food on little serving trays, by the size of her house that overlooked the ocean on Isle of Palms. The house had five bedrooms and there were only two kids in the family. Her father was a businessman, importing Chinese silks and tapestries, so her house looked like an exotic place somewhere far off. Staring at all those colors, feeling the silks in my fingers, I longed to go to where these things were made. I longed to be exotic myself. But

I was only a ten-year-old girl with a ponytail and shabby poodle skirt with the tail that kept coming unglued at the edges.

"How do you do?" I said, curtseying at my mother's request as we stood there at the big front doors. Margaret seemed very popular for being so unknown, girls giggling and running up and down the stairs. I figured having money and being so pretty and blond like she was, was all one needed to make lots of friends. I envied her at that moment.

"Thank you for coming," Margaret said, smiling genuinely at me. "Neat poodle skirt." She was a liar, and I knew I liked her that instant. She grabbed my hand and tugged me upstairs to go look at her new room.

I remember accepting food at that party from a black woman holding tea sandwiches on a silver tray. She was wearing a black dress with a white apron and I thought she looked a little familiar. I imagined Vesey's mother working in a home like this. I was embarrassed as I took the food from her, wondering, *What must she think about us white folks? Does she think we're all this rich? Does she think we're all so different from her?* I knew my answer, of course. In that house full of black servants, I decided to guard my friendship with Vesey from Margaret and the other girls in fourth grade. I knew not to speak of it, lest something unpleasant be said. I decided in that very house on that very day that Vesey Washington was going to be my very own secret. He felt more special then, pressing upon my heart. I never wanted him to think of me the way these servants surely thought of me and Margaret. *I'm different*, I thought. Vesey knew that. There was no distance between us. At least, that's what I told myself.

SEVENTEEN

Co-Cola Bottle in the Sun

Vesey

I REMEMBER THE FIRST TIME I SEEN HER LIKE IT WAS yesterday. I was just a boy.

My father was an oysterman, shrimper. Hardworking man. He used to take that old johnboat down over past the river bend to the waterway, and then on out to the oysters. Me? I pestered him to use that boat whenever he weren't in it, which meant, 'less I was off oystering with Daddy, I was on my own, fishing line in the creek out back. I knew the birds, the same ospreys that kept their nests and had little'uns every year. I knew the fiddler crabs at low tide, how they ran all this way and that. I knew the tides like I knew my own heartbeat. Better, still. So when I seen this girl on the other side of the creek—my very own river—I knew I had to know her too. It was only natural. She was running through my veins.

It was a scorcher that day, but it was early yet. I put my line with a live cricket down in the water and watched that house over yonder, how big it seemed from my side of the river, how the dock would stretch out, asking me to hop on over. Begging, even.

I seen her daddy out there many a time, though I was barely eight year old. Knew not to mess with white folk. Knew it well. Had it bred into me by my father, from his father, and on back to Africa from whence we all came. Knew not to mess with white men—especially not to look them in the eyes. But the girl—she was my age. She was small and harmless, as I knew myself to be. She was sitting with her feet dangled down in the water, the same water that lapped up on my side. We shared that water between us, like blood, or so I thought.

Early one morning I took Daddy's johnboat out in the creek and dared to get closer. Her skin glowed in the sunlight like a shiny penny. I crept near, letting the water lap me up, and there I was, standing in my boat just feet away from her, and I could almost see the light in her eyes as she grinned.

"Hey!" she said. "I saw you last summer. You waved. Do you remember?"

I did remember, too, but the wind stole my voice. Couldn't speak a word.

"You like to fish?" she asked.

I nodded. Gulped. With her white skin, she looked and even sounded different, strange. Then a noise from behind liked to put the fear of the devil in me. Near 'bout fell out the boat.

"Veees-ssae! Get yo' fool-hide back on over here!"

It was Mama, and she ain't sounded angry, not exactly. I could tell by the pitch of her voice—she was something closer to fearing for life.

I told myself we weren't doing nothin' wrong, but couple years into knowing Miss Ally, my mama found out about us two—how we'd sneak off in the boat, how we'd fish and laugh and pass the time in secret. She found out because I weren't too smart at ten year old and seemed to be getting dumber every day. I actually told myself I was invisible when I'd push off from the bank into the black molasses. That no one could see me. I was like that ghost pirate off the coast of Carolina. What's his name? Blackbeard. I was a ghost and the water was my turf, my place in the world. Where I belonged.

Dad-an-howdy, you ought to seen my hide after Mama got aholt of me. I couldn't sit for a week and I don't think that's stretching it none. See, Miss Ally and me was coming back from one of our trips on the water. We'd gone to sit in the breezes over down by the nice big oysters, when all a sudden my father comes on by in a boat with my uncle Percival. I told Miss Ally to duck when I seen Daddy's eyes grow big and white, and his mouth drop open. Why'd I tell her to hide? I don't know. It was a mistake though, and Daddy and Uncle Percival beat me home. They told my mama I was out in our boat with a white girl, and let me tell you, I ain' never heard the things I heard, ain' never felt the whoopin' I felt that day. Saddest part was, I weren't so much hurt on the body but in the heart. How could I get in so much trouble just for being with a girl I considered a friend?

A friend. That's what Miss Ally was to me, but nobody could understand that, could they? We'd talk about fishing and the water and such, but we'd also talk about the other things. Like the clouds up in the sky and how the angels get to sit right up on there, nice and fluffy. And we'd tell each other our dreams. I wanted to be a doctor like Ally's father, Doc Green. Wanted it so much I could see it when I closed my eyes. I wanted to help people. I wanted folks to look at me when I come in the door with a thank-God-you-here look like Mama give Doc Green. Miss Ally would say things like she ain't want to marry and settle down, but she ain't known what she did want to do. Maybe go off to Hollywood and be a star. It sounded silly to me but I never told her that. I believed she could do it if she tried. She was pretty enough. Smart enough too.

Miss Ally told me 'bout this one time her white friends was talking and one of 'em says, "I think it would be the worst thing in the world to be colored. Don't you?" Humph. Imagine that? What did she know about being it anyway? Worst thing in the world.

Miss Ally tells me this while I'm laid back feeling the sun on my face, the boat rocking all this way and that. I sit up right slow and just looked at her. I reckon I'd never thought of it that way—that being colored was the worse thing there was in the world. I knew it then, because it all made sense when Miss Ally looked at me, studying me. "I don't agree with them though," she told me. But I knew she was thinking hard on it like I was. Here she was, a young girl in a boat with the pret' near worse thing in the world.

I still at that age could not understand the differences between us. I don't claim to be the smartest person out there, but dad-howdy, I was a God-loving body just like any white folk. I was.

Least, I thought I was till Mama laid that whooping on me and told me I had no business being with a white girl. Who did I think I was and did I think I was better than everybody else and don't I know she a cracker and we don't mess with crackers lest we want trouble and Mama didn't want no trouble. She done had all the trouble she needed so far. What she left me that day was this: not one more sneaky thing out of me with that white girl or she'd ship me off to go live with my cousins in that one-room house on John's Island with the meanest man I ever seen, my uncle Percival. There'd be no schooling for me, just hard work in the fields day and night.

I tell you, that did it for me for a good long while. It did. It was hard, but I never had any contact with Ally till she started leaving me notes in an old Co-Cola bottle at the end of her dock. I seen it odd-like shining in the noonday sun and come close enough to snatch it and take a better look. By that time I was pushing thirteen and struggling not to get into fights at school. The last thing on my mind was white girls. Until I read those first words I knew were meant for me: *I've missed you. Where have you been? Meet me tonight. I have something important to tell you.*

Well, with the soul of a thirteen-year-old boy pent up in my body, how in creation could I ever resist an invitation like that?

EIGHTEEN

The Radio

Ally
1963

"You came."

"Of course I came."

Silence. Water rippling. "I haven't seen you since . . . It's been a few years." The moonlight shimmered on the black glassy creek. Marsh grass tickled my legs. I could barely see the lights on at home. My parents were already asleep. "I could hear her whipping you that night," I told him. "It was all I could do, listening to it. I cried and cried. Put a pillow over my head."

"Weren't so bad." His looks had changed. Even in the faint light of the moon, I could see he was almost a man now, and his voice was lower. A lot lower. It sent chills down my spine, and I found myself unable to look him in the eyes.

"You said you got something you wanted to say," he prompted.

"Yes, I do . . . I'm sorry."

"Sorry for what?"

"Sorry . . . that we're so different. Sorry that everybody thinks a colored and a white person should go their separate ways. Sorry about what happened to you that night you got caught . . . with me. I think if people just took the time to know—"

"Ally, stop."

"No, really—"

"I said stop." His voice was barely a growl. He clenched his fists and looked around toward his house to make sure no one was watching. Then he whispered, "Things have changed, Ally. It ain't the same. We ain't kids no more."

"What does that mean?"

"It means we cain't see each other." The words hung there in the air between us and then like mist they vanished, taking my breath along with them.

"But why, Vesey? I mean, I don't want you to get in trouble anymore, I don't."

"You cain't know what I go through. You cain't know. I walk to the store and white folk yell at me, call me nigga. I try to go to school, mind my own business, and white kids knock down my books. I see signs that won't let me drink the water, won't let me come into a white restaurant. I'm colored, Ally, and I ain't nothing to do about it. I cain't do nothing. You cain't do nothing."

If I was honest right then, if I was really honest, I knew what he was saying was true because I'd seen it. Hadn't I? Different people, different circumstances, but I'd seen it—people being treated differently, wrongly, because of the color of their skin. And what had I done? Had I spoken up? Had I? The truth pressed my shoulders down.

"I just . . . I wanted to say I'm sorry, that's all," I told him. "And

I hope . . . I hope we can still be friends. I've missed you, you know. I miss going out in the boat and just being with somebody I don't have to impress. We could just sit there and not say anything at all, not *have* to say anything, and nowadays I have to be all proper and perfect and ladylike, and, well, I just miss the way we used to be."

"We used to be kids," said Vesey.

I reached back behind the marsh grass and pulled out a shiny black radio. I turned the knob and a small sound pierced the night air. Then I turned it just a hair louder. It was the Beatles. Vesey stared at the radio.

"Where'd you get that?" he asked, suspicious.

"I didn't steal it, if that's what you're implying. I got it for my thirteenth birthday. It was yesterday, you know?"

"Yeah. I know. That's a nice radio."

"So do you want to dance or what?" I asked him. It was the best thing I'd said in a long time. It made me feel right with the world.

There was nothing but stone and concern in Vesey's face at first, but when Stevie Wonder's "Fingertips" came on, he started bobbing his head a little. Then a smile broke out. A full-out grin. Then something like courage rolled onto his broad shoulders, and he put his hand out to me.

I remember the way his warm hand felt in mine. Strong and capable. Music drifted between us, around us, and up into the cool night air. Lights glittered on the black water, and I stole furtive glances at the sculpture of his cheeks as the marsh grass swirled around us.

Hands down, that moonlight dance with Vesey when we were thirteen years old was the best dance I've had in sixty years.

The worst dance was not long after that, when Margaret

insisted I make Vesey appear. She said she was losing patience with me, and if I didn't produce him soon, she'd have no choice but to tell her parents or our friends at school. So I did produce him. I lured him back to the spot on the riverbank, brought my radio, and when we started shagging, Margaret stepped out from behind a tree.

"Well, well, well," she said. "I don't believe you've introduced me to your friend."

She held her hand out to a rock-still Vesey. He looked at me, eyes wide. "This is my friend Margaret," I told him. He seemed too stunned and afraid to shake her hand, and I was Judas.

I'd betrayed our friendship. I'd betrayed his trust.

NINETEEN

Supper with Old Friends

Mount Pleasant
Ally

"I'VE ALWAYS FELT DRAWN TO VESEY," SAYS MARGARET, watching him wave from the boat. "Drawn to his . . . his, what is that, Ally? Animal magnetism?"

"Forbidden fruit," I say.

"No," says Margaret. "Yes? No. Well, maybe so." Vesey ties his rope and steps up on firmer ground. "Vesey Washington, would you look at you? Looking good, old friend! Looking fine."

"Miss Margaret." Vesey tips his hat. "Been a long time, ain't it? Decades."

"Don't you dare count how many, neither."

"Miss Ally?" He turns to me. "Right nice to have me over. Ain't every day a man gets an invitation for supper . . . with old friends."

"Vesey, you are a sight for sore eyes! I just can't get over . . . I declare, Ally, he hasn't aged a wink! And for us, we have to work so hard to look this good."

Vesey is uncomfortable with this talk. Always has been a

little uneasy with Margaret's forceful nature. I feel protective of him and take him by the arm. "You are my guests for the evening, so I want you to relax, have some ginger ale or sweet tea, something cool to drink. We've got pot roast, you know. I hope you brought your appetite."

"And homemade gravy?" asks Vesey.

"Even homemade macaroni and cheese."

"Lawd, I died and gone to heaven." A look flashes between us, and I plead with my eyes, then mouth the words, "I'm sorry. About the whole heaven thing."

"Not at all, Miss Ally. Not at all. And who is this?" Vesey puts out his hand for Graison, who is standing quietly in Margaret's shadow, taking us all in.

"This is my granddaughter, Graison. Say hello, Graison."

"Hello, Graison," she says.

"Graison is staying with me . . . for a while."

"That's nice," says Vesey.

"I'm preggers," says Graison, taking his hand and shaking it firmly. My eyebrows rise.

"Graison!" says Margaret.

"Well, it's true. They'll know about it soon enough. Not like you can hide it forever. Mr. Washington, I'm staying here with my grandmother until the baby is born. Then I'll be headed back home to Memphis. Back to school and all, I guess."

None of us knows what to say. The child is what, sixteen? A child having a child. Something aches inside of me and I brush it off. "Alrighty then, how about we go on in and eat some supper? I'd like to take a little boat ride before the sun goes down. If you feel up to it, Graison."

"Oh, I'll be fine."

"That okay with you, Vesey? Dinner and a boat ride?"

He nods. "Don't have to ask me twice. Here, let me lead the way."

"As you can see, I have a long ways to go," I say, pointing to the kitchen behind me. We never did have a proper dining room, just a screened-in patio out the back of the house with a concrete floor and aged wood walls. The table is new to the patio, teak, with fruits and little details carved into the legs. "Got this table in Hawaii nearly twenty years ago," I say, patting the wood. "It's turned a little, sitting in the warehouse."

"I think it's lovely out here," says Margaret, stretching back in her chair and crossing her legs. "Love how you can sit here and feel the breeze and watch the water dance." She looks over at Vesey. "You still live across the river there?"

"Sure do."

"How quaint. To still be this close, after all these years."

"Vesey was kind enough to look after Daddy over the past—"

My throat catches and I grab my glass of tea. After a sip I say, "Would anyone like some more macaroni?"

"Don't mind if I do," says Vesey, holding out his plate. I offer some to Graison.

"Not for me," she says. "I'm stuffed." Margaret looks at her granddaughter and at this moment I can see the resemblance, somewhere in the eyes and the forehead. Margaret seems concerned she's not getting enough food for two.

"Graison, have you thought about what you're going to do

once the child is born?" I hear the words come out of my mouth with such ease and familiarity; I don't know what's come over me. Obviously I've ruffled Margaret. She grabs her glass and swigs her ginger ale.

"I'm going to adopt, I guess. We're working with a lady to find a good family."

She says it so matter-of-fact, she might as well be selling a used car on craigslist. "I see. Well, you do have quite a life ahead of you, high school, college—"

"Boys," says Margaret. "It's the boys that got her in this mess."

"Mimi!"

"Well, it is."

"Miss Ally?" Vesey interrupts. "Looks like we got another twenty minutes or so before the sun sets. How 'bout I help you clear the table? That was some good food. Ain't et that well in many a year." He smiles big and jovial.

"That would be nice," I say. "Margaret, Graison, use the little girl's room if you need to. You sure you're up for a boat ride? Mister Vesey, here, can show you the most amazing views and the best places for oyster harvesting. I promise you. You're in for a real treat."

"How 'bout we bring that old radio," says Margaret, "and go shagging in the moonlight like we used to . . . back in the day."

The thought of it takes me back, fully there, and I can almost feel the damp ground beneath my feet, the way Vesey's hand felt in mine, the music fading into the night. My heart skips and I smile at Vesey. I can see it in his eyes. He remembers too.

TWENTY

You've Really Got a Hold
on Me

Ally

1964 WAS A LONG, HOT, HUMID SUMMER. HOTTER THAN
the ones before. I would lie there in damp sheets, the window
open, listening to sounds of night—the frogs and owls, the grass-
hoppers. Every now and then a noise would ripple up from the
water as if a large fish had jumped for freedom.

It sounded like my heart stirring.

I was beginning to think about boys. All the time. I was fourteen years old and pretty much any boy made my heart race, the
way their hands were strong and bigger than mine, the way they
walked and how their shoulders were wide. Their muscles. My
goodness, I was a mess of hormones and Mama didn't know what
to do with me. Not having any siblings at home to play or fight
with, I'd skulk off alone in my room or on the dock with my sketchbook and draw the male figure in my mind's eye. This worried

Mama, and I'd hide the book just so she wouldn't have to get all bothered about it. I never did put a face on those pictures I drew, those strong chests and rippling backs and arms. I didn't put the face on it because it could only be one person: Vesey Washington.

That summer, a strange awkwardness had grown up between Vesey and me. Having Margaret privy to us, I finally understood the taboo of our relationship, harmless as it was in my own eyes. In the South, it didn't matter how things really were; it mattered what things *looked* like. The civil rights movement was well under way and businesses and restaurants had been so-called desegregated, but while the signs on the windows no longer read *Whites Only* or *No Coloreds Allowed*, reality was another matter altogether.

I knew Vesey's life was difficult. I knew it was all because of the color of his skin. Well, that and his mama. I could sense the unrest in whites and blacks alike as I'd walk down King Street or go into a diner. South Carolina had never been a state to simply abide by what the rest of the country was doing or what its federal government was telling it to do. It prided itself in being autonomous in some ways. The people of our town did things in a way they saw fit. Even though John F. Kennedy was dead, the civil rights acts had passed, and protesters were jailed in Birmingham, New York, Rock Hill, and elsewhere, Charleston was a little different story. There were things I saw—shoving, slurs, private conversations in beauty parlors—that never got reported on the evening news or in the paper. Folks didn't just wake up one day and decide their feelings had changed toward blacks, or toward whites, for that matter. There were years and years of deep-rooted resentment built up on both sides.

Being a white girl, I was on one side and Vesey on the other, and the river of justice flowed right there between us, evading us, current taking it on by.

It was still socially frowned upon for us to be seen together, but I would lie in bed and think about him, my hormones racing. I would imagine what it would be like to kiss his full lips. I couldn't help it. I'd never kissed a boy, though I'd been tempted to kiss good-looking Murphy Halsey at the eighth-grade dance. My girlfriends had dared me to, but I wasn't about to go there. Things weren't like they are today. A girl with loose lips brought true shame to her family, and I wasn't about to be someone who brought shame to my mother and father. They'd worked hard to raise me right. And except for the lying about being with Vesey every now and again, it was almost working. Almost.

"I think we should go to Woolworth's tomorrow," I told him one evening as the moon was setting low.

"Why?" asked Vesey, his voice quiet beside me. I could feel the heat from his arm.

"I think we should go in there and sit at the lunch counter. Together." I could picture Margaret's horror at my sitting side by side with Vesey in public.

"Must be crazy," he murmured.

"I'm serious, Vesey."

"No, you ain't, Ally. You talkin' like a fool." His words were harsh and I wasn't used to it. Normally he was so mild-mannered.

"I'm not a fool! I'm not!"

"After everythin' happenin', what with protesters in the streets and the arrests over at the *News and Courier*—"

"Maybe you like being the one who always has people looking

down on you. Maybe you don't want anyone to stand up for you. Maybe you want to suffer your whole life all by yourself and then die a victim, die—"

"Would you listen to yourself?" Vesey was holding on to my arms now, tight. I stopped talking, tears streaming, and looked up at him. There was something in his eyes, a glimmer from the moonlight. I'd never seen this look before, one of anger and confusion—one of true feelings for me, I thought.

Smokey Robinson and the Miracles came on the radio singing "You've Really Got a Hold on Me," and I began to feel the music inside. I began to sway. This song was playing just for us, I knew it. He did too. So I did it then. I stood up on my tiptoes and, with my eyes fully open, touched the edges of his lips with mine. I held them there like soft butterfly wings for a long second, then I pressed up on my toes farther. I pushed myself into him. He didn't back away. He just stood there, motionless, his hands still gripping my arms with the Miracles singing around us. The heat going through us was hotter than anything I'd ever felt before, and when I think back on it now, it makes me go weak in the knees. That kiss was so packed full of double meaning and passion and taboo that I could have swam right into Vesey that second and disappeared forever.

But what we heard next sent the fear of God through my chest like lightning. Vesey's mother had snuck up on the bank behind me, and before my eyes, she wrenched her son off the ground and ripped him away from me. I'd dreamed all summer of kissing those lips and there we were, caught, a Montague and Capulet. The music was still playing as he disappeared from sight, but I could barely hear it over my sobs.

I lay in bed that night, crying my eyes out silently as I could hear Vesey getting whipped on his side of the river, taking the blame for something I had initiated and had, in my heart, been planning since the day I met him. Hadn't I, really? Hadn't I always known it would happen? I didn't mean him any harm, but how could I have been so selfish? How could I have allowed myself to cross that forbidden line?

We were done. It was the death of our friendship. I didn't dare see Vesey anymore, and he didn't try to see me either. I'd been careless, and now my closest friend in life was gone. In the days after, I'd take Daddy's boat out on the water and stare over toward Vesey's house, hoping to see him, to see if he was all right, but he was never out. Once, his mama was hoeing in her garden, and she shot me the evilest look I'd ever witnessed. My stomach began to hurt after that something awful, and it didn't let up until school started. I wondered if she'd hexed me.

The window shades on Vesey's house remained pulled shut. I imagined he'd been shipped off to John's Island to live with his mean uncle Percival. I felt responsible for Vesey's demise. He'd have to work hard the rest of his life with no schooling, no education, no possible way of getting ahead and making something of himself—all because I couldn't get him out of my mind.

I never did understand how his mother knew we were there, but deep in the pit of me, I wondered—or rather feared—that Margaret had somehow tipped her off. That somehow she'd known Vesey really had a hold on me.

TWENTY-ONE

On Education and Freedom

Mount Pleasant
Ally

THE BOAT IS HUMMING BENEATH US, THE WATER rippling up quietly on the sides. Vesey is silent, hands on the wheel. We're in Daddy's cruiser, a sixteen-foot Boston Whaler. It's a little bigger, more comfortable than Vesey's skiff.

"Isn't it beautiful tonight?" I say. I can feel that pot roast dancing in my belly. I'm nervous, gearing up for the big talk. "I do love the breeze on my face, the smell of that pluff mud. Don't you, Margaret? It's the closest thing to heaven for me."

I let the word *heaven* prick our ears, then I take another deep breath. "Vesey, I was out today . . . went over to that new Whole Foods store to buy supper, and you know, I declare, I thought I saw you standing on the corner selling newspapers! Isn't that funny?" A nervous laugh escapes my chest. "Was that you? That wasn't you, was it? It couldn't be."

"It was," he says, steering the boat to the left a little as we pass the oyster beds and head out toward the inlet.

"But you . . . I mean, really? How long have you been doing that?"

"Oh, 'bout six year now."

"Six years!" I grab at my chest. I think of all the places I've been in six years. All the living I've done, the sights I've seen. I think of the poor peddlers begging on the streets. I think of Vesey standing under that umbrella for six whole years.

"But why do you do it?" I ask quietly.

"Must be out of his mind," says Margaret. "I could never set out on the street corner like that and tote all those magazines, all those newspapers, every day in the heat, the rain . . ."

I shoot Margaret a look that could light the moon.

Vesey is calm and smiles a little. He seems to be taking great pleasure in my discomfort. "Sho' is a pretty sunset tonight, ain't it?" he says.

The sky is fire red on the horizon with purples and pinks shooting up and out. The color reflects on his dark skin.

"Vesey, I don't mean to pry," I say, "but I thought you, you know, lived off your land and owned your house outright and . . . Well, what I mean to say is—"

"What she means to say is why in the world would you want to stand there out in the weather like some paperboy?"

"Margaret!" I squeal.

"Mimi, that was rude," says Graison. "Maybe he likes it out there. Maybe he likes selling newspapers."

"I do like newspapers," says Vesey. "Miss Graison, you see that over yonder? That's the old lighthouse. Ain't it purdy? Back in the day it used to keep boats and sailors from crashing to their deaths on these Charleston beaches. Mighty important job, don't you think?"

"Vesey, please. I don't mean any harm," I say. "I just want to know . . . if I can help you in any way. I mean, if you're hurting for money or—"

"Oh, Miss Ally, now. Listen." Vesey lowers the throttle and the boat slows down to a crawl. The engine is quiet and his voice hits me loud and hard.

"My grandfather couldn't read," he says, eyes firm, held on me. "His father, my great-grandfather, couldn't read neither. He was born a slave over to White Point plantation on up in Georgetown. My mother and father couldn't read, and they suffered their whole lives because of it," he says, waving his hands. "But me? I learned to read. Even when I was at Uncle Percival's farm, I got me some books, and I hid 'em, and I read 'em. The Bible, mostly. Weren't much, but I knew . . . somehow I knew that I could make myself a better life if I could only master those books and newspapers. It's how I learnt about Martin Luther King Jr. It's how I knew what was happenin' in Birmingham and Greenville. It's how I realized I was part of somethin' bigger than me and my own troubles. Readin' was how I survived, Miss Ally. And my son gone on over and fought in a war just so people like me could go on being free and learnin' to read."

I turn to look at snails hanging high on tips of marsh grass, but he goes on.

"The way I figure, if sharin' newspapers and magazines with the world on that street corner can help somebody the way it done helped me, well then, almighty, I'm gonna sell those things. You hear? Don't care what I look like doing it. Education, Miss Ally. Freedom. That's what I'm out there peddlin', and I'm right proud to be doing it. Best thing I ever done."

The whole boat is silent as Vesey revs up the engine once

more. Margaret and Graison are stunned still. Tears burn my eyes as I think of this man, this good, principled man I've just offended, who had to grow up on his uncle's farm, struggling for books, all because of me. I'm desperate to be a snail on that blade of grass, small and unseen.

I cannot speak for the longest time, but when the sun dips down below the horizon, and the air chills another degree or two, I manage to say, "I think it's time to call it a night. Would you please take us on home, Vesey? I . . . I'm awfully tired now. Suddenly, awfully tired."

Secretly, I'm wishing I was far away. I itch to be somewhere on the other side of the world.

Part Three

Before I was humiliated I was like a stone that lies deep in mud, and he who is mighty came and in his compassion raised me up and exalted me very high and placed me on top of the wall.

—SAINT PATRICK

TWENTY-TWO
Maharajgunj Road

Kathmandu, Nepal
Sunila

THERE ARE STATUES OF ELEPHANTS IN A PLACE CALLED the Garden of Dreams. Through the gate I can see them, a pair, each with mother and child. I watch as the rain comes down and feel as if I have been here before. I have seen this very garden in my dreams with the pool and the symmetry and the elephants. I did not know it existed, yet here it is in front of me. Everything is gray and wet, and as the rain hits my face, it masks my tears. Oh, how I long to enter the gates of the Garden of Dreams, but it is locked, and I must keep going. I feel as if I am walking backward in time. It is a treacherous journey.

I have grown so tired, and I'm lost now. Every storefront looks alike. Water rolls down my face with the blowing rain and my stomach is empty. But I will not cry. I will keep going. I look in a store window for life and light and move closer. The shop owner sees me and gives me a look, daring me to come in. I move on and hope for a friendlier face in the next window.

117

There is a woman sitting at a desk sewing sequins onto a long piece of pink silk. I close my umbrella and open the door, hoping she will not scream for me to leave. I know I look unclean. I will try to hold my head up and act as if I am of caste. "Namaste," I say.

My shoes are soaked and a puddle of water forms below me on the tile floor. She looks down at it, then up at me. I cannot hide my shame. "What are you doing? Filthy girl, get out!" She stops sewing and stands, throwing up her hands.

"Please," I say.

"Can you hear? Are you so stupid? I have no food!" she tells me, holding the needle in the air. "I have no money. Why don't you beg elsewhere?"

I shake my head, then lower it. I stare at the puddle and say, "I need only to find Maharajgunj Road."

"What? Why?"

I think of telling her. I think of telling her that I have to get to the US Embassy to meet a man who may not even still be alive, but the words do not come out.

She stops yelling for a moment and then says, "You are nearly there." She points with her head. "Go to Lazinpat Road. It is at the gas station. Keep following it north. It will turn into Maharajgunj."

Turn right or turn left? I wonder. She sees the confusion on my face.

"It will *become* Maharajgunj, stupid girl. Just stay on that road. Now go."

I nod and thank her and back out of the store, wishing I had something to mop up the mess that I left on the woman's floor. I watch as she goes to get cardamom to cleanse the place on the floor where I stood and defiled it.

As the rain hits my umbrella again and wind whips my sari around my wet legs, I remember the cruel man. I remember his violence. I feel the Book of the Gods pressed to my chest. I think to myself, *Keep going, Sunila. You are getting closer. You're almost there. I can feel it.*

TWENTY-THREE

Gods in the Garden

Mount Pleasant
Ally

I CAN FEEL KAT WALKING ACROSS MY LEGS. HE'S READY to go out or get food or whatever it is cats do. I groan and roll over. The memories of last night are still fresh, the pot roast, the macaroni, Margaret and Graison, the boat ride. My shame. How can Vesey always sound so perfectly right every time he says something? I mean, here he is on the side of the road in fatigues, and I'm the one who feels rotten and ignorant. He makes everything seem so dignified and worthy. Which leaves me on the other side of that coin.

I don't care to see him today. I think I'll go and see about trying to walk that bridge. Maybe get some exercise and do my own thing. I don't need him.

Daddy. Hey, how about that? It took me a few seconds before I remembered he was gone. I was distracted. Maybe to heal, one needs distractions. Plenty of them.

Of course, I already knew that, didn't I? I've been distracting myself for decades.

A pain, deep and low, shoots through me, and I clutch my stomach until it's properly deadened. Coffee. I need coffee. I roll out of bed, thankful that my hip is even better today, and then head for the kitchen. In a drawer beneath the coffeemaker, I find Daddy's notes and relive them again. I shouldn't, but I do. I stop when I see the one he wrote about her.

Ally, sweetness, I've seen her. She's here.

Time for you to rest now.

Dad

My knees go weak and I hold myself up on the counter. She's there. In heaven. With Dad.

But no she's not, because these notes are phony. Why would Daddy say something like this to me? So I would give up? So I would stop looking for my child . . .

So you can get on with your life, Ally. It's time for you to move on. I can almost hear him now.

My chest feels like it's opening up, a raw, bloody wound. I open my mouth and let out a perfectly silent scream. Then I close it, compose myself, and slowly walk to a chair by the table. I hug my knees and feel the pinch in my hip.

I've been stuffing things down for so long, I barely know what it feels to be normal.

With my coffee I go outside and look at the mess of statues littering the yard. A stone garden. A healing garden. That's what I'll have here. With plants and flowers and places to meditate. I look over to Vesey's house without thinking, and it's as if I've conjured him up—there he is on the water, gliding toward me. How does he do that?

"Mornin'," he hollers, tipping his fishing hat.

I smooth my hair and smile despite myself. I take a hot sip of coffee. "Come back for more punishment?" I say.

"Maybe just more pot roast if you got it."

"For breakfast? You men. You're all alike."

He steps up on the dock then makes his way toward me. "Figured we don't move these statues today, your grass is gonna start growing up all wrong. Doc Green wouldn't 'a liked that. Thought I'd go 'head and fix it now."

"That's awfully kind of you. How 'bout that pot roast first? Give you some energy?"

"Naw, man needs to work on an empty stomach. Helps him work harder. Keeps reward on his mind."

"Okay. Whatever you say. It's your back."

We walk around the yard for a while, me trying desperately to figure out where to put everything and him hoping to not move anything twice. At the end of it all, the shoving, the panting, the ordering around and changing of minds, I've had my second cup of coffee and Vesey is sweating, drinking water without breathing or stopping. He wipes his face and surveys his work.

"So who all you got here?" he asks, leaning up against the house.

"Well, the fountain, here, has cherubs, angels."

"I do know that much, Miss Ally. What about him over there?"

"Him? Oh, that's Poseidon, Greek god of the sea. And next to him is Aphrodite, the goddess of beauty. Also Greek."

"And this one with all the arms?"

"That's Durga, Goddess Mother in Hindu."

"She seems scary to me."

"Scary, why?"

"A woman with that many arms is bound to be trouble. So what about this one?"

I walk over and run my hands over the smooth white stone. "This one is Buddha. You're supposed to rub his belly for good luck. Here. You wanna rub it?"

Vesey backs up, hands raised. "Not really my thing," he says. "I don't need luck. 'Specially not from some fat man." Then he's quiet, thinking.

"What? What is it?" I ask.

"Oh, nothin'. None of my business."

"Come on, Vesey, you know I have no boundaries when it comes to other people's business." We laugh at this sad truth and finally he opens his mouth to speak.

"Well, I cain't help but notice how you got all these gods everywhere. You got a god for this and a god for that. And what's that, an elephant?"

"Ganesha, god of knowledge and reflection."

"I see. Well, I'm just wondering, now, out loud really, does it do you any good? I mean, do these folks give you any peace, these pieces of stone?"

I stare into his big brown eyes, unable to move. Peace. Peaceful. I haven't felt that way in, well, in forever. "There was a place once," I tell him, my mind drifting far away and my gaze out over Spanish moss hanging from trees. "There was a very special garden with statues of gods and elephants. The Garden of Dreams, it was called. It's the last time I was happy. It's the last time I—"

"Now, now," says Vesey, putting an arm around me. "I ain't meant to be pushy. I know how you feel. I've lost . . . Well, I've lost too. But listen, honest truth, you ever decide it's too crowded over here with all these statues, you come on over to my side of the river. It's simpler over there. See that? See right yonder?" He points toward his house.

"What? What am I supposed to be looking at?"

"See that clothesline? Looks like a . . . What does it look like from here?"

"A cross?" I say.

"It sure do."

"You're telling me you worship a clothesline, Vesey Washington?"

He smiles and sips his water again. "Somethin' like that, Miss Ally. Somethin' like that."

I look around at my stone garden and think of what it will look like when I get some flowers planted, maybe a walkway. It will feel peaceful then. It will. "To each his own, Vesey. Now, how 'bout we get you that pot roast? You've worked harder than a, than a—"

"A slave?" says Vesey.

"I wasn't going to say that, Vesey, and you know it. Now, what am I going to do with you?"

"Feed me, I reckon." As we step in the doorway, I glance at the clothesline across the river, and for half a second a crow roosts on it. Then it seems to notice my gaze and flies off into the clouds. Flies away in a blur as if I'd only imagined it.

TWENTY-FOUR

Thieves

Kathmandu, Nepal
Sunila

I AM IMAGINING THINGS, A BOWL OF RICE AND RED lentils. The pigeons are scattered like white ashes in Durbar Square now that the rain has stopped. They are hoping to find food. As am I. The pigeons scavenge while the monkeys roost like kings on their temple. I keep my umbrella above me. It helps to hide my face. I am soaked through, my clothes, my spirit. I see a cow lying on the sidewalk, hoping for sunshine to dry its coat. The cows, the pigeons, the monkeys . . . they have a better life than me and Amaa and Buba. They need not work for their food. They need not always slave away in dust. They are not shunned by those high-caste people who pass by in silk saris and jewels and fancy cars.

I continue to walk for miles, stumbling, struggling for breath.

I can see a long compound across the street. If I were not so tired and hungry, my blood would stir at the sight. Instead, my stomach growls and reminds me I am nothing. Who am I to think

I am anything special? Who am I to think I can possibly escape my fate? They may spit on me if I try to set foot inside. Perhaps I should not have come. I should not have come! I turn and clench my fists around the umbrella. I feel the jagged edge of the book in my sore ribs and remember the faces, remember the gods, the rivers, the pictures. I feel calm again and know I have not come all this way for nothing. For Amaa said it was so. She said I must come here.

"The cruel man is dead, Amaa! He has fallen and is no more. His cold, hard heart has finally killed him!" Amaa does not stir. She stares down at her hands, rough and swollen from smashing rocks so many years.

"He is dead and can no longer keep us!" I say.

"His brother will take over his affairs," says Amaa. "Or his son. We will always be in debt. It will never end. Never."

"I stole the book, Amaa. I took it. The Book of the Gods. I have it here in my hands."

I pull the book out from behind me and hold it reverently out to her. "Do you remember I told you about this? I feel it has secrets about the gods, about me. Look, Amaa. Do you see? There are words here, but I cannot read them. And here? Do you see this face?" I flip through the pages. "This goddess, Amaa. Does she . . . does she not resemble me? Is it not as you always told me, that I am descended from the gods? That I do not belong here? But a great white bird—"

"Sunila." Amaa's words are barely a whisper.

"Yes, what is it?"

She looks at me dry-eyed with a faraway stare. "He thought you would bring us good luck. That you would fetch us a large fortune. That we would finally find favor with the gods and escape this life." She wrings her hands. "You were there, outside a café . . . with a woman."

Time slows and my hair stands on end. I pull the book back and press it to my chest, desperate to keep my feet from floating off the ground.

"Buba was passing by and saw your white skin, saw the woman with her head turned the other way."

"No. Please."

"You must go now, Sunila, while you can. Go."

"How? How could you do it, Amaa?"

She is quiet and then she looks at me. She whispers, "I wanted a child. He wanted to sell you, but I insisted on keeping you as my own. I begged him. I only wanted a daughter, Sunila—you must believe me. I saved you from being sold away."

I look at Amaa and see the lines around her eyes, webs of lies covering her, spreading out on the hard soil at her feet. She has fallen, no longer looking at me. I do not know this woman. I do not know my mother.

"Amaa." The cry escapes my lips.

"It was a mistake. I know this. But I loved you the moment I saw you. And besides, there was no way to return you to her. Buba bargained with the cruel man and gave him the book that was tucked in beside you. It was all to pay down our debt, but then his foot was crushed. We had hospital bills. He always blamed you, said you were the reason we would never be free. I think he was right. You can hate me if you want. Take the book, Sunila. You have always known, haven't you? Just go. Please. Don't look at me in this way."

As I stand, I am risking turning to stone. I see her there, but I cannot go to Amaa. I am unable to feel any love for her at this moment, nor hatred for Buba. I am turning to stone and must leave here quickly. As my feet trample the dust, I shake it from me and swear I will never return here. I clutch the book in my hands and promise to die before I ever return to this quarry.

I wipe the wetness from my brow and fold down my umbrella. I see myself in the windows of the US Embassy, and in the right light I catch a glimpse of her there before me—the face of the goddess drawn in the Book of the Gods. She tells me to open the door. So I do.

TWENTY-FIVE

Escape

Mount Pleasant
Ally

I OPEN THE BACK DOOR AND MOVE TO STEP OUT. I LONG for fresh air and feel the need to visit my new stone garden, but the cord just won't reach.

"Ronnie, don't harp on me. I'm dizzy with it all as it is." I twist the cord around my fingers and look down toward the dock. I'm getting claustrophobic. I've got to get out.

"Because I've pretty much worn out my welcome, that's why. Vesey has no use for me. Every time I speak to him, I stick my foot in my mouth. I'm thinking Bermuda beaches are calling my name. Maybe a little sun, a little relaxation—how about you and Marlene, you feel like joining me? Can you get off of work? We could take a cruise. They have a new ship that leaves the Charleston port, if you can believe that. You wouldn't even have to fly a lick."

"Oh, come on, Ronnie. Don't tell me you and Marlene can't use a vacation ... You're having what? Dental surgery? Wow, that sounds positively atrocious. Well, I guess if you have to have it, you have to have it, but you really should take better care of your teeth. You never did floss when we were married . . . Well, it's gross, Ronnie. All right. All right, honey. Listen, I'll stick around for a few more days, maybe, but I can't make any promises. Daddy obviously didn't know me very well. Imagine thinking I could actually be still long enough to live here. Okay, honey. Love you too."

I unwind and put the phone back in the cradle. It's still Daddy's old white phone, now faded and butter colored. I think of his ear at this very place. How did Daddy feel when he was tethered to the phone and I called him from afar? He was probably busting at the seams to get out of the house like I am.

I escape and enter the sanctuary beside the house. The soil is still dug up in a few places, but the grass seed will cover that up nicely. Pretty soon this garden will be lush and I can bring out a glass of wine and watch the sunset, stare at the statues and think about things, or nothing at all. I lower myself onto a little stone bench with two bunny rabbits holding it up on the sides. Nice bunny rabbits. I can see the water from here and my soul rumbles from construction going on somewhere down the road. I take a deep breath and close my eyes. I hear the pound, pound, pounding of the hammers and open my eyes again. Peaceful. It's supposed to be peaceful out here. I look to the god of wine, Dionysius, spouting water out of his mouth. Is he spitting at me? Is he laughing at my meditation spot? I'll show him. I close my eyes again and touch my thumbs and middle fingers together. "Ohhmm . . ."

No, it's impossible. I cannot sit still. I have to do something, go somewhere. No, do something. I see the boxes and tools still propped up on the side of the house and decide to move them into Mama's old room. Yes, I'm going to set up a batik-making station. A studio. I'm going to learn how to make batiks once and for all. How many years has it been? I can almost smell the wax in that little storefront in Bali. I long to have the dye in my fingers. I'm going to get inspired again and keep my hands busy like they used to be when I had my sketchbook. Back before the Great Sadness.

Forget it all. I'm going to draw again and rewind time.

I bend over to lift up a heavy box and pray to God or the gods or anybody who might be listening. *Oh, please don't let me wrench my hip again. Please just let me do something on my own without having to depend on Vesey or anyone else. Ever again. Let me get this box inside and escape into the wax, the colors, the birds, the mountains, and the rivers I'll paint. Just let me do this one thing, please.*

I need an escape.

Gritting my teeth, I open the door and hold it open with my hip as I pass on through. The gods must have been listening. My hip is okay. I walk by Daddy's La-Z-Boy chair, by the Guatemalan rug and flat-screen TV leaning up against the wall. As if in a dream, I head to Mama's old room to turn it into the studio I've always wanted. I picture notes from heaven falling on me when I open the door, but nothing but empty memories greet me. Mama and Daddy are gone. It's up to me now to create something new in here. I can do it. And I won't feel alone. I refuse to feel alone anymore.

TWENTY-SIX

How It Will End

US Embassy, Kathmandu, Nepal
Sunila

I SEE MY REFLECTION IN THE HEAVY GLASS DOORS AS I pull one to me. I am filthy and cover my face with my scarf. I step into a foyer, a large rectangular room with marble floors. There are statues of lions flanking either side of the hall, and I can tell by the style of them which family has carved them in Swayambhu. They pass down their secrets from father to son. But me? I could carve these lions better than what I see before me. A strange and foreign sense of pride comes over me. I shudder and shake it off. I am a Dalit. I am a woman. I am nothing. I turn to go.

Then I stop and turn back around. *You have come too far.*

Slowly, I approach a lone woman sitting behind a wall. She has long black hair and a fitted green dress. She is of caste. I am afraid to speak. "Namaste," I manage.

"Yes? What do you want?"

I pull out the rumpled old card and set it down before her.

"Please," I say, looking at the card and not in her eyes. "I am here to see this person. Mr. Davidson Monroe." I say it just the way I repeated it back to him many years ago, the way I have rehearsed it in my mind. My stomach churns as I await her reply. My knees tremble beneath me.

She hands the card back to me and says, "I'm sorry, but there is no one here by that name."

I look at the card. I look at her fingers. They are soft and have never broken gravel. "Please. Please. Are you sure? I—"

"Where did you get this card?" she asks. "I can double-check the roster." She looks to her computer and puts her fingers on the keys. I leave the card sitting on the desk.

"Forgive me. I got this from Mr. Monroe himself, a long time ago. Perhaps twenty-five years."

The lady raises her eyebrows. Then she stops typing and folds her hands under her chin. "I see. And you are an American citizen?" She looks at me with pity.

"No. I am not." I am filled with shame for standing here.

"Then why are you at the US Embassy?"

"I—" I shake my head. "I do not know. I am sorry." I turn to walk away.

"Miss," the woman says, "if you'd like to see another consulate officer, you may make an appointment."

"An appointment."

"Yes. Let's see . . . I have next Wednesday at . . . mmmm . . . 1:30?"

She is mocking me. I look toward the door. Next Wednesday. That is five days from now. Five days with no food. I cannot go home; I have nowhere to stay.

"Miss?"

I look at the lady.

"Did you hear what I said? A consulate officer can see you on Wednesday. Shall I put you down for 1:30?"

I feel a draft from my wet clothes and shiver. Then, uncontrollably. "No. Thank you. Namaste."

I move as quickly as my legs will take me to the door and back into the street where I belong. I am unclean. So it is, and so it will always be. But I must survive. I will search for twigs or straw. I will make a broom and sweep the streets of their filth and excrement in the morning with the other Dalit women. But I cannot go back to the quarry. They will kill me if I do.

The rain pours on my umbrella and suddenly it is being ripped from my hands, yet I will not let go. A car has stopped. Two high-caste men tell me to get in the car. I struggle to stand. I have seen what happens to Dalit women who struggle. They are stripped in public and humiliated. They are beaten and burned. And the police do nothing.

This is how it will end. Here on Maharajgunj Road.

I open my mouth to scream, and a man falls to the ground. There is a fight before my eyes. The rain is coming down hard and a third man is here, fighting the other two. They get up and run to their car and speed away.

I fall to my knees, a stone on the sidewalk.

Someone puts hands on my arms and walks with me back to where I came.

"Are you okay?" the man asks.

I cannot speak. I am trembling.

We enter the embassy doors again, but this time I am too stunned to be afraid.

"My goodness, you're freezing. Are you ill, miss? Did they hurt you?" He turns to the secretary and speaks in English. "Marta, please, a towel. And some hot tea for the lady."

The man wrenches the umbrella from my hands and sets it up against the wall. I have never been called a lady before in any language. The towel and tea warm me and I begin to focus once more on my surroundings. I touch my breast to make sure the book is still there. It is. I look straight ahead and see the man's legs. He is sitting on the edge of a desk, arms folded.

"Better?" he says, returning to Nepali.

I nod slightly with the warm cup in my hands. The woman who brought the tea whispers in the man's ear. He is bald and wearing a wet brown suit.

"Really? I see," he says. He studies me. I try to drink my tea. I may not have any for a very long time. "You speak Nepali. I understand you were just here looking for a consulate officer. Yet you are obviously not American, are you? I have to wonder what brings you here. Tell me, how long have you traveled to get here?"

My eyes shift and I recount the days.

"You do speak?"

I count the times I found an overhang or trash bin to rest my eyes. "Four days," I say.

His eyes open. "In the rain? No wonder you're cold. It is too dangerous for you to be on the street." Silence sits between us as I sip my milked tea. The steam wafts up into my face.

"Tell me, why did you come all this way to the US Embassy? It must have been a very important trip for you to make. Do you have matters with the US?"

I am afraid to speak. I bite my cracked lips.

"I'm sorry, where are my manners?" The man unfolds his arms and puts a gentle hand out to me. "My name is Theodore Assai. I'm with the US Consulate. And your name? Please. Look at me."

I look at him and say, "M-My name is Sunila Kunari. I came to see a consulate officer I met many years ago. Mr. Davidson Monroe."

"Ah, I see. And you've come all this way to find out he is no longer here?"

"Yes."

"Mmm. Pity. Tell me, what sort of business would a woman like you—a Dalit, no?—have with the consulate of the US Embassy?"

"I—" I press to stand. "I have taken up too much of your time. I am sorry."

"Let me explain," he says. "I am an American. I was born in America to Nepalese parents. So I have returned to Nepal but I do not believe in the caste system. I do not believe I am any better than you. Do you understand this?" The man looks at his watch. "I am on a break, so it is my time to take up. So tell me, would you like to have lunch? I am hungry and I've nearly forty-five minutes left."

The thought of food makes my mouth quiver, but I am wary of this man. No one eats with a Dalit.

"Good. Marta, I'll be taking tea and lunch in my office today. Please bring enough for two of us. Dal bhat. Oh, and a cold compress for my hand. There was some trouble on the street today." The man helps me get to my feet, holds my rainbow-colored umbrella, and with a curious voice says, "Right this way,

Ms. Kunari. Right this way." The feel of his hands on mine, Dalit hands, untouchable in my society, makes my head swoon. I feel far away from home. The book burns in my chest, and I wonder if this has all been a terrible mistake.

TWENTY-SEVEN

Jasper Farms

Mount Pleasant
Ally
1968

IT HAD ALL BEEN A MISTAKE. A TERRIBLE, AWFUL MIS-
take. I went through four years of high school, fifteen dances,
eight different hairstyles, and countless Beatles songs without
ever laying eyes on Vesey Washington again. All because of my
impetuous nature. My parents never knew anything had happened between us. They saw me sitting on the end of the dock,
pining away as all teenaged daughters did, no doubt. They had
no idea—and they would have had strokes had they known—
that I was missing Vesey. I, Ally Green, homecoming queen to
the class of 1968 at Mount Pleasant High, missed a colored boy.
When I was dating Sam Packard and Miles Dupree, I was actually thinking about Vesey—how he would never say something
just to impress me, how he would speak from his heart about his
dreams for the future, about spiritual things and the true state of
man—how he was real and genuine and everything right.

It was all wrong in everyone's eyes, but I remember sitting there with my feet down in the water, thinking, *If it's so wrong, God, why would you let me feel this way?* A loving God wouldn't make somebody have feelings for a person and then never ever let it be right. Would he?

My religion was wavering, my foundation growing shakier each year, and by the time I hit eighteen and was thinking of leaving Charleston—going off to college, going off to start a life somewhere—I could not bear the thought of never seeing Vesey again. He had grown into the image of a near-god in my drawings and in my heart.

To never see him again? I simply could not bear it.

When you have wronged someone, you live with it. It does not go away. It lingers and stains and hurts and festers. I had wronged Vesey by keeping my mouth shut. I should have rowed over to his mama's house and told her that I was the reason Vesey was caught dancing with me that night. I should have told her it was me who had had designs on him and not the other way around. I should have explained that I was like Odysseus's sirens, luring him to the rocks. To his death.

But I never said a word. I thought it might inconvenience and embarrass my parents. I thought of my own shame and what people might say about me. I thought of Vesey, I did, but in all actuality, I only did what served me best. And by the time I turned eighteen years old, I remembered that little girl I used to be, the little girl who used to be good friends with the little colored boy across that river. I thought of who I had become, who I wanted to be. And then early one Sunday morning I borrowed Daddy's car and headed straight for John's Island. I was going to find Vesey

Washington and set things straight once and for all. I feared he was no longer there anymore, that he'd been drafted or hurt or grown bitter or run off and gotten married. I feared I'd never get the chance to tell him I was sorry, that I could never tell him the depth of my true feelings—that I had cared for him deeply. All these years. Him, and nobody else.

Daddy's '65 Olds rolls along the dusty roads of John's Island, clouds forming at the back of the car. The oak trees hang over me, Spanish moss dripping down and doting on me like an old nanny. I should have come here a year ago. Two years ago. Three. I should have found Vesey as soon as he got moved here. I could have cleared things up. I might have moved on with my life, had some closure, but no. I am still living with his ghost just as if he never left.

I look at my hands on the wheel. Have they changed any since I've become a young woman? I look down again at my chest that has filled out this sweater, then back up into the rearview mirror at my eyes with purple eye shadow and blond hair, curled and smoothed. Yes, I have changed. I hope Vesey likes what he sees. But what will I find in him? Will he be handsome still or grown bitter, living out on this farm? Will he even agree to see me?

There is a sign on the right for the Angel Oak. Mama and Daddy and I drove out here once to see it, a large sprawling fourteen-hundred-year-old tree. Standing there, cradled in its arms, I could almost feel the souls of the Indians who had prayed there before me. I pass the sign and keep on driving. No time for prayer. A deer is standing on the side of the road flicking its tail. It waits and waits and I slow down to a crawl. I honk my horn and it turns back to join its family. I take a deep breath, and then I see it—a hand-drawn sign that says *Jasper Farms*. This is it. I turn into the dirt drive and hold my breath.

Pothole after pothole, at the end of a very long road, I finally see a break in the sky. There's a river straight ahead of me and on the left, a sprawling farm with cotton plants and tomatoes and purple wildflowers as far as the eye can see.

And there bending down to the soil is Vesey.

He looks up and stands, hands on hips, watching me. He squints and when he realizes it's me, he drops his basket and runs toward the car. My heart is about to burst out of my chest! I set the car in park and get out of the door. I go to run to him, but he stops several feet away and scolds, "What are you doin' here?" He looks behind him to see if anyone is watching. His body is a man's now, taller, fuller. His clothes fit him loosely, a long-sleeved white shirt with blue jean overalls. He looks healthy and dark. Better than I imagined.

"Vesey, is it really you? I can't believe how you've changed."

"You cain't be here."

"I won't stay. I just needed—my goodness, it's been so long." I grab my stomach and smooth my dress. I look over now toward the house to be sure we are alone. "I'm, I'm going off to college. In the fall. I got in."

Vesey is silent, watching my face and pressing his hands in his pockets.

"Are you?" I ask. "Are you going to college?"

"Ally, why'd you come here? It ain't good for you to be out here. Ain't you heard all the stuff goin' on?" His voice is low and thick like molasses.

"Oh yes. I'm sorry about Dr. King. I—I don't know what to say really, but it's awful. All of it. I just cannot believe people behave the way they do."

Vesey looks back at the house and folds his arms across his broad chest.

"You don't think I'm like that, do you?" I ask.

"What kinda question is that?" he says. Crows come for whatever is in the basket he dropped, and he shoos them away.

"I'm graduating next week, Vesey. We're going up to visit Furman as soon as I do. I guess I came here because I wanted to . . ." I look down at his dirty shoes and then at my own. "I'm sorry, Vesey. I've wanted to tell you how sorry I am for the longest time, but—"

"Sorry 'bout what? Ain't nothin' to be sorry about."

"Yes, there is! It was my fault. I'm the one who got you into trouble. It was all me! You had to come all the way out here because of me."

"It was bound to happen," he says.

"Yes, it was. And it was all my fault because I—" I look up into his eyes. "Vesey, I've cared about you since the day I met you."

The silence between us is loud and awkward. I want to absorb the words back into my mouth but I can't. It's too late. Confusion comes over Vesey's face and then concern. Crows dance behind him on the ground, cackling at my announcement. I speak again to smooth it all over.

"So are you? Going to school?"

He shakes his head. "Nah. I've got work to do here. It's pretty good work. I like it. Uncle Percival ain't so bad."

"But, Vesey, if you're not in college, they'll send you off to

Vietnam! Not to mention, with a mind like yours you should be going off to college. Didn't you always dream about becoming a doctor? About saving people's lives? My goodness, how many times did you say it?"

"I quit schoolin' few years back," he says nonchalantly. "It was too hard to keep up with the farm and all. We sell on down the road and do pretty well. Got a stand and stay pretty busy year-round."

I rub my arms and feel the weight of it. "You dropped out of school? Because of me?" I am crushed by the unfairness of it all. They'll come for him. They'll send him off to war . . . all because . . . I want to tell him how I really feel. I want to wrap my arms around him and beg him to come with me. I want to stomp my feet and throw a tantrum like a little girl, but I stand back, way back from myself and look at the situation. It's tragic and hopeless and worse than I expected, just as it's always been, no matter how much progress has been made between black and white. I stumble back against the car.

"Ally, don't—"

"I've made a mess of things, Vesey. I honestly had no idea you would have to quit your dreams because of one stupid kiss."

"Please—" He reaches for me.

"No. I can't." I back up and open the car door. I sit down slowly and reach for the keys. "Lord knows I don't want to make things any harder than I already have for you, Vesey. Just know I'm sorry. I'm so, so . . ."

"Ain't so bad," he says, wiping his brow with the back of his hand. His top lip is perspiring. "I mean it—it ain't. And it ain't your fault, Ally Green. It was my decision to quit school. Can you get that through your head? I cain't have you thinkin' it was 'cause of you, 'cause that's a flat-out lie. A flat-out lie."

I smile sadly at him and want to cry. "It was nice to see you again, Vesey. I-I've thought about you. Time and again. I better be getting back before Daddy reports his car missing. Take care of yourself . . . and the farm."

Vesey moves closer and reaches for my door. His hand touches mine for a moment and he gives my fingers a squeeze. "Study hard," he says. "You're gonna do just fine. I know it. Maybe you'll be a doctor like Doc Green. Or maybe you'll go to Hollywood or travel the world like you always wanted."

With one last look, Vesey closes the door and I back up over roots and potholes, turning the car slowly so he can't see my face. I hold my breath and the tears start falling before I reach the end of the dirt road. I am desolate, heaving fully, growing dizzy as I head off for the next chapter of my life.

TWENTY-EIGHT

Fate and Strangers

Kathmandu, Nepal
Sunila

THERE IS A WINDOW IN MR. ASSAI'S OFFICE OVERLOOK-ing a small courtyard. In it, I see birds flying and landing on stone statues. I cannot see the way I used to when I was younger. Squinting down into the dust to chisel fine pieces of stone can age a person's eyes. Though I cannot see it clearly, I long to be out there in the sunlight with the birds dancing. Instead, I am here in a wood chair in front of Mr. Assai's desk. He is looking at me curi-ously and fear nips my insides. Why did I come here? What do I have to say? What proof do I have, and still, what can he do about it? Hopeless I feel. Hopeless.

Mr. Assai pushes a container of food toward me—dal bhat, or rice with steaming lentil soup and tarkari, curried vegetables. The aroma makes me dizzy and my stomach responds by growl-ing loudly.

"Please, eat," he says, dipping his roti into the dal and scooping up a bite. He has changed his suit and is dry now. I am wrapped in a brown blanket.

I see a plastic spoon. Mr. Assai is using his. I always eat with my right hand, no spoon, but I am dirty now. I lift the spoon and approach my food tentatively. Then I scoop a bite and place it in my mouth. It melts on my tongue, and I want to ravage the plate, to inhale it. But I don't.

If only my mother and father could see me now. Amaa would be fearful, as am I, that this is a trick. No one invites a Dalit to have food with them. It is the principle of *jutho* or ritual impurity. I look to the door to be sure I'm not being tricked. That I am not going to be beaten by the cruel man. If Buba saw me, he would scream at me and tell me how ignorant I am. He would tell me I am no better than the hungry dogs who wander in the streets. I put my spoon down and close my eyes.

"Is it not good?" he asks.

"Yes, it is good. Very good," I say. I open my eyes. No tricks. No Amaa and Buba, just this man, eating before me, asking me to do the same. I do not know where my next meal is coming from. I may walk out of here in a few minutes and then what? Where will I go? What will I do? Go back to the quarry?

I eat my food and nearly lick the container clean. I need this food to carry me for whatever comes next.

When we're done, Mr. Assai takes the container away from me and stuffs it in a trash bin next to his desk. He pours fresh tea into my cup and I take it in my hands and sip it.

"Thank you for your kindness," I say.

"It was my pleasure. I'm not used to sharing my lunch with someone as lovely as you."

There it is again. He called me lovely. I am quite uncomfortable. The last time anyone said this he was asking for my hand in marriage, vowing to unite me with a wealthy man if I would only follow him across the border. He would lead me to a better life.

Lovely. I am not lovely. I am poor. Lowly. Unclean. This man is lying. I move to get up, but something keeps me sitting. I have come so far. My shoes are still damp, and so is my hair. *Tell the man*, a voice says deep inside.

"Now, Ms. Kunari, I am interested to hear why you have come such a long way to speak with a consulate officer at the US Embassy. Please, won't you oblige? I am very curious."

The birds fly past the window. There are dark clouds forming where the sunshine was. It is monsoon season. Any break in the clouds only leads to more clouds and more rain. I look to the wall at my umbrella. I'll need it soon.

"Mr. Assai, forgive me, but I do not know where to start."

"Just tell me what prompted you to come here now. You met Mr. Monroe, was it, a long time ago. Why make this trip now? Why today?"

He has leaned back in his chair, one arm up on the rest, his hand rubbing the side of his neck. I place my tea back in the saucer and pull my knees together. I sit up straight and look down into the swirling tea.

"I am a master carver at Chobhar Stone. I have worked there since I can remember, along with my parents. My family is in debt to the man who owns it. It is a sad story. We shall never be free." I swallow and breathe in deeply. I am beginning to shake.

"Several days ago I was bringing in the last of the statues to the owner, as the rains are here. He wanted to take inventory and sell the things I carve. He is cruel and tells me I am no good at carving, but I have seen others' work. He is an evil man.

"When I brought him the last statue—it was the goddess Durga—he looked at it and started yelling, 'Stupid girl! You did it all wrong!' I was so ashamed. I looked down at the ground. The next thing I knew he was silent and staring at me. I was afraid he would strike me, but instead he grabbed his chest and dropped to the floor on his knees. I was terrified and stood there, unmoving. His eyes rolled back in his head and soon the life had left him. I should have notified someone, but instead, I knew this was my chance. I went to the cabinets behind his big desk. There is a book. I have known it since I was a child. The cruel man had me study the pictures when he saw I was capable of carving stone, not only crushing it. He had me study those drawings and I would carve them into stones that the others had prepared. He would sell them, my statues, for a lot of money, but I never saw any of it. I remained in his debt. When I was nine or ten, he took the book away from me and I never saw it again, but oh, I could see it in my mind's eye. I carved the stones from memory." I look up at Mr. Assai and he encourages me to continue.

"I have always suspected there was something special about this book, Mr. Assai. I do not look like either of my parents. They have always told me they found me, abandoned, and took me in as a baby. But Amaa, she told me the truth before I left."

"And what was that? What was the truth?"

I touch the book beneath my sari and close my eyes. I look at Mr. Assai and summon my courage. "That I was not abandoned as a child, but stolen. That my father stole me from a woman in a café. That there was a book, this book, tucked in with me." I turn from the man and reach into the top of my sari. I pull out the book with its worn edges and faded drawings. It is still warm from the heat of my body. I set it gingerly on the table between us, and Mr. Assai looks at it. Then at me. He seems to be studying my face, my blue eyes, my small nose.

Mr. Assai takes the book in his hands. "May I?" he asks.

I nod and prepare to watch his face as he flips through the pages. He will, no doubt, be able to read the words, which I cannot. I feel as if a fire is rumbling up within me. I sit up straighter and put my hands in front of my mouth. I am shaking, but this is happening now. The book, the man, it is all happening. My fate is in his hands.

TWENTY-NINE

Tears and Molten Wax

Mount Pleasant
Ally

"COME TO MAMA," I SAY. I PULL OUT A PILE OF WHITE silk from a cardboard box and feel the softness in my hands. I shake it out, a piece about four feet wide and six feet long. I look at the old green carpet of Mama's bedroom. This will have to go. I imagine dropping wax and dye and all else on the floor . . . but that will come later. For now, we play.

I set two sawhorses up, about six feet from each other, and use stick pins to carefully hold the ends of the silk in place. The middle droops slightly, just as I remember it in that little store in Bali. For a moment I wonder about that woman, the one who was kind enough to sell me all of this. Was she able to buy better equipment? Did she continue to make batiks all these years? Did she live a happy life? How old would she be now, seventy-five? Eighty?

Kat strolls through the door and his eyes grow large as he surveys the silk. His tail twitches.

"Don't even think about it," I say. I can picture him, claws out as he slays my silks, me freaking out. I pick him up and set him out the door, then close it. "Not today," I say through the wood. "We have to build some trust, you and me, before I let you in here. Run on now."

I find the old electric skillet and a packet of wax. I set it in the plate and plug it into the wall. As soon as it begins to melt, I can smell the wax and it transports me back to that store, back to the streets of Bali. I open a window for some fresh air.

What will I draw with the wax? Something like euphoria or adrenaline or both builds up in my veins and I itch with creative desire. It grows so strong I can barely stand it. What have I done all these years? I haven't drawn or painted or sculpted a thing. I haven't used my creative side at all, yet here it is bursting, ripe, dying to come out. How sad to have suppressed this desire. It feels much like the desire for a man, and goodness knows, I have learned to suppress that as well.

The river. I will draw the river. My first batik will have blues and greens and yellows, and I will draw Vesey's house on the other side, the white birds that glide over the water between us. I smile despite myself. To be thinking of drawing again, just thinking about it, brings me so much pleasure. I feel it's a sin to have put this aside for so long.

But then again, it was all I could do. I couldn't draw again. That sketchbook had my life in it, and when it was gone, there was nothing left to draw. There was nothing left in me. I was a dry well. Empty. Parched. Barren.

Is it possible, after all these years, that I've begun to fill up with healing waters again? I shake the past from me and focus on the task at hand. I test out the wax pen and move my hand slowly across the long middle of the silk. I am drawing the line between Vesey and me, yet it is not black and white, only barely there, easily smudged. I think of the reeds by the river and the story of Moses in a basket. I long to draw a wayward baby there, but I push it away. I will draw Molasses Creek the way it is today, the past gone away with the current and new beginnings coming in with the tide.

As I draw with my molten wax, tears fall down my face and leave faint wet spots on the white silk. It is part sadness, part joy, as if finding an old friend. Although I have never in my life created a batik, with this tool in my hand, expressing what is inside of me, I'm feeling closer to home than I have in many, many years. Over the next few hours I succeed in losing myself completely, and only the occasional prick of pain in my hip and in my heart reminds me I have a body at all. That I am not just a part of the drawing that is before me. That instead, I am real, and the master of what is being drawn.

THIRTY

Drawing Clues

Kathmandu, Nepal
Sunila

"WHAT YOU SEE BEFORE YOU IS A BOOK OF DRAWINGS that was with me when I was stolen. I believe the owner of this book to be my mother. My birth mother. I believe that these are her drawings and that they hold some clue as to who I am and where I come from."

"Your accusations are dire, Ms. Kunari," says Mr. Assai as his eyes flip over the pages. "Are you saying you would like to bring charges against your father for stealing you from this woman? For kidnapping? Those are very serious charges, especially in today's climate."

"No," I say. "I do not want to press charges. What is done is done and one cannot go back and undo it. I do not want Amaa to have to suffer more than she does already. What I want, Mr. Assai, is for you to look at this book, to tell me I am not insane, and to help me find the woman who made these drawings. Here."

I take the book from him and flip to a page near the back. "There is a picture of her here. Of course, I only think it is her. Do you see a resemblance?"

Mr. Assai looks at me and then at the book and back. His eyebrows rise. "Perhaps a small resemblance."

"Then look here." I turn the page and show him a drawing of a café. It is still there, near the Garden of Dreams. "Do you see this drawing? It is the very last one in the book. Do you see what is here, near the ground?"

Mr. Assai takes his reading glasses from his desk and places them on his nose. He holds the book away from him. "Yes, I do see it." He takes his glasses off and looks at me with finality. His voice is low and dire. "It is a baby, Ms. Kunari. This sketchbook, indeed, appears to have belonged to an American woman. And there's a baby in this drawing, in the café, just as you described." Mr. Assai pushes his chair from his desk and walks toward the window. He stands there, hands on the sill, watching the rain now pouring on the courtyard and statues. He is silent for so long, I can hear the sound of my own beating heart.

Then a knock at the door startles us both.

"Mr. Assai?" It is the woman from the reception desk. "Your next appointment is here. Shall I have him wait?"

Mr. Assai is far away in thought. He looks at me and then back at the woman. "Marta, I need you to help Ms. Kunari here get set up in the Shangri-La Hotel. Please arrange a room and food and anything else that she needs."

"Sir?"

"Just do it, please, Marta. I'll need to speak with her further.

Get her set up in a room, and tell them . . . Tell them she is of caste if they ask."

"Yes, sir."

"And go ahead and send in my next appointment."

"Right away."

Mr. Assai comes to me and bows his head. "I must be honest. I am not sure whether to believe your story. You may have done these drawings yourself, no? You are an artist yourself."

"No," I say. "I did not do these drawings. It is just as I explained to you."

"Very well. I don't know what we're dealing with exactly, Ms. Kunari. This case may or may not have merit. But I need more time. Please go now with Marta and I will call on you this evening. Don't worry about anything, your meals and room are paid for. Do you understand?"

I nod, but feel as if I'm in a dream.

"All right then. I will speak with you later."

I turn to walk away and face him again.

"Oh, your umbrella, of course," says Mr. Assai, retrieving it for me. I look toward his desk.

"The book," I say. "May I . . . have it back?"

Mr. Assai looks uncomfortable. "I'm afraid I'll need to hold on to this. I'll need to do some research. You do understand."

He can see the fear and mistrust on my face, but I cannot hide it. I have longed to have this book in my hands for three decades and now I am expected to leave it with another man, one I am not sure I can fully trust. One who does not yet believe me.

"Please," I say. "I cannot part with it. Not again. Please understand."

Mr. Assai assesses me. "Then you will not go anywhere. You will not leave the hotel?"

"I will not leave the hotel," I say with as much strength as I can muster. The book returns to my hands and suddenly I am not so afraid.

"Very well. I will see you at seven. And I'll be eager to review this book again."

THIRTY-ONE

Homesick

Ally

August 22, 1968

Dear Sketchbook,

It's the last time I laid eyes on him that haunts me the most. It isn't all the memories of our childhood together, fishing, talking, playing along the water's edge; instead, it's Vesey as a young man now, how he's tall and filled out and not at all the way he used to be as a child. Not the gregarious boy who spouted off all the things he wanted to do with his life, but the one who's resigned to quit everything and just farm.

Just farm. Am I a snob now that I'm going off to college? I suppose it is so. There are plenty of colleges where blacks can go, and I know Vesey is smarter than me. If life was fair he'd be the one going off to school and I'd be the one stuck at home.

How could his mother send him off to live with his uncle after she lost her only other son in Molasses Creek? I'll never understand it. One day, I'll go right over to her house and demand, woman to woman, an answer for how she could do it. But then that accusing finger will point back at me and tell me I'm the reason her son has no future. That she had to send him away from me before I got him into more serious trouble. I know she's right too. I remember what happened to that Musser boy who looked the wrong way at Silvia Draught when she was getting on the bus. A group of white boys jumped off and chased him down the street. Knocked him silly. I only heard about what happened to him later. One would think those boys would get into serious trouble for fighting and skipping school, but the truth fell on deaf ears and all the boys were back to school on Monday, looking like the cats who ate the canary. And bragging about it.

Yes, I know what could've happened to Vesey if I'd continued to be his friend. It would not have been tolerated by a certain segment of society and worse things than farmwork could have happened to Mrs. Washington's son.

I put my pen down. I try not to see him in the cars and trees and clouds as we drive along Highway 26 toward Furman. *You're starting a new life, Ally Green, one where there will be fun and learning... and boys.*

Vesey is there in the field beside the road. In the reflection of a kitchen window.

I close my eyes.

"Margaret, your mother tells me you're thinking of teaching, is that right?" Mama asks. She swivels her head so she can see Margaret in the seat beside me. My mother is wearing large white glasses that point up on the edges so she looks like a cat. Her hair is tucked beneath a brown hat and pinned in place. Simon and Garfunkel are on the radio singing about Mrs. Robinson.

Margaret is drop-dead gorgeous. Her hair is long and wavy blond, her makeup just right with pale lips and smoky eyes. Her miniskirt is so short nothing is left to the imagination. I look down at myself, at my green dress suit with cropped top and big buttons. My mother made it herself. She looks back at me and smiles excitedly. She's trying to cover up her worry and sadness. Her little girl is going off to college. Mama never did.

"I'd like to teach, maybe on the college level," says Margaret, as if she's fully mapped out her existence in this world. "I think that's where the cutest boys are."

"College is not about boys," says my father, glancing at us from the driver's seat. "It's about higher education. You think too much of the boys there and you'll wind up back home in Charleston after a semester or two, working behind a counter."

"There's nothing wrong with working behind a counter," my mother says. "Oh, listen to this nice song. Jesus does love you more than you will know. Did you know that, girls?"

"Don't worry about me, Dr. Green," says Margaret. "I've always been able to keep my grades up . . . even when I was dating the captain of the football team. And there was no one cuter in our school than Graham Scups, was there, Ally?"

I look out the window as we pass a family in the car next to us. There's a little girl pressing her doll up to the window for me to see. "No one cuter," I say.

"I could have been Mrs. Scups," Margaret goes on, "but to be honest, he was always a little dull. I need more excitement. I *need* to go to college."

Margaret crosses her legs and peers out the window. Then she turns to me wide-eyed and grabs my hand. "Ally, I just can't wait!" she whispers. She puts her fingers up to her lips and acts as if she's smoking a joint. She watches my father to be sure he's not looking in the rearview mirror at her shenanigans. My stomach cramps up and I have to look away.

"I think it's wonderful you two get to room together," says Mama. "That way you already have a friend. You won't get home-sick nearly as much, Ally. You'll go off having sort of a built-in support system." She's quiet after that, pretty much for the rest of the trip. I wonder if she's imagining herself moving away to live in a dorm room and earn a degree.

"I—it'll be fun," I say to no one in particular. Then I cross my pale legs and lean my face on the cool glass of the window. After so many miles down the road, I cannot get the rich color of Vesey's skin out of my mind. For a moment, I wonder why in the world I'm going off to college when I belong back in Charleston.

Yes, I do belong there. With him.

THIRTY-TWO

Evolution of a Co-ed

Ally

January 29, 1969

Dear Sketchbook,

Getting a college education means different things to Margaret and me. I've realized, after so many parties and dates and nights in which I have to sit out in the hallway or sleep in a chair in the dormitory common room, that Margaret has come to college to find a rich husband. After she's done having her fun with the suitors, that is. But me? I suppose I'm here to better myself, or to find myself. It's easy for me to get on with my studies and classes because it gives me something to think about other than Vesey. The longer I study, the more removed I feel from him. Imagine not reading about Greek mythology, The Odyssey, the cosmos, psychology. My mind remains titillated and extremely busy and, truthfully, Vesey Washington has faded into the background. Until it comes to boys, that is. Boys, silly college boys, who drink too much and pound their chests and grope at me, only make me wistful for a gentleman like Vesey Washington. The distance he kept from me. The intimacy of our conversations. His genuine, pure heart. These college boys pale in comparison in more ways than one.

June 5, 1969
Dear Sketchbook,

Our freshman year at Furman is over and Margaret has talked me into staying in Greenville and getting a job for the summer. I know that if I go home to Charleston, I'll be thinking about Vesey, looking across Molasses Creek to his mother's house. Not to mention after the freedom I've experienced living on my own, I'm not sure I want to come back under Daddy's roof. Under his rules. He was so disappointed when I told him I wasn't coming home, and I know for a fact Mama was heartbroken, but they've never been parents to force me to do anything I didn't want to do. Why would they start now? I'll be making my very own money working at a craft store downtown, and Margaret has a paid internship at a local radio station. She's long given up her desire to teach and is moving on to more exciting things like music and dancing and rock-and-roll.

June 15, 1969
Dear Sketchbook,

I've been fairly truthful about our summer existence, except that when Daddy came to move us into our loft apartment I neglected to tell him two of Margaret's friends would be living in the extra bedroom. I also neglected to tell him that these friends happen to be strapping young men. Mama would die a thousand deaths over that. But I have evolved. It's honestly no big deal—living with members of the opposite sex—what with the liberation of birth control and my not minding cleaning up after them. Somehow, I've become a regular home-away-from-home-maker.

September 20, 1969
Dear Sketchbook,

Summer has come and gone. Men walked on the moon for the first time. A war is being fought on the other side of the world. A bus full of our Furman friends drove up to Woodstock and had the time of their lives. But me? I stayed back at our apartment and worked at the craft store—still timid due to my upbringing, I suppose. School has started again and I am officially a sophomore at Furman, but to be honest, I feel tied down by the books, by all the rigmarole.

Margaret's finding it harder to adjust to a schedule again. She was gone basically the entire summer, traveling with boys, sleeping out, and occasionally working. She had more than a working relationship with several of the folks at the radio station and would come home telling me how groovy so-and-so was and how lame I was for not wanting to date his friend, what's-his-name. Margaret and I are growing more and more different as evidenced in our attire. I've retained the simple shirtdresses I went off to school in while her colors have grown bolder, patterns wilder, dresses skimpier. I'm more Jackie Kennedy and she's more Jane Fonda in *Barbarella*. But I'm not a stick in the mud. I'm not. I do let loose occasionally.

I date boys and drink too much and smoke whenever I feel like it. I've been on my own, making my own rules, with no parent to tell me what to do for a full solid year . . . but my lack of boundaries has begun to feel as stifling as a boundary itself. Is that possible?

My head simply isn't into school anymore.

December 2, 1969

Dear Sketchbook,

Something dreadful has happened. Last night they held a lottery for the selective service. We were all gathered around the television in our dorm room, anxiously watching as numbers were called. Girls whimpered as soon as they heard the birthday of a brother or cousin or a friend who hasn't already been drafted, but by the time they hit number seven, September 14th, I was the one doing the crying. Vesey's birthday is September 14th. And his number was called.

THIRTY-THREE
Daddy's Girl

1969
Ally

DADDY!" I HOLLER INTO THE PHONE AS SOON AS HE picks it up.

"Baby, what is it? What's wrong?"

"It's the draft, Daddy! Have you seen the draft on television?"

"'Course I have. Your mother and I are watching it now."

"But all those boys, Daddy! All those people have to go over to war and fight and kill or be killed!"

Daddy is silent. He's letting me vent and listening well as he always does. He's fairly used to my hysterics.

"It's not fair," I whine.

"It's as fair as they can make it, honey. It's a random drawing. Nothing's fair about wartime."

Words catch in the back of my throat and my eyes begin to burn.

"Ally? You all right?"

I try, but I can't speak.

"Is it your friends? I realize you might have some boys there whose numbers got called tonight. Is that what this is?"

"Mmmm," I manage. "Yes, it is a friend, and Daddy, everyone's been talking about going up to Canada or . . . or who they might know, or, well, some folks are saying that you have to get a physical first and if they find something wrong with you, why then you don't have to go to Vietnam at all."

"Yes, I suppose that's somewhat correct. In certain circumstances."

"So, Daddy. I have a huge favor to ask." The silence between us hums a long minute. "I want you to see if there's any way at all you can help a dear friend of mine."

"Ally, you know I can't do that. I can't fake something. That would be unethical."

"This war is unethical, Daddy! It's not ethical to—"

"Honey, calm down."

"Daddy, promise me you'll help my friend. Okay? Please! He's . . . he just can't go off to war. Thirty-three thousand American boys have been killed already! I would die. I would just—"

"Ally, tell me who your friend is," says Daddy. The wind has shifted. His words are slow and calculated.

"Just promise me, Daddy."

"I'll do no such thing. Now, who is it? Who has captured my daughter's heart so much that she would ask her father, a doctor, to bend the rules? I certainly haven't heard you talking about any one particular boy."

I bite my bottom lip until it bleeds, and then finally, I breathe it out. It's time I stood up for him. It's time, once and for all. "It's

Vesey, Daddy. Vesey Washington. Remember the boy who used to live across the creek from us?"

The words I spouted are long and snakelike and seem to be wrapping tentacles around my throat, squeezing tighter. I can hear Daddy breathing, thinking, but nothing else. Nothing until—

"Ally, Vesey doesn't need my help."

"Why? Because he's black, Daddy? Is that it? Yes, he does need your help! His birthday is September fourteenth!"

"Ally, slow down. Vesey doesn't need my help . . . because he's already gone. Far as I know he enlisted two months ago."

My body burns and turns still like stone, and the phone slips out of my fingers, falling with a thud to the ground. I sit down on the edge of the bed and hear Daddy's voice calling to me from the floor. "Ally? Ally, you there?"

But I'm already gone. Like Vesey.

Already gone.

THIRTY-FOUR

Up in the Air

Ally

May 2, 1970

Dear Sketchbook,

Daddy has not said one word about why I would be so worried about Vesey. Apparently, he has no idea how I feel about him. I am positive he'd have something to say about that if he did. Perhaps he understands we are childhood friends and go way back. Perhaps he always knew I snuck around, spending time with Vesey, and he just never said anything about it. Come to think of it, maybe he knew everything. Maybe Mrs. Washington gave him an earful when she sent Vesey away and told him it was all my fault. Maybe Daddy knows all of this, all our history together, but he lets me lead my own life anyway. Or maybe he knows nothing at all. Yes, that's probably it. Whatever the case, I've asked him to please keep a watch on the Washington house and listen for wailing or other signs that Vesey has been killed at war.

Killed at war. Oh please, God, don't ever let me have to utter those words about Vesey. April Cunningham's older brother came home in a box three weeks ago and honestly, I don't know how she can stand it. She's going to try to finish this semester, but bless her heart, I don't know how she can study for exams in this state.

So far, no signs of mourning have been reported by Daddy, so I hold my breath as I write this.

Margaret is getting married. She's dropping out of school to marry a senior who's very wealthy and going off to med school at MUSC next year. She'll be going back to Charleston to begin her life as a married woman, probably will have some kids. I guess I saw this coming, but I never imagined that a woman like Margaret, so free-spirited, would ever agree to settle down. She says she's gotten all her wild days out of her system, and in a way, I suppose she's right. Maybe that's what's wrong with me. Maybe I haven't taken enough time to go wild and be free and just live life. All I know is, my head is nowhere in school right now. I don't know how I'll ever pass my final exams. I don't know how I'll stand a summer at home or how I'll manage college again in the fall without Margaret here.

A girl on the hall downstairs, Brigit, is leaving school to become a stewardess for AirAmerica. She says she'll get to travel all over the world for free, get to meet new people, get to live the glamorous life of a beauty queen, really. She said I'm pretty enough to get a stewardess job, too, and I'm seriously considering it. I've already sent off an application and am awaiting a reply.

My heart is on the other side of the world in Vietnam.

Vesey is out braving the world and fulfilling his patriotic duty, but me? I'm just bored and sheltered. I've got to get out of here. I've gone absolutely stir crazy.

July 4, 1970

Dear Sketchbook,

It's official! I am going to be an AirAmerica girl! They have the cutest little outfits with knee-high boots, stylish short dresses, and adorable hats. I leave for training in Dallas next week and am excited to be studying again. It's been awhile since I've felt that way. Mama and Daddy are not pleased, to say the least, but again, they're letting me make my own way. "Make my own mistakes" is the way they put it. But I know what I'm doing. I'm getting out there. I'm not sitting still. My life is going to be full of exotic travel and adventure and I'll be all too busy to miss Charleston or Vesey Washington. Goodbye, Furman. The world is my textbook.

Happy Independence Day to me!

November 1, 1970

Dear Sketchbook,

I took my first real working flight today from my home base in Atlanta to Tampa. I was nervous, wondering if I'd spill a drink on someone's lap or forget something important when showing the passengers how to fasten their seat belts. Not everyone would do it, mind you, but with a little prodding, they acquiesced. A particularly difficult gentleman in seat 7C asked me if I'd like to have cocktails with him when we landed, but I got out of it by saying I was meeting my sister and only had a short time to spend with her. But thank you, anyway, and hope you fly with us again soon.

We've been told to say this last part when trying to smooth over uncomfortable moments with the opposite sex. That wouldn't work with a woman, you see. There was a woman flying with her husband today who seemed to look at me disapprovingly, as if I was doing something wrong by serving her husband a drink. I most certainly am not doing anything wrong. I'm a grown woman. This is my job. I get paid to be kind to the passengers and wear this cute little outfit. So I've done nothing at all wrong.

And yes, of course, the men are going to be attracted to us—we're all single young ladies with skirts that rise up to the North Pole when we bend over or help a passenger with his bag in the overhead. But we're making a living and a good one, I might add, one that with hard work and many miles will bring seniority and perks and maybe even more.

Brigit is convinced her husband will fly our airplane someday. Well, the future Mr. Brigit, anyway. She hasn't met him yet, but some of the girls think it would be romantic to have a gorgeous passenger in the back row, to bring him a pillow or a cocktail, and then, when their eyes meet, voila, love at first sight.

I told Brigit that if that happens she'll have to quit flying. She says who cares; she'll have the man of her dreams. Marriage is grounds for being let go from the airline, as is pregnancy. I've heard many stories about girls who've been fired after letting the airline know they were pregnant. I suppose it's fair, but maybe it's not fair at all. I'm not sure yet. All I know is that the pilot we had flying our aircraft today, Robert Friedberg, was so handsome and capable, I felt very safe in his hands . . . well, having his hands at the controls, anyway. Between you and me, he could land on my airstrip anytime. That's sort of a joke between us AirAmerica girls.

Now for the mundane: Tampa was very nice as far as airports go. It was sunny, of course, and a couple of us girls just sat out on the cafeteria veranda and soaked up sunshine.

And for the more exciting: I called Mama and Daddy tonight and told them I think I'm going to like this job. They seemed genuinely happy for me. I could tell at the end of the conversation, though, that my father was unusually quiet, so I asked him what was wrong.

"Nothing's wrong," he said. "I just thought you might like to hear that there's a lot of shouting going on tonight at the Washington house across the creek."

"Shouting?" I asked, heart stopped.

"Yes, and dancing. He's back, Ally. Your friend Vesey? Looks like he came back in one piece from what I can tell from over here with my binoculars."

I couldn't speak. I just couldn't speak. Finally, I mustered, "Thank you, Daddy, thank you! I . . . That's good news."

Good news is an understatement. Can you believe it? Vesey's back! And he's alive! He's served his time, and oh, how badly I wish I could be there to welcome him to Mount Pleasant. He may need all the welcoming and dancing he can get, because from what I've seen and heard, there are boys coming home to jeers, not cheers, and worse. I saw a couple soldiers in the airport today, having just come home from overseas, and a woman actually spit on them as they walked by. It's not right, any of it. They're still people, these soldiers. And they've just been through hell.

But thank God Vesey survived it all. He always has been a survivor. No matter what this life throws him.

My goodness, I do miss that smile. I'm flying out to Chicago tomorrow, and I'm excited about the trip, I am, but honestly, part of me wants to go—needs to be—home.

THIRTY-FIVE

Shangri-La

Kathmandu, Nepal
Sunila

I AM THINKING ABOUT HOME. I AM THINKING OF AMAA and Buba and what he must be doing to her now that he knows I have left. He's never been a kind man. He's never loved Amaa, from what I can tell, and certainly, he's never loved me. He once made me sleep in the rain for two nights when I was twelve years old and had just been promoted, if one can call it that, to a carver instead of a stone crusher.

"She thinks she is too good for us. She thinks with her skin and blue eyes that she is some sort of goddess, someone high caste, someone special. But she is not special. She is like the dogs that roam about. She should sleep with the dogs."

And sleep with them I did. I suffered a terrible sickness in my lungs after that and when I was finally well and home from hospital, we only had more debt to pay off. Buba hated me all the more.

I am thinking of home, of our hovel, our tiny tent with its

walls that keep nothing out, the water, how it comes in beneath and leaves muddy puddles where we should be sleeping. I am thinking of home now, because I am in the Shangri-La Hotel, and this must be how the gods live. This is nothing at all like home.

There are two beds, big enough for a family of six people, in this one room. There is a television set that seems to send me into a trance when I push the button and hear the people talk. Time moves quickly when I watch it. I have to keep turning it off for fear my time in this room will be gone when I blink my eyes. There is a working toilet and a bathtub—not for sharing—only for me. And no one is watching. I have bathed already and although the water was warm and there was sweet-smelling soap to use, I was anxious. I felt someone would break into the room and yell at me to get out. They would say, *Who do you think you are? You filthy dog, get out of this room. You are stealing it, you little thief!*

I have heard these words many times in my life. To not hear them makes me uneasy. I know they are coming. I try to stay prepared.

There are two mirrors in this room in the Shangri-La Hotel. One is by the television across from the beds. When I sit on the edge of the bed and watch the newsman telling about the tragedies in Kathmandu, I see myself in the mirror, and it startles me. I cannot get used to seeing my image. She is older than I remembered. Before my bath, I saw myself in a dingy pink-and-orange sari. It is now clean and drying on the bar in the bathroom behind me.

I am in a white towel that covers little of my body. I, too, am clean. My skin is mottled with spots on my forehead and neck, but the rest of my body, the part that lies beneath this towel, is much whiter than Amaa's body. I have seen Amaa nude many times, and her skin is the color of roasted beans. But beneath my towel—I dare not peek—my skin could be from the tops of the snowy mountains of Nepal, where that white bird should have left me, instead of dropping me into the filth of Kathmandu.

My heart jolts. There is a knock at the door. It will be Mr. Assai asking to see my book again. Fearful, I feel the hanging fabric of my sari, but it is still wet. I run out of the bathroom and make sure the latch is still fastened. I open a door to a very small room. There is a bar with hangers on them and a long white robe. I put it on and feel even more like a thief than before. But the odor of the fabric is of the finest powders, and I smile inside despite myself.

When I'm ready, I open the door, but instead of finding Mr. Assai before me, there is a woman holding a tray with domes of silver and a little vase of flowers. I nearly faint with delight when I smell the food. My stomach rumbles and the woman sets the tray on the table near the curtains. "Would you like to see the view?" she asks me.

I did not know there would be a view, but she pulls back the curtains, and there, on the ground below, is green grass and colorful flowers and tailored gardens. There is a man-made river flowing through the stones and trees, and it seems as if it is all sculpted from drawings from the Book of the Gods itself. As if I have opened the pages and finally managed a way in.

THIRTY-SIX

The Invitation

Ally

IN THE SUMMER OF 1971, I'D EARNED TWO WEEKS' VACA-
tion and decided, after traveling nonstop for work, to come home to
Mount Pleasant and rest with Mama and Daddy. Mama filled me
with butter beans and fresh corn and vegetable soup, things I had
been missing. But I went easy on it all. I couldn't afford to gain any
weight for fear they would not let me fly. There was a girl I knew
who had reached 130 pounds and the airline made her step on the
scale before they let her board an airplane. It was shameful to watch.
I certainly didn't want to have to go that route, so I ate lightly and
did the exercises we'd been trained to do. Mama seemed thrilled to
have me home, but there was some distance between us. I suppose
now that I was a woman, she didn't know me the way she once did.

Daddy and I would sit for hours on the dock and fish. I still
loved fishing and acting the tomboy as I always had. This fancy
girly-girl life I was leading was great fun, but I loved to stick on an
old pair of blue jeans and go barefoot through the grass.

One morning as Daddy and I were setting up shop on the end of the dock, we saw a boat coming toward us. I nearly fell over when I saw Vesey Washington. He was a sight for sore eyes, handsome and so bright-eyed. He had no visible wear and tear from the war, and I imagined him to be just as he had been before he left.

As he docked, I ran to him and put my arms around him, right there in front of Daddy.

"It's so good to see you!" I squealed.

Vesey pushed back and smiled. "Good to see you too, Miss Ally. Good to see you too. And Doc Green?" Vesey reached his hand out for Daddy's and Daddy shook it heartily with both hands. My heart nearly overflowed with joy. I had certainly thought about Vesey every now and again . . . Oh, who was I kidding? Every new city I went to, I thought to myself, *Boy, wouldn't Vesey love to see this!* As I stood on the foggy San Francisco Bay. As I saw the skyscrapers of New York City. As I walked through adobe houses in New Mexico. I thought of him every step of the way and brought him with me, in my heart.

So seeing him in person was beyond belief. I'd been waiting and plotting how to set out and find Vesey without Daddy getting suspicious of my motives, yet here he was. He'd come to me by water, as if I'd dreamed him up. He was a vision.

"How have you been?" Daddy asked him.

"Doing real good," said Vesey. "Thank you. Good to be home."

"I hear you went off to Vietnam. Is that right?"

Vesey's smile faltered and he looked at his feet for a second. "Yes, sir, I did."

He waited to see how Daddy would respond and tears sprang

to my eyes when Daddy eyed him hard and said, "Welcome home, son. You did your duty. Your parents must be awfully proud."

I don't think I've ever wanted to hug my daddy more than I did that minute, but instead, I said, "How about some iced tea? Vesey, would you like to come sit up on the porch?"

Vesey looked at Daddy for permission and Daddy nodded. "Come on up and set a spell," he said. "I'd like to hear how your mama is doing."

"Oh, doing right well. Feeds me all the time." Vesey smiled and patted his lean belly. "She thinks I'm wastin' away."

"And your dad?"

"Daddy's good. Still oysterin'. I been workin' with him a good bit. I can bring you a bushel anytime you like."

"That'd be nice," said Daddy. I left the two to go grab the iced tea and when I came back, something was different on Daddy's face. I set the tray down and offered each man a glass, then I took one for myself and sat on a rocking chair, crossing my legs just like they taught us in stewardess school. It didn't have quite the same effect in my blue jeans.

"Miss Ally, Doc Green says you been flyin' all over creation."

"Yes, I have. I'm a stewardess now on AirAmerica."

"Well, that is good work. Ain't sure how you do that flyin' though. I seen enough of it in the army, and every time I had to hold my breath."

We shared a laugh and I felt so silly, like a schoolgirl with a crush. The two most important men in my life were there with me on the same porch and it was nearly too much. I sipped my tea and smiled, unable to speak.

"So how long are you home for?" Vesey asked me. My heart

skipped, imagining him asking me to get together with him, to go fishing like old times or maybe more. Dare I imagine more?

"About another week," I said. "I go back to Atlanta on the eighteenth."

"Oh," said Vesey. He looked genuinely disappointed, and I was sure in that moment that he had feelings for me too. I'd always wondered. He'd never out and out said it or shown it, really, but I knew deep down he must have felt the same for me.

Then Daddy said, "It's too bad you'll be gone for the wedding."

"What wedding?" I asked.

"Vesey, here, just invited us to his wedding in two weeks' time. He's marrying a girl . . . What's her name again?"

"Beulah," said Vesey, his eyes beaming. "She's a great gal, great cook. Her daddy owns the farm down over next to my uncle Percival's. That's how come we met."

If ever there was a moment when the world seems to melt away and you wither down to nothing but a crack in the cement, it was that moment for me. I choked on my iced tea and Vesey moved to pat me on the back, but I had to get up and leave. I had no control over what I might say or do, so I excused myself, faking a smile until I made it to the bathroom, and there, in the privacy of darkness, I bawled my eyes out. When Daddy came in to check on me, I couldn't speak. He told me Vesey had gone on back to work and then he stood at the door a long time without saying anything. Finally, Daddy walked away quietly and I turned on the light. My face was distorted and red and streaked with makeup. I climbed down into the dry cold tub and stared at my backward reflection in the faucet. Everything was distorted and backward and wrong.

When I came back out much later, I grabbed my sketchbook and found Daddy on the dock. I sat down Indian-style and started sketching Daddy holding his fishing rod. He looked at my puffy eyes but didn't say one word. I loved my father then something fierce, and I drew him well, a profile in his fishing hat.

Neither one of us uttered Vesey's name again for the rest of my trip home that summer. Both Daddy and I knew it would have been more than I could have stood.

THIRTY-SEVEN

Rude Awakening

Ally

ROBERT FRIEDBERG AND I BECAME AN ITEM IN OCTOBER of 1971. He bought me a drink in the Dallas airport and then another and soon we began spending all our layovers together. He was charming and handsome, and something about his flying an aircraft just hypnotized me. I'd seen those controls. I'd imagined myself trying to learn everything he'd had to learn in order to fly, and if I thought about it, it made my head swim. He carried all of us safely in the air. It was a lot of responsibility and made him all the more attractive to me. Robert Friedberg, the cutest pilot to ever fly the friendly skies, was interested in me, and he proved to be the perfect antidote to thinking about Vesey Washington.

By this time, Vesey was married, and he and Beulah Washington were farming away as husband and wife, digging in the soil, selling their produce on the side of the road. I could picture them. It was quaint, really, and I was happy for Vesey. Truly, I was. I was glad he finally had a happy ending to his life. There you have it. I was no longer responsible for his happiness or sadness—not that I ever had been, but I'd carried the weight of it, for sure. I felt as if I'd finally been set free. Knowing Vesey would never be mine allowed me to give myself fully to another man.

Robert and I flew quite often together, and although I'm fairly sure we weren't exclusive due to the talk among the girls, I knew he had feelings for me. He told me as much, maybe not in words, but through actions. He would buy me flowers and put his arm around me in broad daylight in the airport. He would tell me how beautiful I was. Looking into Robert's eyes, I believed him and was falling for him hard. As hard as I could, anyway.

And then one morning, we were to fly to San Francisco and back to Atlanta in one day. I woke up happy next to Robert and went to the bathroom to get ready. I remember starting the water in the shower, and as the steam filled the room, the room started to spin. Before I knew it, I was running to the toilet and vomiting, something I just never did.

I looked at myself in the mirror then, thin, pretty, terrified. I'd tried using the Pill, but it was putting weight on me and I was afraid they'd start weighing me in before flights and telling me I'd gotten fat. That they wouldn't let me fly anymore. But now I was pregnant and that was definitely worse. I was twenty-one years old, single, and scared to death to tell Robert about it. If he knew, he might feel responsible to tell the airline. One word and I'd be out of a job. So I decided to keep it to myself until I formulated a solid plan.

That was by far the longest day of flying I'd had in my first six months as an AirAmerica girl. But as the days and weeks went on, it seemed I was running out of time. I'd have to do something, to say something to Robert quickly, because if I waited any longer, the whole world would know about my indiscretion, and I'd be out of a job *and* a cute pilot boyfriend, not to mention the father to my unborn child.

THIRTY-EIGHT

Dusty Files

Kathmandu, Nepal
Sunila

MR. ASSAI, THE US EMBASSY CONSULATE OFFICER, AND
I are sitting in the restaurant of the Shangri-La Hotel. It is outside on the lawn, and the chairs and table are carved out of wood
that seems to grow up out of the ground. The view behind me
is the hotel itself, but beyond Mr. Assai, I watch the trees and
flowers and water flowing, as if paradise lies just beyond his
shoulders, almost in my reach. The moon is rising higher still,
full and orange, casting warm light on my hands. They itch to
hold a chisel and busy themselves. I am anxious, yet there is a
hope inside me I have never felt before. For what I am hoping,
exactly, I am unsure.

"Ms. Kunari, thank you for meeting with me again," says
Mr. Assai.

"No, thank you," I say.

"Are you comfortable here? Are they treating you well?"

"Oh, very much so. I—I have never had such . . . Yes, I have been treated very well, sir. Better than I deserve."

"Good. That is very good. I took the liberty of doing some research before I came to see you this evening. It seems I may have found something . . . worthwhile." I search his face and he reaches across the table. "May I hold the book, please?"

Slowly, I lift the sketchbook from my lap and place it in his hands. I take a deep breath. "Please, what did you learn?"

"Do you know in which year you were born?"

"Yes. Well, no. I am either thirty-eight or thirty-seven. Possibly thirty-nine. Amaa told me I was several months old when they found me. Or rather, when they took me. I—I do not know what to believe, Mr. Assai. Perhaps I was born in 1971 or 1972. I have never truly known. I remember as a child that in the month of December, Amaa would hold me close at night and put a dot of rice yogurt on my forehead for good luck. I've always considered my birthday to be in December."

Mr. Assai nods but his face remains untroubled as he opens the book. He makes grunting noises every now and again as he flips the pages or mutters, "Aha . . . I see." I do not know what all of this means. The server brings us two cups and saucers and a pitcher of milked tea. I pour a cup for Mr. Assai with shaky hands and then a cup for myself.

"This is very interesting, Ms. Kunari," says Mr. Assai, stirring his tea. "I am eager to tell you what I'm reading here."

"And I am eager to hear. Please. Go on."

"First, I should tell you what I learned in our embassy files this afternoon." He closes the book and sets it in his lap, then he leans forward and places both hands on the table. "I wanted to verify the things you mentioned to me earlier, not that I didn't believe you—that your mother claims you were taken from a woman in a café."

My heart falters and I'm unsure what to do with myself. I take my spoon and stir my tea.

"Ms. Kunari, this sketchbook appears to have belonged to an American, based on the written words. So with that, I looked back to see if there were any reported kidnappings of American children in Kathmandu in the early 1970s . . . assuming your age, of course."

Mr. Assai smiles and is quiet for a moment, and the big orange moon behind him makes him glow until it seems he may burst into flames. I put my hands to my lips and bite on my finger.

"Ms. Kunari, indeed, there was an American child reported missing."

The server comes by and asks if we are ready to order, but I am unable to speak. Mr. Assai sends her away.

"This book, Ms. Kunari, the one you brought me, the one you said was found with you when your father took you, this book"—he holds it up in front of me and taps the worn black cover—"appears to have belonged to a young woman from the United States, the same woman who reported to the embassy that her child was stolen from a café in Kathmandu in December of 1972."

I let out a tiny squeal and tears begin flowing down my face. Mr. Assai reaches forward and gently brushes the tears from my cheeks. He smiles at me compassionately, encouragingly. "Ms. Kunari, there is so much more to be done to confirm all of this, and I don't want to get your hopes up too soon, but I believe you do have an American mother out there somewhere. I believe you were born an American citizen and that you were kidnapped and raised as a Nepali. And I'm going to do everything in my power to make sure justice is served in this case."

I put my hands over my eyes and begin shaking although it is warm and dry now. The rains have stopped. "This will require a lot of work and time, and even more patience. So I will need your total cooperation, Ms. Kunari. I'll need you to stay here at the Shangri-La until I come up with further evidence. We will, of course, take care of your payments here. You will not incur any debt. May I count on your total cooperation, please?"

"Yes, of course," I say. But inside, I feel strange, as if I have walked off and left a shell of myself sitting here. As if the ground is shaking and I am desperate to hold on. I have always been untouchable. I am Sunila Kunari, daughter of Amaa and Buba, master carver of stone. I am a Nepalese worker. I was born in debt. I am a member of the lowest caste in Nepal, a Dalit. I am not worthy to be sitting here in this hotel café with paradise within my reach. I am not worthy to have this man telling me that I may not be who I've always thought I was but am instead an American citizen. I do not know what this means.

Part of me wants to scream for joy. It feels right in my bones. But in many ways I need to run and run and run, all the way back to Amaa. I want to tell her that I forgive her. I want to lie in her arms again and listen to her singing. I want to go back and chisel the stones that have never brought me freedom.

I want to thank the gods for what is happening at this moment. But I am too confused to be sad or to be happy. I simply *am* right now. Torn.

"Thank you," I say to Mr. Assai.

"We will get to the bottom of this, Ms. Kunari. Mark my words. Now please, let us have some food and then I'll need to take this book back with me. May I do that? May I take it with me?"

I grab at my chest and stare at Mr. Assai. It is more than I can handle. I am unable to fully trust this man, yet I must trust him. It is too late not to trust him. I realize I have come too far, crossed some invisible line, and now I must continue traveling this journey, for to turn back now would mean the death of me.

I am different now.

Somehow, I am different than before.

THIRTY-NINE

Steak au Poivre in Paris

Mount Pleasant
Ally

IT'S VERY DIFFERENT NOW, MY ARTWORK. IT HAS TAKEN
on a sophisticated, exotic air it never had before. With the silk
beneath my fingers and the smell of hot dye in my nostrils, I feel
whole, as if my entire life has been to get to this moment, to making this batik, this scene of the river with indigos and blues and
greens and bright sun yellows. When I look back on my life now,
for just an instant, it all seems to make sense. When I am doing
this artwork and engulfed in this creation, my life seems to have
had a purpose—to get me here—the good, the bad, the people,
the loss, all of it. Though I can't understand why I need to be here
exactly. It's just a feeling.

Maybe I'm breathing in too many fumes. That's it. I go and
open the window to let some fresh air blow through. Daddy would
be pleased to see me in this room, making my way. I wish with
all my heart he could see me now. He would say something like,

Ally, girl, just look at you. I always knew you'd come back, always knew you'd come to your senses. I hoped you'd move on with your life one day and realize you don't have to go traipsing all over the world anymore to find happiness. That she's been here with you, all along. There is a time and a place for everything under the sun, sweetheart. There is a time to search and a time to give up searching. It's time that you stay home.

I stop. I put my brush down on the table beside my dyes. I should not have allowed myself to imagine Daddy's voice. It's too soon. I feel as if he might come to the door any minute now and want to see what I'm working on.

There is a scratch at the door. I go to open it and find Kat at my feet, eyes bright and purring. I smile at the little booger.

"I don't mean to shut you out, Kat. Come here, you old boy." I bend down carefully and lift him up. The hip is so much better that tomorrow I'm going to walk that new bridge. I am. The cat and I go find Daddy's La-Z-Boy to sit in. We settle and I stroke his soft fur. He purrs and my soul just rumbles. I lift him up to me and rub my face on his side. I kiss the top of his head and rub his ears just the way Daddy used to do. Kat leans toward me as tears drop down my face, and he licks my cheeks with his dry scratchy tongue. It makes me cry all the more, having this little cat love me. I've never done anything to deserve his affection, yet here he is giving it to me freely. He's lonely too; I understand that.

"It's you and me, Kat. Just you and me. Don't run off now, all right?" Another pang of sadness strikes my gut as I imagine Daddy here after Mama died, and me, flying off to anywhere-but-here. I left him all alone, didn't I? Was that selfish? Did he understand? "Thank you for being Daddy's friend," I tell the cat.

"I imagine you were just what the doctor ordered by the time you set up house here. You were a stray, weren't you? Little skinny, scrawny thing. Look at you now. Are you some sort of angel cat? Hmmm? Someone to comfort the afflicted?"

The words coming out of my mouth only bring more grief. *Where are you, Daddy? Where are those messages, the real ones you promised you'd send me when you got to heaven? What else did you tell me that was a flat-out lie? That my heart would mend after losing Constance? That I could get on with life and just forget about her? That I could forget I'd had my only child stolen from me and go on to live a normal, productive life?*

"You were wrong, Daddy," I say, looking out the window at the sunlight glistening on water. "I know you meant well, but you were so wrong about so many things."

I lay my head back and close my eyes. I remember how wrong Daddy was about Robert Friedberg. Daddy believed him when he said he would marry me. He believed him like a fool.

I remember the night I told Robert about my pregnancy. It was 1972. We were having dinner by candlelight in my little Atlanta apartment. I had made his favorite, steak au poivre and pommes frites, although the potatoes were not fried but roasted. A pilot and stewardess need to stay fit.

I could barely eat a bite, but I watched him ravage his plate and tell me about the little café in Paris where he had the very best steak au poivre, and he looked at me, took my hand, and said, "We'll go there someday. I can't wait to take you to Paris." After a while, Robert noticed I wasn't eating and asked if I wasn't feeling well.

I came right out and said it then, no pussyfooting around.

"I'm pregnant."

Robert put his fork and knife down. He looked up at me. He bit his lip.

"Are you sure?"

I began sniffling and he knew I was serious.

"Oh boy," he said. He wiped his face with his hand. His eyes darted back and forth across the table. "How far along are you?"

"About ten weeks."

"Ten weeks?! And you waited till now to tell me? Is it . . . Whose is it? Is it mine?"

"Of course it's yours, Robert." He was quiet for a minute, soaking it all in.

"Well, what are you going to do?"

I blinked at him. "What am I going to do? What am I going to do? I—I don't know. Why don't you tell me what you want to do?"

In the pit of me, I had dreamed of this moment, when I would tell Robert the news of our baby, and he would know that I was his forever and would confess his love for me finally. He would come round and sweep me off my feet and hug me hard and tell me how happy he was, how I should just forget the airline, that he would take care of me now. That I didn't have to worry about anything. That he would be the happiest man alive if I would just agree to be Mrs. Friedberg.

Instead of getting down on one knee, Robert got up and walked to the other side of the room. It grew cold around me. After a few minutes of silence, he said, "I know this place, in Paris, where a girl can go and . . . and not have to worry about having some quack without a license . . ."

My heart sank. In that moment, seeing Robert there, all the love I'd mustered for him fell down by my feet and I knew I was in this thing alone. I had already decided to have the baby. I had decided to love this child on my own. I would have to go home to Charleston with my tail between my legs and live with Mama and Daddy so I could raise this baby, but I was going to do it. I was going to give up the so-called glamorous life of travel and make my way back home.

Seeing me silent, Robert came to me and put his hands on my shoulders. "It'll be all right, kid. Don't worry. We just can't let the airline know or . . . or you'll be out of a job, right? And me, well, I doubt they'd look too friendly on me getting you into this . . . position."

Into this position. I wanted him out of my apartment. I wanted him out of my face. Any attraction I'd had to him before was gone and to look at him made me sick. "I'm not feeling well, Robert. You understand. How about we call it a night. I'll see you at work tomorrow?"

Robert studied me and faltered. "Oh, okay. I, um . . . so you're all right . . . with this? You're . . . We'll make plans to get you to Paris in a week or two. Just leave everything to me, all right? I know what I'm doing here. It'll be the best thing for everyone. And then we'll go to that little café and get that steak au poivre I was telling you about. It really is to die for."

"That sounds swell," I said, dismissing him. I smiled and pushed him out the door. He kissed me on the lips before he left and, honest as a heart attack, I felt nothing for him. Nothing at all. It was like kissing a brick wall.

FORTY

The In-between

Kathmandu, Nepal
Sunila

"I'm afraid we've run up against a bit of a brick wall," says Mr. Assai. He is holding a file and tapping it.

"Please," I say, "sit down." There is a balcony outside my hotel room at the Shangri-La. Over the rail I can see the gardens and hear the water trickling in fountains. There are tourists to Nepal, Americans, sitting at a table below us eating lunch, and I want to run to them and ask them if they know my mother.

"I've spoken with the police about you. We have confirmed our records. In December of 1972, a woman by the name of Alicia Green worked with the embassy, with Kathmandu police, and with the Nepali military to try and find her baby. Flyers were put up all over town near the Malla Café where the alleged kidnapping took place. She and her father—apparently he came here after the event—offered a reward of one hundred thousand Nepali rupees to anyone who had any information that would lead to the return of the child."

I straighten my back and shift in my seat. This is painful to my ears. I am picturing this woman and her father frantic to find her child. "And did anyone come forward?" I ask.

"No," says Mr. Assai. "No one came forward. The money was never paid out. Nothing ever turned up. And I need to be honest with you. In the beginning of the search, the police suspected the mother was lying. So did embassy officials. You see, Americans are supposed to register themselves and their children with the US Embassy upon arrival for many reasons, for safety, mostly, but she did not. She admitted she was here in Kathmandu, running away from something in the US."

"Running from what, exactly?"

Mr. Assai opens the file and flips through pages. He stops on one and looks at me before he reads. "Ms. Green claims to have come to Nepal for rest and to get away. When asked what she was getting away from, she replied, 'A broken heart.' Then she erupted into tears." Mr. Assai closes the file. "Apparently, this woman was troubled when she came here. Perhaps the father of the child had left her, abandoned her? There isn't much else in the file."

"So the brick wall—is this the brick wall you mentioned?"

Mr. Assai sets the folder on a little table between us. He leans forward and clasps his hands.

"Actually, Ms. Kunari, the issue I'm finding is . . . Well, without speaking to your mother and father here in Kathmandu, without getting a confession from them, I'm afraid everything is just hearsay. There are no facts. Surely your story has merit and it certainly seems to be true, but I'm afraid that without some facts, everything in this case is coincidental. I certainly cannot try to contact Ms. Green in South Carolina—"

"Wait. You have found where she lives? You have found her?"

Mr. Assai's mouth falls open and he does not speak. Then he nods and says, "Yes, I have located this woman."

"And she's still alive?" I ask, hopeful, heart racing.

"Yes. She is. Though her father is recently deceased. The one who offered the money for your return."

"Deceased," I repeat. I breathe in deeply and picture his ashes swirling up into the air, being released into the Baghmati River to flow along the water until transported to the holy Ganges.

I stand and look out over the trees. The sky is dark and bringing more rains. I do not want to cause more trouble for Amaa. I do not want her arrested. I am torn. I clutch my sari and feel my heart beating.

"Ms. Kunari, I must tell you that I have looked over this woman's sketchbook. I believe that she did indeed have her child stolen from a café in Kathmandu. I believe this woman has suffered immeasurable loss. As have you." I turn to look at him and a tear escapes. "We need to gather some evidence, Ms. Kunari. We must now talk to your parents and get the truth from them. If your mother loves you, as you say she does, she will do this for you. Only then will justice be done."

I know what he is saying is correct. I excuse myself, leaving him on the balcony, and walk into the hotel room. I splash water on my face in the bathroom and look at myself in the mirror. My cheeks are fuller. They have been feeding me well here. I do not look like Amaa or Buba. I look like her, the woman in the drawings. She, too, looked at herself in the mirror. Only she drew what she saw. She saw sadness and loneliness, confusion. I see it in my own eyes. Perhaps she saw me in the mirror the way that I see her in mine.

I pat my face dry with a clean towel and firm my shoulders. I am not the same woman who left the quarry. I am like a spirit who has left a body. I am in that in-between when the spirit may choose to return to the body, to linger here on earth. Mr. Assai is like the loved ones holding vigil over my death, encouraging me to go on to my ethereal next world.

Yes. I will go. I will not return to the quarry the same as I was before. I will go with Mr. Assai and we will speak to Amaa and Buba. The cruel man is no longer there. I have nothing to fear with Mr. Assai at my side. We will go and I will continue my metamorphosis. I am changing into someone else.

"I will take you to the quarry, Mr. Assai. You may ask the questions you need to ask."

"Good," he says. "Very good, Ms. Kunari. You are a very brave woman, the likes of which I have not seen. We will do this thing together, you and I. We will find the truth. You deserve as much."

My old life is dead to me. I turn and picture my white ashes falling onto the Baghmati riverbed, commencing their long, winding journey to the Ganges. Flowing home.

FORTY-ONE

Falling in Love

Ally

I WENT HOME TO LIVE WITH MAMA AND DADDY IN
January of 1972. I told AirAmerica that I was expecting a child
just fourteen months after starting that job, and of course, they let
me go. I had broken "airline policy." I did not say who the father
was; I simply apologized, packed up my belongings, and came
home to live with Mama and Daddy on Molasses Creek. I was
doing the right thing, keeping my baby, no matter how difficult it
was making things. A single woman having a child was frowned
upon, but not altogether unseen in those days. The free love era
had brought with it some children, and I was beginning to see
there was nothing free at all about love. Love was about sacrifice
and giving and loss. I could see that now.

My parents were gracious, as I knew they'd be. They never
condemned my choices; they just remained quiet for the first few
weeks. I remember going to the grocery store with my mother
and hearing her whisper to an acquaintance she'd run into that

my husband had gone off to war. I knew the depth of her shame in that moment, listening to those lies, but I understood she was doing what she needed to do. As was I. Mama never said anything negative to my face, and I acted as if I didn't know how hard she was working to cover up my indiscretions. Daddy kept on working, seeing his patients from a little office he kept now near Shem Creek with another doctor. I didn't see him nearly as often as when he was visiting patients' homes, so Mama and I spent time together. It went something like this:

"Honey, have you had enough breakfast? I can make you some more toast."

"No, I'm fine, Mama."

"How about some grits. You don't need to be getting hungry. You feelin' all right? You're looking kind of pale."

"Mama, please, I'm really fine."

She would stand there, rubbing her apron nervously. "Well, it looks like it will be a nice day. How about I set you up some cushions on the porch chairs and you can read or draw. Whatever you like. Get some fresh air."

"That sounds fine, Mama. Thank you."

I can't say there was any substance to our conversations. I can't say that Mama seemed comfortable with me being home. She just doted on me to excess. A few months into living there, when my belly was swelling, I understood she was acting this way as a comfort to herself, so she could *act* and not have to talk her way through this pregnancy. But as time wore on, I realized Mama was actually getting excited about the baby. I had been an only child, and now there was going to be another one in the house. Mama, I realized, was nesting, something I had not quite begun. It seemed our house was too small for two mothers, and she was doing a fine job for both of us.

Robert knew I was keeping the baby. It was my body and I was doing with it what I wanted. He was nice about it, albeit scared to death, but I assured him no one would know the truth about his involvement. He relaxed in this and told me what a brave little girl I was. That he would be there to help out in whatever way he could. At about six months my stomach was the size of a small basketball and my limbs and rear were growing in proportion to the food Mama was feeding me. I hadn't seen him since I left Atlanta, but it was then Robert decided to pay us a visit.

He had flown into Charleston and was on a short layover. It wasn't as if he made the trip especially to see me. There he was, flowers in hand, as my father opened the door. We'd been expecting him, but I don't think my parents were quite prepared for how handsome this man was. Honestly, he looked like a movie star, Robert Redford or someone equally as cute, and the baby seemed to be squirming in my belly when I saw him again. I wondered if I really did have feelings for him. Maybe I did. He was coming to see me, after all.

Mama nearly tripped over her own two feet as she waited on him with iced tea and little cucumber sandwiches. If I didn't know better, she seemed flummoxed and flirty. I suppose Robert had that effect on people.

He and Daddy sat on the back porch and talked about airplanes and flying and such. Daddy said he'd always wanted to fly, something I had never once heard him utter, and I remember wondering if he was lying or if there were really things I did not know about my father.

After a supper of chicken fried steak, asparagus, and roasted baby potatoes, Mama served her famous key lime pie, and with all the fussing and goo coming from everyone's mouths, you wouldn't have known there was an elephant the size of Texas in the middle of the room with us—namely me.

Filled with muscadine wine and key lime pie, the handsome and dapper Robert looked my father in the eyes and told him he thought he and I should get married. He turned to me and said with dimples shining, "How 'bout it, kid?"

I gasped and Mama grabbed at her chest and Daddy reached out and shook his hand.

"Is there a ring too?" Mama squealed as if this was happening to her and not to me.

But I knew there was no ring. This was not a premeditated marriage proposal; it was probably the last thing Robert ever intended to do. And that angered me, seeing Mama and Daddy all happy and hopes up and wrapped up in him. Something in me knew Robert was a fly-by-night. He was impetuous by nature and a true romantic and honestly believed whatever he was saying in the moment. Until he changed his mind later. The problem was he didn't have a loyal bone in his body. I knew how many girlfriends he had. I knew he couldn't become a one-woman man overnight. I knew his career and his flyboy lifestyle were too important to him to give up, and so instead of having him break Mama and Daddy's hearts later, I took the bull by the horns right then and there.

"Thank you, Robert, but I just don't think you're ready for marriage. Or me, for that matter. Thank you for asking, but my answer is no." Then I stood up and walked away before anyone at the table could utter a word.

I didn't cry, but I looked out the window as I walked back to my room. I saw the marsh grass blowing and the water rippling in the current. I saw Vesey's mother's house and the permanence it had on the riverbank, in my life. I had given up my career, my body, my dignity by getting pregnant with Robert, and I wasn't about to give my future and my heart to him too. I could see him for what he really was. Too good to be true.

Right or wrong, I was going to do this thing on my own, have a baby. I was bringing this child into the world and I vowed, then and there, to do everything in my power to protect it from smooth-talkers like Robert Friedberg. I grabbed my belly and held on tight, and in those quiet moments, I fell in love with my child.

FORTY-TWO

Collecting Evidence

Kathmandu, Nepal
Sunila

I AM IN A CAR WITH MR. ASSAI AT THE WHEEL. HE
pauses to let a cow cross the road and then manages to ease in
and out of people and bicycles and rickshaws. It seems everyone is out in the street tending to work and other errands before
the rains come again this evening. I look at his hand gripping
the stick shift. I have never learned to drive a vehicle, though I
have seen men driving on buses. I always like to see what people's
hands do while their eyes are on something else.

When I carve, I must look at my subject, but every now and
again, when I have done something so many times, I can look
away while my hands continue working. I can look away and forget that I am a slave to this piece of stone. Even if it is becoming a
beautiful angel with outstretched wings.

How can I love the stone and hate it at the same time?
Because it is a piece of me. I know nothing else. How can the ox

stand having the yoke put upon its neck day after day after day? Because it is all it has ever known. Nothing more, nothing less.

I study Mr. Assai's face. He has not spoken in many minutes since we left the Shangri-La Hotel. I want to tell him, *Thank you for believing my story.* I want to thank the gods for planting this seed in my heart long ago. I've always known there was something about me, yet the truth has always eluded me, much like a horse with blinders. The world is there for it to see if it could simply turn and look at it, yet it has not the courage to turn and to look.

"We are getting near," I say after a while. The streets are dirtier here. The walls of the buildings grayer. There are children with dusty bare feet standing on the corners, and as we pass them I think to myself: *How many of you are meant to be here? How many of these children have no future but to break stones or to be broken? Which of you will be lucky and find favor with the gods as I surely have?*

No, I am not lucky. I have never been lucky. I have been a curse. My throat closes on me and I close my eyes. I breathe in deeply until I am able to open them again.

"Are you all right?" asks Mr. Assai.

"Yes," I manage.

"You are welcome to wait here in the car if you feel it's too much for you. They may speak to me on my own. It is a possibility."

"No," I say. "I must go with you. I must be there to see the looks on their faces."

"Very well. We will go together, and when we have what we need, I will take you directly back to the Shangri-La Hotel. You are happy there?"

"Oh, very happy."

Yet part of me feels I am being tricked. Mr. Assai is taking me back to the quarry and leaving me there. My parents will never admit to their wrongdoing, and I will appear to be insane. The cruel man's son will never let me go. I will stay here and die here as we all do. As we all must.

The sound of pounding greets us, like birds chirping. Some are hard at work already. When the rainy season comes, people are hungry. They cannot make their wages, for the stones are wet and the dust turns to mud. There is a storehouse with some shelter overhead and some stone on the top remains dry. These are the stones fought over in this hungry season. We walk past mothers with naked children strapped to their backs. We pass old men crouched down and talking to themselves. The people recognize me after a few moments, yet they do not recognize me. I am clean. I have no dust on my clothes or hands or feet or face. I am with a man, a very important-looking man. No, it could not be Sunila, they think to themselves. And we walk on toward Amaa's tent.

I stand there silently taking in this desolate place that is my home. Now that I've seen the Shangri-La and slept in its bed, tasted its fine food, and bathed in its clean water, I am shocked that I have not seen this place for what it is before. I open my mouth and utter, "Amaa?"

There is a rustling sound within the tent and when the cloth swings to the side, I see Buba with no tunic, and unkempt, gray taking over his beard. His eyes pierce me. "You," he says.

"Namaste," I say, nodding. My father spits in my face.

Mr. Assai moves forward and moves me aside. "Mr. Kunari, my name is Mr. Assai. I am with the consulate office with the US Embassy."

Buba looks at the man and shrinks. Fear is in his eyes.

"What is it?" I hear my mother's voice in the tent and my heart melts. I want to hold her again.

"Amaa?" I say. "Amaa, it's me. Sunila."

"Sunila!" My mother wails and comes to her husband's side. She does not pass him, yet falls to her knees, arms outstretched when she sees me. "I thought I would never see you again. Oh, my child, my Sunila."

I go to her. Of course I go to her. She is all I've ever known about love. She is all I've ever had in my life. I love this woman, no matter what she did to have me. She is the only family I have ever known. I bend and pull her to me, fearful at first that Buba will strike my face, yet he is too afraid of this consulate officer from the US Embassy. I have brought a shield beside me.

Mr. Assai holds out identification for Buba's eyes and Buba holds his hands to his sides, perfectly still.

"Mr. Kunari, I have some questions to ask you about something that happened a long time ago. Ms. Kunari, Sunila, here, has come forward with a book of drawings." He looks toward Amaa. "It is my understanding that you, Mrs. Kunari, told your daughter she was taken as a baby from a café in December 1972. That she was not abandoned but stolen. Is this true? Did you say this to your daughter?"

Amaa stands slowly with my help and is no longer crying. Her hands shake as she holds on to mine. "It is true," she says, finding the courage to look me in the eyes.

My father flinches beside her. She dares not look at him.

"Thank you, Mrs. Kunari. Mr. Kunari," says Mr. Assai. "It is very important that you listen to me carefully. You will see I have not brought the police with me. Yet I do need a statement from you. Your daughter, against my own encouragement, wants to protect you and does not want to press charges. But in order for her to find her own mother again, for justice for this family to be served, I need you to tell me the truth of what happened. You understand, I have enough evidence to have you jailed at this very moment, but your daughter is saving you. Do you understand this? Now please, tell me your involvement in stealing this child."

Mr. Assai pushes an old newspaper article toward Buba, and I open my mouth to tell him that he doesn't read, but I stop myself. I close my mouth.

Buba is battered, but a proud man. He looks down at the paper and says, "Yes, I am the one who stole the baby. She was in a café in Thamel. I wanted to sell her for money, but my wife insisted we keep her. I should have sold her away when I could. She's brought nothing but bad luck since the day she was born."

Then he spits at my feet, and the ground falls out beneath me. I stumble and Mr. Assai holds me up.

"But you have no proof," says Buba, smiling. "So what if I say it? I could be a crazy man. You have nothing against me."

Amaa grows still and looks down at her feet. She pauses for several moments and then backs through the doorway. "Amaa! Please don't go!" I wail, but she has disappeared. Mr. Assai holds firmly to my arm and holds his gaze on Buba. In the next moment my mother is quietly joining us again. I look at her and see the tracks of her tears, though she is not upset; she is firm. She pulls her arms out from behind her back and hands Mr. Assai a package wrapped in paper and tied with twine.

"Here," she says. Buba looks at her. "You will find your proof," says Amaa. "You will find when you open this package that the clothes are there, the very clothes she was wearing when she was brought home to me thirty-eight years ago. She is telling the truth. My daughter, Sunila, tells the truth. She is a good child. Always a good child."

Amaa puts her rough fingers up to my face and strokes my skin as if looking at me for the last time, as if studying every new line and silver hair. In her eyes she is empty, yet at peace. She puts her hand down to her side and I know in my heart that this is our final look, our final moment together as mother and daughter. She has done all she can do, and now—now the rest is up to me.

Part Four

He that cannot forgive others, breaks the bridge over which he himself must pass if he would ever reach heaven; for everyone has need to be forgiven.

—George Herbert

FORTY-THREE

Can't Take It with You

Mount Pleasant

Ally

IF IT WERE ALL UP TO ME, VESEY WASHINGTON WOULD never have to work again. Look at him there, loading his cart up with newspapers and magazines. He keeps it hitched to a bicycle and stuffs that rainbow-colored umbrella down in the mix. Hauls it all the way down the road like a mule till he gets to his intersection by the Hardee's. I've watched him. It's sort of a spectacle. I try to act as if I don't see him from in this house. I sort of peek out the windows. I don't know why I'm still uncomfortable with his stand, but I am. There you have it. He shouldn't have to sit out at that stand and cater to people as they drive by. Trust me, I know catering to people. I was in the service industry for nearly four decades, saying, *Welcome aboard,* and *Have a nice flight,* and *May I get you anything, sir?* and *Yes, sir, I'll get you that pillow right now,* and *Yes, ma'am, I do like these outfits,* and *No, they don't make me feel at all patronized by men. I like my job. I enjoy the people. I love to fly.*

Ughh. I do love to fly, or rather, I love getting to my destination. I love the *idea* of going where I'm going, the dreaming about it part. I used to love seeing that same look on my passengers' faces. I loved sitting with the little children who happened to be flying alone. I would take them under my wing and take great care of them. I considered them my own child until I got them to the ticket counter in the next airport and saw the reunion with their parent or grandparent. And all of us were relieved.

All in all, I think I've had the right career for me. Flying away was my vice as well as my bread and butter. This sitting still, even though I've made Daddy's house my own as much as possible, is not all it's cracked up to be. When I'm not working on my batiks, I'm going stir crazy. I feel as if there's something else I need to do!

I look at them out there, my batiks hanging on the back porch, blowing in the wind like prayer flags, sending offerings up to the gods. They've turned out better than I'd imagined, and I have been busy. When I'm creating, I forget my own existence, but when I'm not, I feel something stirring in my soul, this itching under my ribs I cannot satiate. I grab my cell phone from my purse in the kitchen and head out for some fresh air in the stone garden. I go to sit by a particular statue that has always made me think of her. An angel with outstretched wings. I dial Ronnie's number and wait, eyes closed, birds singing around me, squirrels gathering nuts at my feet.

"Hey, it's me," I say. "Y'all home today? Great. Uh-huh. Yeah, I've made a couple more. I'm going to send you one of Molasses Creek. I think Marlene will like it. It has these big white birds and . . . well, maybe she can hang it in the dining room. It'll go well with her blue walls.

"No, no, I'm fine, I just . . . well, I'm feeling that itch again, Ronnie. No, not that itch, you doofus, the one where I need to go flying. I'm . . . thinking of getting away for a while.

"Mmm-hmm. Yes. Yes, I know, but . . . well, Margaret's busy with her granddaughter. Not like we get together all the time. I have lunch with her every now and again, but I declare, spending time with Graison makes me . . . well, it makes me sad, I guess. Seeing that belly and all. Knowing she's going to miss her baby someday. It hurts, Ronnie. I want to save her from herself. And from the rest of the world."

I walk back inside and grab a tissue on a sideboard in the kitchen and dab my nose as I listen to one of my oldest friends, if ex-husbands count as friends. Ronnie met me after my Great Sadness and he was just what I needed, always cheering me up. Shame I never did give him a child though. I'm fairly sure he was shooting blanks. I suppose children for me or Marlene just was not meant to be.

"I realize, Ronnie, that it has been a long time, but I'm different now. I'm not crippled emotionally like maybe I used to be. I just . . . well, Vesey has his own life and I do too. It's just too quiet over here. I'm gonna tell him I'm leaving. No, I am. Maybe Aruba or Hawaii. Someplace warm where I can wear my bathing suit and not give a darn who's looking at me. Someplace they give me little umbrellas in my drink and I—

"Okay, Ronnie. You can try calling me tonight, but I tell you, I'm not gonna change my mind. I believe I am the best judge of my mental health. But thank you, sweetie. I know you're just saying what you think is right. Uh-huh. Uh-huh . . . Oh, listen, I've been missing this mirror Daddy used to have in his bedroom. We'd put these little notches on it every year on my birthday to show how tall I was getting. I was thinking of having you send that back for me if it's no trouble. I . . . Well, from Daddy's furniture in the warehouse. I was just thinking about it the other—

"What do you mean? Are you kidding me? Are you sure?" I fall down into a chair at my oversized kitchen table. "But then where is it? Did they send it to the wrong place? Oh no, Daddy! He'd have a heart attack if he knew his stuff was gone!"

I get off the phone with Ronnie after I beg him to go and double-check. My mind is a blur. Eyes shifting, I think back on that moving day a few months ago and how out of it I was because of the pain medication. Did I even tell those movers where to take Daddy's stuff? Did Vesey? Or did they steal it right out from under me and rob my daddy blind!?

I am so heated I don't know what to do with myself. I grab Daddy's boat keys hanging on the kitchen wall and make my way to the dock where I proceed to climb in, start the engine, and glide fifty-five feet over the water to Vesey's side. It's over in a split min-ute, and I tie up on his dock and barrel toward his house. I could have driven over but it would have taken too much time. I need answers. I feel sick to my stomach. I feel robbed, stolen from, and there's nothing that stabs me worse than when I feel like some-thing important to me has been taken. I've been violated.

"Vesey!" I holler. He'll be able to tell me. He'll be able to ease my mind as he always does. "Vesey, yoo-hoo. It's me, Ally."

Still no answer. I get closer to his little house and think of climbing his steps to knock when I see a door open to his shed where he keeps his bicycle. I go to the doorway and flick on a light. It's been a good long while since I've been here. Vesey's usually the one to come over to my house for suppers or coffee and cards on the dock.

I grab my chest and hope I'm not having a heart attack. There before me, stuffed from wall to wall and floor to ceiling, are my Daddy's things—all his furniture and knickknacks. Everything he ever owned or accumulated. The little table I had when I was a girl, the one I sat at and had tea parties with all my stuffed animals and dolls—that very table is perched upside down in Vesey's shed!

This feels worse than a death. Vesey is the person I've lived my whole life loving. He's the reason I ran off to the airline in the first place, the reason I ran into Robert's arms and got pregnant, the reason I ran off to Nepal with my daughter to get away from the pain of watching Beulah carrying Vesey's own child, and the reason I lost my own. Vesey. He's always been the cause of my reactions and now . . . now I find out he's a fake? He's a thief and a liar. He's no better than society deemed him to be long ago.

Maybe I am a bigot. Maybe I'm no different than all the others who came before me.

Heartsick, I lean out the door and scream bloody murder; it's a sound I should have made years ago when they stole my child. It's a sound I should have made months ago when Daddy left this earth. It's a sound that comes out from someplace deep and foreign inside me, and I scare myself with it. It's the same scream I listened to when Vesey's mama lost her youngest son in Molasses Creek. When the sound stops, I hear an echo far off. I run around to the front of Vesey's house, and there, lying on the dusty ground face-down, is Vesey Washington. His bicycle and cart are still standing.

Without thinking, I rush to his side and tears flood my eyes as I turn him over and see white dirt like ash covering his face. His eyes are closed, and at this moment, I do not care if he stole all my daddy's stuff. He can have it! All of it! This is Vesey Washington. This is the little boy who lived across the river from Daddy and wanted to be a doctor like him when he grew up and never got the chance because I stole his future from him with a single kiss. Yes, this is the same Vesey I've always known, and as I hold him in my arms, crying his name, I understand one hundred percent why a man like this might have stolen from my daddy. *Oh, I understand, and I forgive you. I do.* Because the truth is still there between us in black and white. No matter what he's done, no matter what he might do, he's always had a hold on me.

"Vesey? Honey, speak to me," I plead.

I wipe his face with a wet washcloth and watch as the ambulance pulls up. A man and woman in uniform get out and approach us.

"Thank goodness you're here!"

The man takes my place holding Vesey and says, "Sir? Can you hear me?" He holds his wrist and feels for a pulse. The woman grabs the stretcher out of the back and brings it to us. Everything's happening so fast.

"He's breathing," he says. "Pulse is good."

"Oh, thank God!" I cry and stare at the crosslike clothesline in the yard.

"You're gonna be just fine," I say to Vesey. Then, turning to the paramedic, "I'd like to ride with him if I can."

"Are you family?" The question seems silly to me, obvious, seeing the difference in our skin, but this is a young man in his twenties and times have changed here in the South. We could be family. We could be. "Not family, but neighbors. We've always been neighbors. See? That's my house there, my boat. Well, it is now." The man is quiet. "Do you know what's wrong with him? Is it his heart?"

"I don't know yet. Did you see what happened to him? Does he have any history of heart disease, diabetes?"

"No. I don't think so. But I don't really know. His parents did die pretty young. He'd been trying to get this bicycle and all that heavy stuff loaded up and . . . and maybe it was just too much for him."

The man looks at the newspapers and then at Vesey with recognition. "Ah, the newspaper guy. I know him. Well, come on, Mr. Washington. We're gonna get you to the hospital. Take good care of you."

The next thing I know we are riding down a dirt road, bopping along in the back of the ambulance, and I am praying that Vesey can wake up and speak to me. I'm not sure who I'm praying to, maybe to God, or maybe to Daddy in heaven, or maybe, maybe to Vesey himself.

"Please wake up. Just please, wake up for me." It's the mantra I say to myself and to Vesey for miles and miles to go.

FORTY-FOUR

Elusive Hope

Kathmandu, Nepal
Sunila

FOR THE MILES WE'VE TRAVELED, I HAVE HELD THIS
package in my hands. I cradle it, unable to open the twine just yet.
I am not ready. I will wait for the moment when I can be ready.
When the truth of who I am now meets the truth of who I once
was. My fingers squeeze and the paper crinkles.

"You did very well, Sunila," says Mr. Assai. He glances at me for
a moment, taking his eyes off the road. He has called me by my first
name. Mr. Assai grips the wheel with both hands and says no more.

"The newspaper article," I say. "The one you showed to Buba,
may I see it?"

"Of course." He motions with his head to the backseat, and
there I find an old newspaper folded on his briefcase. I unfold it,
seeing pictures and words I cannot read. Some words I have worked
out from necessity over time, but I cannot take the article and read
it aloud. It would never work.

"The newspaper is a fake," says Mr. Assai. He pauses and I'm stricken, waiting for him to continue his explanation. "I realized your father may not read . . . since you have some difficulty." He reads my face and holds his hand up. "No, it is nothing to be ashamed of, I assure you." He glances at me reassuringly. "I do have the original newspaper in my files, but I didn't want to bring it with me in case your father, well, destroyed it somehow. He didn't, but I wanted to be cautious. The newspaper you are holding is not even from the correct year."

I set the paper on the package and think of the humiliation my father would feel if he knew he'd been tricked. If he knew he'd been made a fool of. Satisfaction fills my lungs as I'm sure it does Mr. Assai.

"I'll be happy to show you the real article when we get back to the embassy."

"We are not returning to the hotel?" Strangely, the quarry we just left felt foreign to me, but the Shangri-La has become my home in just a short while. I am comfortable there. I long to go there now.

"There is much to do, Sunila."

There it is again, my name.

"I hoped we could take lunch in my office again and . . . and work. I'd like to see what's in that package, wouldn't you?"

I swallow and nod. "Yes. Yes, I'd like you to be there when the package is opened. I—this has been a difficult time for me, you understand. Difficult and wonderful at the same time. There is hope in my heart, Mr. Assai." My face flushes and I look at the side of his. "There is hope for the first time in my life. I would not feel this way if I had not come to you. But part of me is unwilling to think that this will end well. Part of me is sure I might wake up from this dream still covered in dust."

"I am glad you have hope. It is good to have hope. But I will tell you that what we're embarking on here is not a simple thing. We must stay determined and vigilant in the days and weeks to come. There is much to do. I need you to stay focused."

We remain silent as the road winds us back to the embassy. We pass the Shangri-La Hotel and the Japanese Embassy and then, as the guard opens the gate, Mr. Assai drives me into the compound of the US Embassy. I am but one small person in this great place. I look at Mr. Assai and wonder why he is helping me in this way. How can he bear to be near someone like me? An untouchable. As I step out of the car holding the package from Amaa tight against my chest, a part of me, that new American part of me, holds hope that this has all been a terrible mistake. My home is not here in Nepal, but somewhere far away, beyond the quarry, the dust and the rubble. I look to the sky as if searching for the great white bird to come and undo his error.

Kathmandu, Nepal
Ally
1972

"You can't undo what's been done," says Daddy, sitting on the edge of the bed. "You can only move forward. Please don't freeze up now. There's too much work to do."

I hear his words, but my spirit has drifted out over the balcony of my room in the Shangri-La Hotel. I watch as it drifts down over the green lawn, past the stone statues, and over the little river and trees. I am far away from home.

Why did I come here? I can barely remember now. I can barely remember how long I have been here in Kathmandu. Part of me thinks I never had a child, that I'm just dreaming it up. When I do dream at night, there's no child in my dreams, only me. I'm flying; I'm flying and have forgotten to put my seat belt on. The air is turbulent and people are screaming and I can do nothing at all to help because I'm scared beyond belief. I look for my purse but someone's stolen it. Someone's taken my keys and wallet and money and identification and everything that is me. I can hardly stand in this turbulent plane. My everything has been stolen, gone, and then I see Robert's face in the cockpit. He looks at me with teary eyes and takes the plane down into a nosedive. We're falling faster and faster and I'm screaming and just before we hit the ground, my screaming wakes me up. And I find I'm here, in Nepal, my everything has been stolen, and I am in a nosedive in turbulent air. Beyond fear. There's no child beside me. She's been taken from me. My world, stolen. And maybe it wasn't a dream at all.

Daddy gets up and paces the room. "Can't believe we haven't heard anything yet. What are they doing? Why is this taking so long? They said a reward would get people to talk, didn't they? Maybe we haven't offered enough money. I'm going to tell Monroe to double it as soon as I see him. Maybe that'll do it. That's got to do it."

We've been told to stay here and wait for word from the embassy. The consulate officer, Davidson Monroe, is coordinating with the police and the military to find Constance, but I'm losing hope. Since she was taken, I don't think I've had any hope.

There are no leads. But she's out there. Oh, God, why would someone take a baby? I pray that they are treating her right. Please keep her healthy and safe, I say. I've never been much of a prayer, but now the pleas flow easily over my lips. I just wish someone, anyone, was listening.

My father kneels down in front of me and looks me in the eyes. "Ally. Ally? Honey, we will get through this. The police know what they're doing, and it hasn't been that long. Seventy-two hours isn't so long. They say there's a good chance they'll find her and bring her back. Don't give up hope, honey, okay? Don't give up." Daddy stands, looking leaner than I remember. He clenches his fists and grabs his jacket and hat. "Well, I can't sit here. I'm going to go look for her myself," he says.

I want to stop him. I want to remind him they told us to wait here for the call, but I can't get my mouth to work. I don't know how Daddy will get to where he's going or where he's going exactly. I just let him go and turn back to the stream on the lawn of the Shangri-La. I watch as it travels over little rocks, and far, far away, I remember Molasses Creek. I am a child with my feet in the water once again, a girl dancing on the riverbed with Vesey. A young woman with a large belly, seeing her reflection in the rippling water with no one beside her.

I am here in Nepal. With Daddy but alone. If they don't find her, I don't think I can ever return. How will I ever be able to look at the water of Molasses Creek knowing my spirit is out here roaming on the other side of the world?

FORTY-FIVE

Where Did All the Time Go?

Charleston
Ally

"Vesey. Can you hear me?" I squeeze his hand. They've run some tests and he's stabilized, resting quietly, but we still don't know what's wrong with him. I can't stand seeing these white sheets on him. Can't stand the wallpaper in here or the artificial lights casting a fake white glare.

Seeing him like this, laid back and unmoving, Vesey looks old. I've never thought of Vesey as old. I've always thought of that tight, plump skin, those muscles, that teenaged boy. He'll look better when we can get him up and out of this place. He doesn't belong here. He doesn't belong in some sterile institution. He belongs outdoors with the fresh air and birds and nature. He belongs on Molasses Creek. This place—this is just all wrong.

The door opens and a doctor walks in.

"Mr. Washington? Mr. Washington, are you coming around?"

I look to Vesey and he struggles to open his eyes. When he does, he's alarmed and moves to sit up but I hold him back. "It's okay, Vesey, I'm with you. Miss Ally's here. You collapsed at your house, honey. But you're fine now." I turn to the doctor. "Have you found out anything?"

"We have. Does he have any family that you know of?"

"Why, yes, a sister and a daughter and her family here in town. Another daughter in Greensboro. His parents are deceased. His son . . . I think they've already called his daughters. I expect they'll be coming in soon."

"Good. Well, I'll go ahead and tell you our patient here has had a myocardial infarction or what you might know as a heart attack. Quite a serious one, at that. You were lucky you found him when you did. Apparently, he was in full cardiac arrest. Mr. Washington, how are you feeling right now?"

He leans in and looks at the monitor showing Vesey's heart-beats. To me it looks regular, but what do I know?

"A heart attack," I say.

"I'm afraid this has weakened your heart a great deal. The chances of this happening again are . . . well, they're very high."

"Again?"

"I'm afraid so."

I look at Vesey, who is now staring out the window. I lean down and kiss him on the cheek. "What do these folks know, any-way? Right? Welcome back, honey."

I motion for the doctor to step out into the hallway.

With the door closed, I look at him, arms crossed on my chest, and say, words beginning to fail me, "I understand he had a heart attack. I'm understanding that. But I can't understand how. Vesey is one of the healthiest, strongest men I know. Don't let his age fool you."

"It's not a matter of age, Ms. . . ."

"Green," I say.

"Ms. Green, your friend is very, very ill. From his records, he's had high blood pressure for quite a while now."

"High blood pressure?"

He flips through his chart. "The records indicate the last time he was in here was due to fainting. Looks like he has trouble staying on his regimen."

"Wait a minute. When does it say he came in here last? Does it say who brought him here?"

"It does. It looks like it was his doctor, Dr. Reid Green. Some relation?"

I nod and fight the fog coming over me. "My father," I say.

My father knew Vesey was ill and he never told me. No one ever told me.

"He should be resting comfortably now. He's in good hands."

"Thank you," I say, and the doctor walks away.

Back inside the room, I sit down on the chair beside the window. Vesey is still staring out, so I look to see what he sees. There is a flock of black birds in the crisp blue sky, flying in V-formation high above the trees. They all descend on one huge oak.

"Sorry you got to see me like this," says Vesey, his voice low and grumbly. It's wonderful to hear that voice again though. It soothes my soul.

"Oh, it was worth it to see you wearing that cute little gown." I smile and he does too, barely. "How bad do you feel?" I ask him.

"Bad. Like a truck ran over me. But ain't nothin' I cain't handle."

"I think your daughters will be here soon."

"I wish you hadn't called them."

"Why ever not?"

"Oh, don't want 'em frettin', all worried and carryin' on."

"You men. You're all alike. Daddy was the same kind of stubborn, wasn't he?"

"He was, he was. Good man, he was."

There is an awkward silence created by me trying to figure out how to begin this conversation. Where's a nice car ride when you need one? "Well, listen, Vesey, the doctor told me you have high blood pressure. Was Daddy treating you for that?"

"As best he could. I'm a terrible patient, Ally. I'd rather let nature take its course."

"Oh, Vesey." I'm ruing every last pot roast and pork dinner I've made him over the past few months. I wish I had known.

"Ally?"

"Yeah?"

"Time. Where'd it all go? Sure has gone by fast, ain't it, and where'd it all go?"

As he looks in my face, I see it, the years cropped up on us, shrouding our faces yet gone with the wind.

"Not sure, Vesey. Just not sure."

"You're a good friend," he says. "You know that? A real good friend."

I want to say the same thing back, or anything at all, but silence lingers and fills the space. I nod with watery eyes.

"I don't want to stay here, Ally. I want to go home," he says. "Whatever my family tells you, I need you to get me back home."

"We'll get you home soon enough. Let's get you fixed up first."

"No," says Vesey. His voice is steel. I get up and walk to the window. I'm not ready to let him go. If he comes home, he'll die there. I know it in my heart and it crushes me. "Promise me, Miss Ally. Promise me you'll make sure I get home, no rehab place, no more hospital. I need you to promise."

This man has never asked me for anything, yet always given freely to me, to Daddy, and now he's asking me for this one thing. A major thing. My insides feel like the shreds of batik that Kat sneaks in and leaves behind. I'm quiet, playing with the fabric of the curtains as I watch the pine trees outside the window swaying in the wind. It looks like it's getting cooler.

"If it's what you want," I say, but I can't face him. "I'll take you home. You know I'd do anything in the world for you. That's what friends do."

The glass fogs up with my hot breath and I work hard to keep my shoulders from trembling. Work hard to keep my tears from falling. I have to be strong for him now.

After the nurses come in and take all his vitals and look all serious at him and curiously at me, Vesey seems especially tired. Looks like he might go to sleep, but I don't want him to. Part of me worries he won't wake up.

"We got to get you back on your feet," I tell him. "I was hoping you could help me get some of Daddy's furniture back in the house."

"Does that mean you found it?"

"I did find it. Right before I found you laid out on the ground." I turn to him. "Vesey, you know I don't care, but I'm just wondering . . . Did I not tell you to have it sent to that warehouse in Georgia? I thought I did, but I don't remember."

"No, you told me to do it. Gave me the address and everythin'."

"So . . . why didn't you?"

"Well," he sighs, "I took liberties. I figured you'd change your mind on it. You usually do. About important stuff . . . and small stuff . . . It ain't a bad thing, just who you are. What with you grievin' over your daddy and all, I figured you'd rue sendin' his things away and then I could be the hero, you know, say lookee here. Look, it ain't gone after all. Maybe it was selfish."

"How do you know me so well?" It comes out more as a statement than a question. I am touched beyond belief that this man knows me so deeply, flaws and all, and still considers me a friend. How could I have ever questioned his motives? I'm a heel.

"Because we go way back, I reckon." He winks at me weakly. "Way back to before time."

"Yes, I suppose we do," I say, turning back toward the window, trying to keep my eyes from filling up. "We go way, way on back."

Vesey
1959

"I seen you sittin' over here," I say to her, waving. "Wonder, you wanna fish with me? I got two poles, some big ol' worms."

Miss Ally's quiet, and I itch behind my head.

"Or I can come back," I say.

"No. No, I'd like to go. I'm just finishing up this picture. Wanna see?"

Miss Ally turns this book around and shows me a picture of a snail shell she done with her own hand. It's big and pretty and the snail is setting right there on the dock beside her. "How you learn to draw like that? You think you can teach me?"

She smiles, which causes myself to grin wide.

"Right now?" she says.

"No. Not now," I say. "We goin' fishin' now."

She looks at her house and thinks a minute. Then she turns round and says, "Okay."

Truth be told here, I been thinkin' about Miss Ally a whole lot since that last boat ride. Things ain't been so happy on over to our house these days and I like to see somebody smile. I like her smile. I help her in the boat and she puts her drawing book under her rear and then nods at me she's ready.

"What would you say if I told you I was gonna have me a nice house someday, over yonder," I say to her. I point and she looks at my hand. "See that there? See how the land juts out, on past the oyster bed, on out beyond Molasses Creek? I'm gonna settle my bones there someday. I can see it now, big ol' house with a big porch and rocking chairs and commodes that don't get stopped up. I'm gonna have me a great big house, a mansion even, just like your house. Then I'll 'vite you over someday."

She stops looking off at the spit of land and turns back to me. "I'd like that. I can see your house there right this very minute. We can have a party. I'll bring over some . . . some sweet tea. And some Co-Cola cake."

"I like Co-Cola cake. And boiled peanuts."

"And Charleston Chews."

"Mmmm. I'm gettin' hungry." Mama had been real distracted

in the days since my brother died and we didn't get regular meals no more. I had me a piece of bread and a little cold piece of chicken that morning. I had me the idea of fishing so I could eat some fish that night. These days I was having to plan ahead. I planned on having some fish all cleaned and ready for her to cook to make it easier on her. Mama'd had it pretty hard.

"Here now," I said as we settled the boat and I hooked her worm for her.

"I don't mind doin' that," she told me. My heart fluttered. A girl who don't mind hooking a worm. I handed her the rod and cast my own and we sat there as the warm sun baked our backs and the tops of our knees and heads. We caught three fish total, one for her and two for me, but when we got back home she told me to hold on to all three of 'em.

"I don't know how to clean 'em and I wouldn't know what to tell Daddy." She turned serious all a sudden. "I don't think he would like me coming off like this."

I didn't know what to say. I thought that was understood between us, that my folks didn't want me with a white girl and her folks didn't want her with me. So I didn't say anything. I just set her off on the dock, looking over her shoulder to make sure her mama and daddy didn't see my boat. When nobody came a-running, I held my pinky finger out and she hooked it with hers and we both smiled and spit on the dock. It was our secret handshake. I liked having a secret handshake. I liked having a secret friend named Miss Ally. It helped me get through the dark days.

FORTY-SIX

Enlightenment

Ally

THE YEAR 1973 HELD SOME OF THE DARKEST DAYS OF MY
life. There was no light whatsoever. I remember the flight home
from Nepal. I remember sitting there in a comatose state, looking
out the window and seeing little lights down below, so dim, so
scattered. Every tiny light meant people, and where there were
people, there was the possibility of someone who had my child.

I'd named her Constance because with my wandering spirit,
she was the one constant I was going to have in my life. I had committed to having her on my own. I was committed to loving her
and raising her and being her mother forever. But I had failed her.
Her name had been a cruel joke. I'd jinxed myself—and her.

I'd been too stubborn. Why couldn't I have settled for Robert
and become a housewife and mother? Why did it matter so much
that he'd have girlfriends on the side? Why couldn't I have just
fallen in love with Robert and not cared any more about Vesey's
life? So what if he was married and had a child? I should have been

okay with that. I didn't own him. I didn't have to run away. I didn't have to be so cowardly. Dang it all, I should have told Vesey a long time ago the way I felt about him, that I didn't give two cents what people would say about us being together. To heck with people. Yes, to heck with them.

It was people who talked me into leaving the States with my child. Many of my friends, now hippies, some of the same ones at Furman who had trekked to Woodstock, wound up hitchhiking through Europe with the purpose of reaching India and Nepal. I would run into them and see the stars in their eyes. They told me I had to go, and so I went to Nepal, desperate for peace in my spirit. Like my friends and the Beatles, I went seeking enlightenment.

I knew I needed some sort of help when I drove by Jasper Farms in the hopes of spotting Vesey and saw Beulah instead with her growing belly, how she looked so pretty and happy. I was eaten up with jealousy. I loved my child and should not have cared about another woman, another child being born to Vesey. I hated the way I felt. So I thought it was time to get over it all and bought a ticket for me and Constance for Kathmandu. I thought I was doing something good for our future, despite my parents' plea for me to stay. I was not going to hitchhike through Europe like the others. I was going to skip all that and go straight to the enlightenment part. Then I'd come home a new woman, a better mother, and the thought of Vesey having a family wouldn't hurt me a bit.

I came home a different woman, all right.

The only thing certain in those days when I came back stateside was I didn't want to live without my daughter. The only reason I didn't do myself in was the fact that I believed she was alive out there. She was alive and the only thing I could do for her now was to keep breathing and hoping and looking for her. The Hindus in Nepal believe in reincarnation. Depending on your past life, you come back in either a higher caste with more luxury or a lower caste with more suffering. I was beginning to wonder what sins my past life had committed. They must have been pretty terrible. I was paying for them now, suffering greatly. One minute I'm sitting in a café reading the menu with my child next to me, and the next minute she's gone. Vanished. I had *lost* my child.

We'd searched all of Kathmandu. I went to that café almost daily in the last few months after they said it would be nearly impossible to retrieve her then. That in cases like this, a baby might be sold to a black market adoption agency. That she had probably already been adopted out. That she could have been adopted back into the United States somewhere to some unknowing loving couple. Someone who'd have no idea she was kidnapped and my child. I clung to this possibility because the alternatives were grimmer.

I went back to Molasses Creek, but only to see Mama. She had lost her luster, her joy. But I didn't really grieve over that. I was in a dark, dark place, far from enlightenment. She doted on me constantly to the point of obsession. But Daddy, for some reason, got the brunt of it. Daddy had aged a good ten years in the months he'd been with me in Nepal. Mama insisted on feeding him to fatten him up on home-cooked meals, but I noticed he wouldn't eat his rice anymore, even when we had pot roast and gravy. He'd just shove it off to the side of the plate. Mama looked worried about him, but I knew why he did it. He'd eaten too much rice in Nepal.

I left home after a few months. I applied for a position as a stewardess on another airline, Worldways, and started over again.

I tried to reset time and forget Robert and Constance had ever happened to me. It didn't work and was especially hard when I was having to be so nice to everybody. There wasn't a nice, happy bone in my body anymore and I wasn't fooling anyone. I was reprimanded a few times, came close to letting loose on a passenger or two, but I flew. I flew and flew and hardly took any time off. I racked up those miles as fast as I possibly could, passing the time in the air, in another city every day. I was based out of Atlanta again, but worked hard to avoid running into people I once knew. People who knew the old me.

I did see Robert again. I saw him in an Atlanta concourse and ducked, but it was too late.

"Ally!" he called to me. I turned and there he was, handsome, dressed in his uniform, same stripes, same everything. As if nothing at all had changed in his world. "How in the world are you?" He was so nice, so friendly, so blissfully unaware of what had been going on in my life. I'd never sent him any news of Constance's birth. In fact, after he asked me to marry him and left Mama and Daddy's house that day, he'd given up easily. Never called. Acted just the way I knew he would.

"You look great," he said. "Are you working? Worldways . . ." He read my name tag.

"Yep, Worldways. More international flights."

"Great. That's great. You look great." He rubbed his hands. "The last time I saw you, you—"

"I lost the baby," I said. It just came out, and I wasn't lying a bit.

"Oh. Oh, I'm sorry," he said. His face looked genuinely pained. I imagined he liked the idea of knowing there was a child out there who shared his genes, that he was satisfied just knowing he'd helped bring a child into the world. That was good enough for him. But for me, knowing there was a child still out there, somewhere, was mind-numbing-crazing obliterating. It drove me to distraction. Part of me thought it would be easier if she had died. Can you imagine a mother thinking that? But at least I would have been able to grieve something definite. The fact that she could still be out there, that someday I could pass my child and not even know it, made me study people hard. Every family, every child I saw who was about her age as she turned one and two and three and four and ten and twenty and thirty . . . Well, the not knowing was the hardest part.

The not knowing still is the hardest part. But at this stage, not knowing is better than the alternative, I think.

I take the notes Daddy painstakingly tacked up on the ceiling for me and call Kat to follow me into the bedroom. I lie down on my side and turn the lamp on. Flipping through the notes one by one, I trace the letters with my eyes. Daddy's hand was here. He wrote this. He was right here. I find the one he wrote about Constance. The one that says for me to rest now, that she's up there in heaven with him, that I don't have to search the world over for her anymore, and I smile. Really I do, because I know what Daddy was trying to do. I'm his child, and he was trying hard to protect me, but he failed, just like I did. He failed and I failed and I'm grateful he doesn't have to deal with the abysmal loss anymore. Now it's only me here. Me and Kat.

I set the notes on the nightstand and turn out the lamp. Kat snuggles down on my feet, and I lie there in the dark thinking of Vesey. His daughter is with him, spending the night in the hospital. I said my hellos and then left them to talk things over, and now they're talking, teary-eyed, grim. I am hoping she can talk some sense into him. If we can just get him on his feet, then I'll stay on his behind about his medication. I will. And I won't let him ride out to his stand anymore. It's just too much for him. Never should have been doing it in the first place.

Yes, maybe they can talk some sense into him, although it sounds as if Daddy wasn't even able to do that. Of course, Daddy never could talk any sense into me either. Maybe Vesey and I are more alike than I ever suspected.

I close my eyes and picture Vesey in the hospital bed, looking all pale, which, for him, is saying something. And not anything good. Tomorrow I'm going to walk that bridge for Vesey. I'm going to finally walk right over the thing, over the water, over to the other side—a vigil for him to get well. And then I'm gonna tell him how nice it was and how he needs to get well so he can come walk it with me. That at this stage in my life, after just losing Daddy, I simply cannot bear, will not bear to lose my oldest friend.

FORTY-SEVEN

Getting Ready

Kathmandu, Nepal
Sunila

THE SECRETARY TO MR. ASSAI KINDLY BROUGHT US DAL
bhat, but I cannot eat. I sip my tea and watch as Mr. Assai works
at his computer. His food sits untouched on his desk. Mr. Assai
stares at the computer screen, then taps the keys and furrows
his brow. His chair swivels and he goes to search through a file
cabinet the color of rain. His fingers walk along the papers and he
pulls something out. He goes back to the computer and taps some
more keys and waits. Then types some more.

I sip my tea and cradle Amaa's package. I think of Mr. Assai.
He seems to be a very good man. He is awaiting my instruction as
to when to open the package. I sit here and cradle it as one would
hold a baby. Gently I rock it back and forth and I close my eyes. I
am in that café in Thamel. I am sitting there with my baby beside
me and in an instant, she is gone.

The paper crinkles and I stop rocking. I can feel my mother.
She is out there, the woman who suffered this. I should open

the package. "I'm ready," I say. "I'm ready now." I look to him for approval or instruction. He simply stares at me and reveres the package as one might an offering to Ganesha.

"Very well," he says after a long silence. "When you are ready. If you would rather me do it—"

"No. It is for me to do." I look down at the twine and remember Amaa's gnarled, rocky hands as she gave it to me. "This, I must do."

Mount Pleasant
Ally

"Vesey, honey, you can't do this by yourself, you know. Somebody's gonna have to keep an eye on you."

"No nurse. No nurse, and that's final." Vesey tries to push himself up in the bed and fights hard not to show he's in pain.

"Then one of us will do it. I'll stay with you, Daddy."

"Ally, help me here. I've already told you girls, it's all fine and dandy if you want to come and visit, but I been living on my own in that house since Beulah gone and by 'mighty, that's the way it's gonna be till I see her again."

My heavens. How he loved his wife. I have to catch my breath.

"Daddy's gotten more stubborn over the years," Deidre says to me.

I smile at Vesey's oldest daughter. She's thirty-eight, the same age my daughter would have been. It is because of this child, right here, that I left this place and took my baby into harm's way. But looking at her now, I guess it's useless to hold it against her. I don't hold it against her that she looks just like Beulah either. That the face I'm looking into now is the same face Vesey's loved all his life. It's as if Beulah's eyes are staring right at me and I understand. It's not me. It never was me. It was Beulah all along. Vesey loved Beulah Washington. He still does. He found true love while I was only dreaming of it. But she's not here anymore. She's gone. And he's here with me.

Deidre, this grown-up child, this swollen-eyed girl, looks to me and says, "Miss Ally, Daddy's being pigheaded . . ." She stops and wipes a tear from her eye. Vesey is directly behind her on the bed, eyes closed. She whispers now. "I don't know what to do anymore. I don't know what to do except to give him back to Jesus. I got to put all this in his hands."

She clutches a cross hanging from her neck and looks at me to be sure I'm with her. I am.

"But I'd feel a whole lot better if I knew you were keeping an eye on him like your daddy did. Maybe come by every now and again when you can."

"Deidre, don't give it another thought. You know I will be there for him. I will. He's . . . very special to me."

Deidre takes my hand, and with eyes filled, she squeezes it. Then she leans into me, lifts up on her toes, and whispers into my ear, "I know. You two go way on back."

Charleston
Vesey

I am lying in this hospital bed, watching my daughter with my oldest friend. They are alive and here and I should worry about what will happen to them after I'm gone. I can feel it coming, closer and closer, but I ain't afraid. I've never worried about dying and going to heaven. How could I worry about meeting Jesus face-to-face? How could I worry about seeing Beulah again and Mama and Daddy, my son, my little baby brother? It's the ones left lingering here that I should be worried about, but for some strange reason, in this moment I'm not. I can feel it down deep in my spirit, the words surround me, fill me to overflowing, *Everything's gonna be all right.* Yes, it is. I'm at peace.

I close my eyes and I am on the porch again with Doc Green. He is ailing and needs the fresh air. I come to him most every day for how many years, I can't count. We rock in chairs and talk about the weather. We talk about the vegetables growing. And we talk about Miss Ally.

"Vesey," he says to me one day. "We've known each other for a long time."

"That's right," I say.

"And in all that time you've been looking after me, making sure this old man is okay."

"You done good for me too, Doc. It go both ways."

"You're a good neighbor. You're like a son to me, Vesey." The chairs stop rocking. "I want you to know that—that if I ever had a son, I would want him to be just like you."

I don't know what to say. I right near choke up. If only my mama could hear this.

"She has feelings for you, you know. My daughter. Ally cares for you. She always has."

"I thank you, Doc. I always cared for her too."

He looks at me then and sits up straight. He turns and leans close to me. "You and I both know . . . she has deep feelings for you." I look down and fiddle with my hands. "And, son, I know you well enough. I know you only had eyes for Beulah. Am I right? 'Cause if I'm not right, tell me now. I need to know the truth."

"Oh, Doc Green." I shake my head and turn away. I bite my lip. "Miss Ally . . . Miss Ally, I cain't explain what she is to me. I don't have the words for it." I firm my shoulders and look back at him. "But it's always been Beulah. And it always will be. I never meant to hurt your daughter. I just don't return—"

"I know. A father knows these things." Doc Green sits back in his chair and watches the water crawl. "I just wish I could see her happy, is all. She's been through so much, Vesey. So much. Always running, always searching and finding nothing. Listen, I have a favor to ask."

"Anythin'," I say. "You know that. Anythin'."

"After I'm gone, she'll come back for a while. I need you to see to it she stays. I know it deep in my soul, my daughter will never be happy until she can stay in one place and stop running."

We're quiet.

"Do you hear me?" says Doc Green.

"I hear you, sir."

"So you'll do it?"

I take a deep breath and imagine the grief Miss Ally will suffer when her father passes on. I think of my own grief. I look at him and open my mouth. "I'll do my best, sir. I promise. I'll do what I can."

I open my eyes and see her now. Ally is in the right place. She's home now, and I'll stay here as long as it takes for her. I'll stay here until she's ready.

And then I'll go.

Kathmandu, Nepal
Sunila

"Should I go?" asks Mr. Assai. "Would you rather be alone when you open it?"

"No. Of course not. Please stay."

Carefully, I pull the twine off the edges of the package. It is soft and not in a box. The paper next. I turn it over and find the opening, slip my hand in, and peel the paper slowly. What I find is a small white hat, yellowed from age, and a dress with rainbow colors, much like my umbrella. I feel the softness in my fingers and tears spring to my eyes. They rush down to the cloth as I pull it to my nose, inhaling myself, the person I was thirty-eight years ago. Not who I have become but the one I was when I entered the world, as intended. I imagine my mother's smell in this cloth and my tears combine with it to form an intoxicating odor. My head swims. I close my eyes and see a river flowing. A single river that reaches all the way around the world and back again. I am in that river. I open my eyes and see Mr. Assai. His eyes are filled. He is smiling and nodding.

"We will find her now," he says. "I cannot believe it. We have what we need."

FORTY-EIGHT

The Bridge

Mount Pleasant
Ally

I NEED TO KEEP GOING. I WILL NOT EVEN GIVE THIS SILLY
hip another thought. It's barely a mosquito nipping at me. Look
at these people on this bridge. I mean, they run, some of them,
they try their hardest, they walk in packs, arms swinging, young
people, old people, black and white people, everyone in between.
This is a bridge of humanity, this new Ravenel Bridge, a godsend
to the area. It bridges the banks of Mount Pleasant, the All-
American City, and the Charleston peninsula, the Holy City.

I push on higher and higher. I will get there, I will. Nothing
can stop me now. Can people see him on my face? Can they see
Vesey oozing out of my pores? I feel my heart pumping hard, poor
little thing. *Keep going, you sweet heart. Keep pumping. I'm sorry I
haven't treated you well. I'm so sorry I've neglected you. I'm so thankful for you. So sad Vesey's is wearing out.* What a gift I have. Why
haven't I ever thought of this little pumping organ before now?

I'm on a pilgrimage. I'm almost there. Almost there. The first tower is coming up. I can get to it, I can. I pump and I pump and I slow down and catch my breath then pump my arms again. Every step I'm taking is a step my daddy used to take. He'd walk to this first tower. This bridge was his friend. I am close to Daddy up here with the wind whipping my hair all around and the cars and traffic whooshing by me, with the people nodding hello with heavy breaths. I am connected on this bridge. I see myself from behind, from above, from in front of me. I see my little self on this bridge in this one little place in the world, and I see it's where I should be right now. In this moment, I am finally living in the moment. I am not trying to be somewhere else, someone else; I am here. Like one of those maps you see in the shopping malls, I am here. And I like it.

My legs are taking on a life of their own. They are carrying me, dear things, up and over. *I love you, little legs, even though you aren't so little anymore and I've never been especially nice to you. I love you, no matter what you look like now. You are pulling me, carrying this old gal across the river.*

It reminds me of something. Yes, my recurring dream about the elephant and the great white bird. Am I beginning to understand it now? I'll need to think on that later, but I think it has something to do with me. I am so connected to the water, to the river, to all the rivers in the world. Is the elephant finally crossing over?

I reach the first tower and join a couple with a baby carriage. They worked hard to get this carriage up here. Look at them, young, happy, their whole lives ahead of them. I look out over the harbor to Patriots Point and the peninsula. I am walking toward the Holy City, toward oodles of steeples and life on the other side.

My hip is aching, but I refuse to care. I will push through the pain and carry on. I have the strength of my daddy inside me, the love of a friend pulling me on. I look down into the water and see a tiny boat. A man on the boat looks up and waves to me. He can actually see me all the way up here. I am connected with humanity like I felt when I was standing on the Ganges, when I saw the Wailing Wall in Jerusalem, when I threw a shell into the water on the beach of Normandy. I have seen the world and the world has seen me, and now I find myself here, aching, older, filled with grief and loss and strangely with hope for the first time in my life, strangely with hope. Hope for what, I haven't any idea, but there it is, plain and simple, like the nose on my face.

I look up and see the white birds flying over me. *Stop and sit awhile*, but they keep on flying. They don't need to land on my back to push this elephant to the other side. I am walking willingly for the first time in my life. I am taking these steps because I take them for Vesey. He can't die on me now. He can't, and he won't. With each step he's getting better and better. I know it. Better and better. Better and better. I say it over and over until I can see the end in sight. I'm almost there. Holy City, here I come.

My feet plod heavily down the side of the bridge, and I know I have finished my miniature marathon. The feeling is hard to explain. Beyond amazing. As high as the clouds. We agreed—Margaret and Graison and I—that they would wait for me across East Bay Street, so I don't have to do it all over again and walk back. Not sure I could do that. When they see me, they get out of the car and clap for me. I bow, obliging, a sweaty, tired curtsy.

"You did it, girl," says Margaret. "You really did it. I'm proud of you."

"Next time you're coming with me," I holler.

I cross the street and hop into the back of the car. I listen to my breathing and feel the blood coursing through my veins. I swig from my water bottle and rest triumphantly, panting. I am sixty years old with a bum hip, and I conquered that bridge. Yes, Vesey's gonna be just fine. I feel it.

"Graison, how you feeling, honey?" I ask. "You look cute as a button in your little outfit."

"Real good," she says, turning from the front seat and trying to smile. Her belly's a cute little basketball.

"Something wrong, girls?" I say. "Y'all are awfully quiet. Normally you two make my ears bleed."

The silence persists until Margaret shifts in her seat and grips the steering wheel. Her fingers turn white. She looks at me in the rearview mirror and I can only see her eyes. "We went to the hospital before we came to get you, Ally."

My heart stops.

"I don't think you have time to take a shower, sweetheart. We got to get you there now. Vesey's asking for you."

FORTY-NINE

Oh, Won't You Stay

Ally

I HOPE I'M NOT TOO LATE! MY HEART IS POUNDING. I HIT
the ground running as soon as we get to the hospital, and Margaret
and Graison go on to park the car. When I step inside the elevator,
I watch my shiny self in the cool gray metal doors and close my
eyes. I feel my way back to the wall and lean against it, holding
on to the rail tight, feeling faint. Then I pray, something I haven't
done in a very long while. *Please let him be okay. Please let him live.
Don't let me be too late. Please. Please. Please. Amen.* Maybe it's just
begging, but it passes the time to the third floor.

When I find Vesey's room, there are three women in there—
his sister, Marcie, and his two daughters. Marcie pushes herself
out of her chair and comes to greet me. I can't hear the machines
beeping anymore.

"Glad you came, Miss Ally," she says. I have a flash of Marcie
as a little girl. I see her sitting in the dark in her living room next
to Vesey the very first time I ever met them. I see her touching

my blond hair as if it was pure gold. And here she is now, a slight woman, about my age, pretty and dignified. And saddened to the core. "He's been asking for you for a while now. I think it's . . . Well, go on."

I turn from her and walk to his bedside. I acknowledge his daughters, who dab their eyes with tissues. "Let's go on out in the hall," says Marcie and the other two follow. It's such a kind gesture, my heart swells.

Vesey looks thinner than yesterday. I can see the bones in his face. His skin is even paler. I reach for his hand and sit down next to him. I fight, I fight, I fight not to cry. Not now.

"Vesey? Vesey, it's me, Ally."

"Ally," he says, eyes still closed. "Wondered when you'd come for me."

"I—I don't know how to get you home—"

"Don't worry. I'll get there." Vesey opens his eyes and looks into mine, shiny tiny marbles. "Listen, I need your help."

"Anything, Vesey. You know that. Anything."

"I don't want no big deal when I'm gone. No newspaper, ceremony . . . no tears." He looks at mine and I wipe them away. "I lived a good life, done lots of things, learned and farmed, had family and friends. Always adventure, always good. Never, never regret."

"Oh, Vesey." I let go then and fully surrender.

"Shh, honey, every man got to go, and I can't wait to get to heaven. You hear me? Gonna see your daddy there," he whispers. "Gonna tell him you're all right. Might just send you a note when I get there too. Maybe from both of us. Never know."

"Vesey, I have something to tell you. Something I should

have said a long time ago." He looks at me with tired eyes and I move closer. "Since the day I met you, I knew there was something special between us. You're the only one in the world who makes me . . . Vesey Washington, I love you. With all my heart. Do you know that? I'll always, always love you."

"I love you too, Miss Ally. More than you know."

"No, you don't understand. I—I'm gonna miss you. Please don't leave me, Vesey, please. I'm—no. I'm sorry. It's selfish of me, and I'm sorry. It's okay. It's okay to go."

"Miss Ally, my life wouldn't have been right without you in it. It was better because of you. Richer because our lives entwined, and I am grateful. I thank God for you."

The words are like a sad symphony in my ears. What I wouldn't have given to have heard those words long, long ago.

"Now I got to ask you something else," he says, his voice labored and slow. "You 'member that spot on past the oyster bed? Where I wanted a house?"

"Of course I do."

"I want you to scatter my ashes there. Where the river run out beyond Molasses Creek."

"Vesey, please don't talk like this. I can't—"

"Look at me," he says. I lift my head and tears stream down, unhindered. He tries to smile for the both of us. "Everythin' gonna be all right. You know that? For me, for you. You gotta trust me on this. You got to stay on Molasses Creek."

"How do you expect me to stay when Daddy and you—"

"Promise it, Ally. For me."

I don't know what to do. I don't want to lie, but I can't imagine being able to look across the river and know he's not there anymore. But this is Vesey, and he never asks me for anything. There's only one thing to do. I reach down and take his hand. I lift it up so it's right there in between us, then I wrap my pinky in his pinky. Like old times. "I promise. I'll stay."

"Good. Good." We sit for a while like that, hand in hand, until I hear a whisper escape his lips. It sounds like, "I'm free . . ."

"Oh, Vesey. No." I watch as his eyes close. "Vesey," I whisper, but his hand in mine tells me he's already gone. "No, no," I whimper. I lean over and with my fingers gently outline his warm face. I touch his forehead, his cheeks, his chin and I study him, the way I used to when I'd draw him. Something warm wraps around me like a blanket and the tears stop. My head clears. "You are part of me, Vesey Washington. The best part of me, and I'm sending it on up to heaven with you now. So go on, friend. Go on home." I kiss his cheek and linger there for a just a moment, then stand and back away dazed and empty, part of me soaring straight up through the clouds.

FIFTY

Dear Ms. Green

Kathmandu, Nepal
Sunila
One week later

MR. ASSAI IS AT HIS DESK, RUBBING HIS EYES. HE HOLDS his hands there for a moment and then sits back in his chair and looks at me.

"How do I tell this woman that we've found her child after thirty-eight years? How does a person go about doing something of that magnitude? Forgive me, I'm talking to myself out loud. But do I write her a letter? Dear Ms. Green, we are happy to inform you that our investigation has concluded and we've found your daughter. No. Our investigation was concluded three decades ago, but somehow, she has found us just now. Sunila, I must tell you. I've been moved by your story. Very moved. I—"

"Perhaps you could call her on the telephone?" I interrupt.

He smiles at me. "The telephone? Yes. Yes, hello, is this Ms. Green? The Ally Green who was in Nepal in 1972? Yes, well, this is Mr. Assai, consulate officer with the US Embassy in Nepal. I am calling you with a bit of good news. You see, we've found your daughter and she's alive and well. And she'd like to see you." He turns to me. "You would like to see her, correct?"

"Oh." I try to let the words come but my head is nodding for me. "More than you know."

His face erupts and he slaps his desk with two hands. "I'm just so happy for you, Sunila! You deserve this." He stands and walks to me, then sits on the edge of the desk. "I think a phone call would be in order, don't you? Would you like to talk to her? I would translate, of course."

I bite my lip and put my head down in my hands. It is just too much. "Please," I say. "You talk with her. Talk with her and . . . and is it too much to ask to arrange a meeting? You've done so much for me already. I don't want to—"

"Of course, Sunila. It's not at all too much." He catches my eye and I feel my stomach grow warm. "But let us get past this step first. We must make initial contact."

I smile as if light is growing inside me and must come out. "Yes. Initial contact."

I watch as he moves back to his desk and lifts a file with papers. He flips through until he finds what he wants, then pulls the telephone toward him. He lifts the handle. He dials the numbers. A strange look comes over his face, one of eagerness and confidence and fear all at once. He sits up straight as he can and turns his eyes from me. We wait and wait. I clench my hands. I grab the clothes I wore as a baby and lift them to my nose again. I close my eyes and try to remember my birth mother, but nothing comes. Nothing at all. I wait, and I wait, until Mr. Assai sets the phone down again and says quietly, "I just realized . . . it's about 2:30 in the morning there. I am not thinking straight. I cannot call her now." He shifts in his seat and takes a deep breath. "But do not worry. I'll call later this evening. And I'll keep trying. I'll keep trying until she answers the phone, and if that doesn't work, I'll think of something else. I will. A letter, perhaps."

I nod. Of course, this was too good to be true. The tears come again. Once strong and parched, I now cry at the simplest things, as if I'm brimming over. I nod again and try hard not to show my disappointment, but it is there. It rises up slowly and threatens to push away my newfound hope. I firm my shoulders and ask, "Would it be possible for me to go back to the Shangri-La Hotel now? I would like to be alone for a while." This request, to be alone, is not one understood in my society, yet it is the way I feel now.

"You . . . want to go back? Of course. Of course you can. You must be very tired after all you've been through. I should have suggested it. I will take you back to the hotel myself."

"I would like to walk," I say. "I would like to walk and think."

Mr. Assai looks uneasy. "Well, you may, of course, though I wouldn't want anything to happen . . . Now that we are so far along, I cannot bear the thought—"

"I will be fine, Mr. Assai. And thank you again. Please, tell me if you make contact . . . with my mother." The words sound so foreign in my mouth. I think of Amaa and what she must be doing now. She is most likely beyond tears and gone on to a place of stone. My heart breaks for her.

"You have my word," says Mr. Assai.

"Please take these for safekeeping," I say, handing Mr. Assai the baby clothes. "You will need them in your conversation, no?"

"I am sure if it is her, she will have them ingrained in her mind. It is how we will know if we have found the correct Alicia Green."

"Namaste," I say, palms pressed flat in front of my chest, honoring the god in him. "Thank you, Mr. Assai." I turn and head out toward the streets of Kathmandu. I want to find my hope again and will walk until I have found it.

FIFTY-ONE

Newspaper Man

Mount Pleasant
Ally

WHAT KIND OF MAN DOESN'T WANT A CEREMONY TO mark his death? What kind of man doesn't want any fanfare, any record, really, at all that he was here? That he walked the earth like the rest of us? A man like Vesey, that's what kind. A good man. My friend.

I cannot look over there and not see him. I see him everywhere—the house, the dock, the boat, the river itself, all black and rich, the yellow sky.

There is no obituary in the *Post and Courier*, just as we promised him, but somebody caught wind of Vesey's death, and the letters are pouring in.

Dear Editor,

How saddened I was to hear of Vesey the Newspaper Man's passing. He always had a word of wisdom for me when

257

I bought my afternoon paper. I must have bought a thousand from him over the years. Once he told me there was an angel watching over me and it helped me through a very rough time. He was someone stable in my life. I could always count on him to be there. I will miss seeing that rainbow-colored umbrella, and I will miss a dear friend.

Dear Editor,

One time Vesey came across the road to the Wendy's parking lot to help me with a flat tire. He saved me that day and I made it to my interview on time. I got the job, by the way, and I have him to thank for it. His corner will always look empty without his stand.

Dear Editor,

A very special fixture in our community has left our fair town. May I be the first to suggest we put up a small memorial on that corner to honor Vesey Washington, who shared the good news with all of us every day.

At the top of the page, there is a photograph of the empty street corner with the Hardee's sign behind it. The ground is littered with flowers and notes and a single rainbow-colored umbrella.

I am beyond crying.

I'm sitting on the back porch with Kat beside me. I rub his head and set the paper down on the table. I watch how the breeze makes the marsh grass swirl. I lay my head back and close my eyes to think of him. I can still feel him, you know. And I can still feel Daddy. They linger here like the glow of glory on Moses's face.

But they'll fade away, that feeling of having them with me. They'll fade and then I won't be able to stand it anymore.

I rest for a good long while out there, listening to the rustling of the trees. Then I get up and take my sadness to the stone garden. I walk to each of the statues, all the gods and angels and heavenly things, hoping for some comfort. Then I stop when I get to the elephant god Ganesha. He is supposed to be the Remover of Obstacles, the Lord of Beginnings. Looking at him, I think of the elephant dreams I had. *Was I dreaming of you, Ganesha?* I wonder. *What does it all mean? All of it. And why didn't you move until the white bird came along?*

In the distance I hear a noise, a ringing, and I realize it's my phone. I don't feel like answering, I really don't, but I look over to Vesey's side of the river and there is a white bird sitting on his clothesline cross. The way it sits so still, so majestic, makes me rise, and as if being pulled, I run fast as I can back into the house to answer the call.

FIFTY-TWO

Shout to the Sky

Kathmandu, Nepal
Sunila

I HAVE MADE IT ALL THE WAY BACK TO THE SHANGRI-LA Hotel, holding my hands together, feeling that they have become softer with the lovely lotion in my bathroom. I am now queen when before I was lower than the pigeons. I see people around me who look me in the eyes as I walk by. They actually look at me, some of them scornful, others lustful, most indifferent. Who am I in this strange world? What is this America I have heard about? What sort of people live there? I have seen some Americans come through our quarry. They leave with statues. I watch my work load up on their trucks and rarely see a rupee for it. All those hours, all that work. Very little in return.

Yes, my hands are softer now after some time away from the quarry. I reach for the door and enter the lovely hotel with its arches and flowers and statues on tables of gods of comfort. I feel as if I never want to leave this place. It has become my home. My

American mother is already here, already in this place. I feel her in the Shambhala Garden and in the pool built of bricks and tiles, in the birds and in the flowers. I hear her heartbeat as I lay in the soft bed, a bed all my own, one I do not have to share. I see her face in the mirror after bathing—*her eyes, are they blue as mine?* I wonder.

I think of the reddened eyes of Amaa. They once were bright but now drag and wrinkle. She is scorched by weather and years of living with rocks and with Buba. A deep longing grows fast as a shoot of bamboo and strikes my breast. *Amaa.* My heart is aching. I miss Amaa. I know that what she and Buba did was not right, but I do know that she has loved me. Now that I'm gone, she has nothing at all.

Perhaps I do not need to find this other mother. Perhaps I need to rescue Amaa and let her come live with me here at the Shangri-La Hotel forever. The son of the cruel man will have taken over the business. They will indebt my parents for my running away.

Perhaps I should simply go home. Back to the quarry.

I sit at the little desk in my room and look at myself in the mirror. There is a woman on the television telling about the Indra Jatra festival coming soon, eight days of dancing and feasting by Hindus and Buddhists in honor of Lord Indra, the god of rain. But I do not feel like celebrating. I put my head in my hands and feel the table under my elbows, the hair in my fingers. The stillness of my soul. I am in an in-between land. Not here or there.

I think of taking a nap now that I am clean. I lay my head down on the soft pillow and let my mind wander. I see darkness and then glowing blue light. I am remembering a fortune-teller on the side of the road today as I was walking from the US Embassy. She was an old woman, dressed in a yellow sari, clouds in her eyes.

She grabbed my hand as I walked past her and I pulled away, fearful. But I saw that she was blind and I stopped, and the woman said to me, "You have come a long way, child. You are searching and have found yourself. If you shout to the sky, do the birds not scatter? Shake the dust from your feet and you will journey over the mountain." I looked up and saw the snow-covered mountains behind her where Amaa used to point and say I was born. *Up on the mountains with the gods,* she would say. I think of the Book of the Gods, of the images ingrained in my mind. Of the stone angels and rivers and faces. I have memorized them all and yet the image I retrace now is of her.

I rest in peace, but just as I drift away there is a loud noise. It frightens me and I sit up quickly. There is a light on the telephone on the table in my room. Someone is calling me. Who would call but Mr. Assai with news of my mother? No one else knows I am here. My skin crawls. I put my finger to my mouth and bite hard so I won't have to scream. Slowly I lift the telephone to my ear and somewhere between my heartbeats I whisper, "Yes? Namaste."

FIFTY-THREE

The Call

Mount Pleasant
Ally

I GO TO GRAB THE PHONE AND SEE THE STOVE OUT OF the corner of my eye. I have to do a double take because I thought I saw something. I think I was hoping to see Vesey again, making okra and rice. But there's nothing but my sadness lingering like a ghost. I am half a woman now, depleted, soul gone off to who knows where. I pick up the receiver on the gazillionth ring expecting to hear Margaret maybe. I'm surprised to hear a man's voice. It's a voice with an accent and I feel as if I'm having déjà vu. I can taste certain things and smell certain things I once did. The man says, "Is this Ms. Alicia Green of Mount Pleasant, South Carolina?"

Oh great. I run in here for this? What's he going to sell me, a website in India or maybe—I go to hang up but something stops me. "Yes, it is." I'm cold and ornery.

"Good, very good. This is Theodore Assai, consulate officer with the US Embassy in Nepal."

Nepal.

"I—I'm following up on the case of your missing daughter, madam."

I cannot speak. My mouth is wide open, but nothing is coming out. The blood is draining from my head and my limbs and I feel my way to Daddy's La-Z-Boy chair. I sit carefully and hold my breath. I cannot take any more bad news. God, if you are real, please, what do you have against me? Am I that terrible of a person? Am I some sort of Job?

"I—okay." It's all I can muster.

"Ms. Green, I realize what you must have gone through many years ago with the loss of your daughter, and I want to convey my sincere sympathies."

Sympathies. His sympathies. I lay my head back and push the lever down. I recline and roll over into a fetal position, the phone resting on the side of my head. It's happening. I have waited my whole life for this day. She's dead. Daddy was right. He wasn't lying about the heaven thing.

"Madam, are you still there?"

"Yes, yes, I'm here."

"Well, what I would like to tell you is that we may have some evidence in that case. Some . . . Well, would you mind, if you don't mind, do you happen to remember what your daughter was wearing at the time of her abduction?"

My mind is shattering, a glass windshield in a rainstorm. I'm having to go back there. I don't want to go back. I've only just lost Vesey. I've only just lost my father. I don't want to go back, and yet there it is, as fresh as if it happened just yesterday.

I have just been to the Garden of Dreams at the Kaiser Mahal

palace, billed as an "oasis of peace." I carry my child and show
her the beautiful fountain pool, the stunning architecture, the
statues of elephants in the courtyard. She likes the elephants and
reaches out to them. There are two matching statues of a mama
and baby elephant together. I let her touch the baby as I say the
word "baby." She is happy with this and smiles. I am beginning
to feel peaceful. I've realized in Nepal that with Vesey, ours is an
untouchable love. It never will be. I am beginning to accept it.

I am sitting in the Malla Café nearby. I have just drawn the
place, the waiters, the tourists, the umbrellas on the tables, the
baby, and I am pleased with myself. I am so engrossed in my
drawing. I tuck the sketchbook down into the bassinet, and I look
at my child for the very last time. She is sleeping and I don't want
to wake her. What I wouldn't give to have just picked her up. She
is sleeping and has the sweetest little baby-doll face and hands. I
smile and turn away, reaching for the menu. I am scanning it and
turn when I hear a commotion. There are glasses breaking to the
right of me. I watch as a waiter bends down to pick it all up and
when I turn back around, something is wrong. Out of the corner
of my eye, I see a very blank spot where the baby just was. There's
nothing there. She's vanished.

I moan a little and whisper hoarsely into the phone, "It was
a dress. My mother made it. It was tiny and frilly with stripes all
over."

"Yes, yes, and was there anything else, I might ask?" The man's
voice sounds almost apologetic. I remember these embassy men.
I remember them all with their kind voices and useless questions.

"A diaper for sure and a hat, I think. A little cotton hat. White.
Very simple. I was afraid she'd catch cold if she didn't have a hat.

My mother had ingrained it in me, and I promised my mother I'd keep one on her. I . . . had to promise."

I hear a deep intake of air on the other side, and I feel my face grimace and tears start to stream from my eyes straight down into my ear. Daddy's note keeps going through my head:

> Ally, sweetness, I've seen her. She's here.
> Time for you to rest now.
>
> Dad

Daddy, where are you? I need you now. I'm getting the call. After all these years, I'm getting the dreaded call.

"Ma'am, thank you for cooperating. I realize this has been difficult for you, but I wanted to be sure."

"Sure . . . of what?" I am near death, I think.

"Well, madam, I wonder if you're sitting down? If you would like to sit down."

I clench my jaws and then relax, my body humming. "Sir, nothing good ever came from a woman sitting down. I'll have you know I am lying down. Is that good enough? She's dead, isn't she? She's dead? Get this over with. Please."

"I apologize, but that is not why I am calling you."

I stop. "It's not?"

"No, madam. I—" The man seems to be choking. He clears his throat. "I am very happy to tell you that I believe we have found your daughter. And your daughter is alive and well."

I hear blood humming in my ears now. Sparks are flying in the back of my head and I worry I may be having a stroke.

"What did you say?" I ask.

"I said we have your daughter, and she is very well. Very much alive."

"Constance? Are you talking about my Constance Green, missing thirty-eight years now?"

"I believe I am. Yes. Although she goes by another name now."

"Another name? What is it?"

"Sunila."

"Sunila?" The word drips from my tongue. I sit up slowly and my face tears apart from side to side. "Sunila? She's my Constance? *My* baby? Are you sure? My child is alive?"

"It appears so, yes."

I begin to wail, a long, loud wail that comes up from years of darkness. I cannot stop. I cannot move forward. I am stuck in this longest cry that begins in my toes and explodes through me.

"My baby? My baby! Oh my, no, no, this can't be happening!" I know I must be scaring him to death, but I just can't stop. When the screaming dies down, I put the phone to my ear again. I am beginning to hyperventilate and feel faint. I may disappear at any moment. "Will she . . . is she there? Right now?"

"No, madam. Not at the moment. Sorry. But if you would like, I will contact her and we can arrange another phone call . . . together?"

I stand up and run to the kitchen drawer. I pull out a piece of paper and pen and with shaky hands say, "Yes, yes, I—may I have your number, just in case—"

"Yes, it is Theodore Assai, US Embassy, zero, nine nine seven . . ." I scribble in illegible handwriting on one of Daddy's prescription pads. I picture them falling from heaven all over me. And when I get off the phone, I am laughing and in some sort of strange euphoria that is oddly similar to grief. It's that same out-of-body experience. My spirit is still soaring up through the clouds, but there is blood rushing through my face, hot and wild. I'm sweating.

I run outside and look for somebody, anybody! I look left and right and run around the statues like a madwoman, then out onto the dock toward Vesey's house, but he's no longer there. So I lift my hands into the air and yell up to the sky, "Yaaaaaaaaa-hooooooooo, she's alive, she's alive, Vesey! Daddy, my daughter's alive! You hear that? They found her they found her they found her they found her oh God oh God oh God oh God . . ." A flock of birds scatters above me and changes direction as I fall to my knees. I cry like a baby then, and mouth just running I start praising a God I've never really known. I tell him how wonderful he is, how wonderful *this* is, how amazing, and how I can't believe it, and for the first time, even though Daddy and Mama aren't here and even though Vesey isn't here, for the first time ever in my life, I know that they are with me, and I feel loved. Wrapped up, snuggled up, warmed up, lift-you-up-in-the-air kind of happy—truly, wholly loved.

FIFTY-FOUR

Awakening

Kathmandu, Nepal
Sunila

"Yes? Namaste."

"Hello, Sunila?"

"Mr. Assai?"

"Oh, good, you are there. I was worried something had happened to you on your walk. I was afraid I . . . Sorry. Are you awake?"

"Of course. Yes."

"Good. May I come over to your hotel and meet with you? I know it is late."

I pause and swallow. I whisper, "Did you contact her?"

"Oh, Sunila." Mr. Assai's voice cracks and I hear him trying to get the words out. I fear she may be dead by the sound of his voice and my heart sinks. My shoulders turn to stone.

"Sunila, I did indeed contact her. We have spoken, this woman and I, and I am quite positive that she is the same woman who lost her child at the Malla Café in 1972."

I open my mouth and a tiny noise escapes. I take a deep breath and try to remain calm.

"I realize it is late," says Mr. Assai, "but with the time difference, this . . . this would be a good time to call."

"You would like to call her again?" I ask carefully. "Tonight?"

"Yes. I would like to. She is expecting us. She is overcome with joy, as you can imagine. She thought that you were dead, Sunila. She . . . she is quite overcome. I feel it is important to go ahead and speak with her as soon as possible."

Tears are streaming down my face and I feel strangely as if I have been lifted up off the bed and am floating somewhere near the ceiling. I want to reach through the phone and kiss Mr. Assai. I want to wrap my arms around him. "Oh, thank you, Mr. Assai. I do not know how to thank you. I—thank you."

"I am heading out the door now. Why don't you get yourself ready? I will be there in twenty minutes?"

"Twenty minutes." I look at myself in the mirror beside the television and see nothing but a glowing blur of a figure. "Yes. I shall be ready. I—yes." I break into a smile and then feel as if nothing could wipe it away. These feelings are truly foreign in me, as foreign as my own American mother. Yet at the same time, it's as if I've only just entered my skin. As if this is the feeling I have been destined. This must be what a child of the gods feels like every moment of her life.

Mr. Assai is wearing the same brown suit he had on earlier, but his tie is pulled down and his top buttons undone. His head is shiny and radiant, though his face appears much more tired than the first day I met him. He breaks into a smile when I open the door and he pulls his hand out from behind him. He is holding wild orchids and curly bamboo for good luck. I take the flowers from him and nod. "Thank you." I have never had flowers given to me. Is it possible for a person to be as happy as I am now? It is almost frightening.

"Please, enter." I set the flowers on a table by the windows and turn around to Mr. Assai. I put my hands up to my face and press my cheeks. Is this really happening? Are we going to speak to my true mother? Mr. Assai pulls his other hand from behind his back and gives me the Book of the Gods along with a newly wrapped package.

"It is the same your mother gave to you. I have rewrapped it. These things belong to you."

"We should have tea," I say, and I pour two cups of hot milky chai that was brought up by the hotel. "Yes. We should have tea."

The two of us sit down gingerly, sipping the tea with shaky hands. I look at him and ask, "What did she sound like, my mother?" My face must be glowing. My ears burn.

"She sounds . . . happy," he says. "She was very cautious at first, as you must understand. She was expecting only bad news when I told her I was from the embassy in Nepal. It was very sad. Very sad indeed."

"But then she was happy?"

"Sunila." Mr. Assai puts his teacup down on the table. He presses his hands together as if he is praying and closes his eyes. "I was not prepared for the depth of her emotion. I have never experienced . . . Are you prepared to speak with her?"

"I . . . I would like to speak with her, but I will not know what to say, I'm afraid."

"You do not have to say much. She will hear your voice. It will be enough. She will hear it and know that it is you, that you are her daughter. Yet I feel . . ."

Mr. Assai looks off and stands to go open the curtain. He looks outside over the gardens and I ask him, "Please, what is wrong?"

"Nothing. I—I am hopeful that this is true. It is happening, but part of me—"

"Yes, part of me as well," I say. "Part of me believes nothing this good could ever happen to me. I am happy, Mr. Assai. Truly happy. Yet there is still a part of me that protects the other. I have lived a life of hardship. I know this now after meeting you, after seeing this hotel. I know that I am not one to deserve this happiness and must be borrowing this life for a short time. I am prepared to go back, you know. I am prepared. I want you to know."

"No, Sunila. Please do not cry. I—I feel responsible. I have grown very fond . . . I simply want things to go as they should for you. You deserve a bit of happiness in this life. I am grateful simply to witness this reunion. I never imagined I could care this way about . . . about a case. I'm sure it's highly improper."

A case. I am a case to him. I firm myself. "Mr. Assai. If I may, would you please tell me, to which caste do your parents belong?"

"I told you I don't believe in the caste system."

"Yes. But I imagine your parents do. It is not easy to forget one's place in the world."

He is quiet and looks pained. Finally he says, "Vaishya."

"They were business owners?"

"Yes."

My heart stills. "Thank you. Thank you for your honesty."

I set my cup down on the table and after a deep breath I say, "All right. I am ready now. Let us call Ms. Green in America and let me hear the sound of her voice. I will know then. I will know if she is my mother."

FIFTY-FIVE

Great White Bird

Charleston
Sunila
Three weeks later

I AM IN AMERICA. MR. ASSAI AND I FLEW ON A GREAT
white bird to get here. I watched the tops of the clouds until my
eyes closed. I flew up where the gods must live. I have never been
so happy. As we sat next to one another, at times Mr. Assai's arm
would rub against mine, and when the airplane would shake, he
would touch my hand and calm me. I like him very much. I have
never had someone treat me so kindly. Except for Amaa. I am a
very long way from home.

The houses here are far apart. There is green grass everywhere and no temples or monkeys or cows in the street. There are
large cars as we drive down the streets. There are great trees that
hang over us and a bright blue sky that welcomes us here.

We arrive at a house and my stomach tightens. I hold my
chest and smooth my sari. It is beautiful blue with gold sequins

like the Brahmin wear. Mr. Assai bought it for me for this trip and I am grateful. Grateful for everything.

My American mother lives in that house. It is a gray house with trees and grass and stone statues to one side. Statues. Behind the house, a river flows. I am meeting my mother in this house, at this moment, for the first time in my life.

I breathe heavy.

"Are you okay?" Mr. Assai asks me.

"I think I am." I sit in the car rented by Mr. Assai. He did not have to come all this way for me; he could have stayed in Nepal. I am greatly indebted to him. I turn to Mr. Assai and say, "I am happy you are here. It is right that you are here today. I am . . . grateful for all you have done."

"I am doing my job," he says. The words spread between us. "What I meant to say is, it is my honor to bring you here. I am honored, very much so, to be here."

Ally

I am a mess. I look in the mirror and straighten my pearls, tuck a piece of hair behind my ear. I pucker my lips and blot my lipstick, then wipe all of it off. I'll want to kiss her. I hope she lets me kiss her. I don't want to mess up her cheeks.

I am bursting out of my skin right now.

I never imagined that I'd be okay after Vesey was gone, but I am better than okay. I feel him with me like I never felt before. He was always across the river, but now, now he lives on in my heart. He's had something to do with this, pulled some strings,

I am sure of it. Because she's coming. My daughter is coming home to me today! Nearly forty years in the desert, wandering alone and lost and parched, and now, now I have entered some promised land. I feel as if I am home for the first time in my life. All the pieces have added up to bring me to this moment, wearing these beautiful shoes and cream-colored dress that Margaret bought for me to wear today. She is here with Graison in the other room. They are drinking iced tea with Ronnie and Marlene. All my dear friends, my whole family is here now. We're just waiting to see her.

God, if I haven't said it today, thank you. Thank you for all of it. The years of wandering. I don't mind them now. I see how they were useful. Look where you have brought me. How much more grateful am I now that I have lost and found. How grateful I am. How unworthy I am. How unlikely.

I have not felt a stitch of pain in my hip since I heard her voice on the phone. It was as if the sound of her voice had the power to heal me from thousands of miles away. I am living pain-free today. Free from the pain of losing her, of losing Mama and Daddy and Vesey. I am free from the pain of loss for the first time in my life, for I am overflowing with gain, and it is truly a miracle. I never thought I would see this day.

Kat jumps up on the bathroom counter and arches his back. He wants me to pet him. I do and turn on the faucet for him so he can drink a little trickle of water. Wild thing. He loves to do that. Why is it that this tiny trickle thrills him more than the big bowl of water I leave for him by his food? There is something special about water falling from the sky. I realize that now. "Sweet boy. Are you ready? She's coming any minute now." I turn the water off and rub his head and kiss it. "You're a good kitty cat, you know that? I am so glad you're here. I love you, Kat."

I enter the living room again and see my closest friends in the world. Ronnie and Marlene are beaming at me, arms around each other, tea glasses in hand. I'm so glad they could make the trip from Atlanta. Ronnie leaves Marlene's side and comes to take my hand. "You look beautiful," he says. "Better than I've ever seen you."

"Yes," I say. "I *feel* beautiful right now. Oh, Ronnie, I'm shaking. I'm—I'm . . ."

He grins. "I'm shaking too, you know. I used to lie there in bed at night and listen to you cry yourself to sleep. I used to pray for you, just for the pain to turn bearable. I never imagined in my wildest dreams a miracle like this could ever happen to a person. What you're going through, Al, it's changed my whole life, I'm telling you. Me and Marlene? We just can't believe we get to share this day with you. Thank you for letting us be here. I've been in such a good mood, I told Marlene I'd buy her that fancy sewing machine she's always wanted."

"You are a dear sweet man, Ronnie Stits. The best husband I ever had." I wink. "And I don't know what I would have done if I hadn't married you. You saved me. I was a shell of a woman and a terrible wife, I'm sure. But I probably wouldn't be here today if it weren't for you."

Ronnie kisses me on the cheek and then looks me hard in the eyes. "I'm happy for you. Really." He walks back to Marlene and hugs her tight.

Margaret comes up to me now. She is wearing an understated outfit of black pants and a soft yellow blouse. This woman, who has never been understated, is today for me. She wants me to shine. She put me in this outfit from Gwynn's and insisted on buying it for me. She cried when she saw me wearing it in the store. She is a good friend, no matter what she was like when she was younger. We're all different, aren't we? Morphed into something better, I think. I am thankful to have her in my life all these years later. She is officially my oldest friend now, and to me that's something I don't take lightly.

"You're gonna do fine," she says to me. Dimples line her cheeks. "I promise we'll try hard not to scare her off. We'll stay way in the background, all right?"

I shake my head okay, but words are failing me. This moment feels like destiny.

"They're here!" Graison yells from the front door. She's peeking out the sidelight, bulbous and positively glowing from pregnancy these days. I inhale and the room grows deathly quiet. I smooth my dress and clear my throat and run over to the coffee table, pulling out a handful of tissues. I close my eyes and fold them in my hand. I blot the corners of my eyes. *Oh Vesey, Mama, Daddy, are you seeing this? Are you here? How I wish you could have lived to see the day.*

Sunila

I turn and look out the window of the rented car. "What if my English is not good?"

"You have been working very hard, Sunila. You will do just fine." Mr. Assai turns the keys and the car goes quiet. My heart beats.

"It is very good to meet you," I say, practicing my English. "My name is Sunila. I am your daughter."

"Good, that is very good. Shall we go now?"

Mr. Assai gets out of the car and comes around to my door. He opens it and helps me out by holding my hand. I want to keep holding his hand, but I do not. I walk slowly over brick and moss and climb the stairs, holding my sari. I stand there facing the red door, and I turn to look at Mr. Assai one last time. He is nodding. The door opens and I feel I may fall to the ground. My head is light and my heart is lighter. There is a woman at the door in black and yellow and I see her, though I do not recognize her. I had always imagined that if I met my mother I would know her instantly in my heart and from the pictures she drew. But I do not know this woman. My heart begins to tear.

Ally

Margaret opens the door and stands there waiting. She steps out onto the front porch. I hear her talking, but I cannot move. My legs and feet are positively frozen. My daughter is outside that door. My daughter is outside that door! Something grabs me and I run, arms outstretched, all polite demeanor vanished. I am a ravaged mama tiger and I see my child. There she is! She is a woman now, not a baby, with dark hair pulled back neatly and a beautiful blue sari to match the glory of her big blue eyes. She is nearly glowing, a gold aura around her. Yes, this is my child! I would know her anywhere. She is even more beautiful than I ever could have dreamed of, and I melt, simply holding my arms out to her, shaking. "You are here, aren't you? Is it really you?"

Sunila

The woman in the milky dress with hair to match down to her shoulders is lovely. She is truly lovely. She is my mother; I know it in my heart.

"Hello," I say in my best English. My voice is shaking. "I am Sunila. I am your daughter." She says something to me but it is too fast and I cannot understand. She is holding her arms out to me.

Ally

Oh, heaven have mercy, I want to grab her and squeeze her up! I want to erase all the years and miles between us. But I am afraid to scare her off. She doesn't know me. I am just a sixty-year-old American woman, a stranger to her. But my arms will not return to my sides. I have entered some tunnel where all I can see is her. She looks at me with tears in her eyes and her hands go up and press her cheeks. She wipes her tears, sweet thing. Then she looks to the man standing beside her and he nods.

Sunila

Mr. Assai smiles at me encouragingly and motions for me to move forward. So I take a step and take this woman in my arms, a warm, lovely woman who gave birth to me, who suffered all these years for me—and feeling her in my arms, I no longer feel my own sorrow for the past but hers. She is in my own skin now, and we cry and wail to the sky as a flock of geese honks above us and scatters our joy until it rains down upon us and washes us as one to the river. There cannot be more to life than this moment.

Ally

I could die a happy woman right now. I could. All is right with the world because my daughter's in it. She's finally home. And so am I.

My daughter is wrapped around me, squeezing tight. I can barely breathe. I am laughing and crying. We hold each other and rock and wail, and as we stand there on the porch with all my precious people watching, we become one again, flesh to flesh, and I know in my heart, if I ever had any doubts—this is the reason I was put here on this earth, for this moment, for this child. For such an amazing time as this.

FIFTY-SIX

Crossing Over

Mount Pleasant
Sunila

IN NEPAL, WHEN A PERSON DIES, HE IS CREMATED AND
the ashes taken to the river to scatter in hopes that the soul will
be cleansed as the Baghmati River turns into the Ganges. I am
watching my mother do something similar for a friend of hers. He
lived across the river and was very special to her. It has been some
time since he died, but she is only now taking his ashes to scatter.
She says she is finally ready.

"This is what he wanted," she says. "I told him I would do this."

The urn is a small round porcelain container. She holds it to
her chest and I can see the pain in her eyes. She looks at me and
smiles. "It's never easy to say good-bye to someone you love, is it?"

I shake my head. I am thinking about Amaa. I am thinking of
her having to work every day of her life . . . without me. I do not
know how she can bear it or how she can remain with Buba. But
Amaa has never seen the likes of the Shangri-La Hotel. She has

never seen America with its trees and people and houses pushed apart. She has never been able to walk out of the place where she slept on a warm bed, filled her belly, and laughed happy tears, to go out back to a river flowing with birds and grass and green and blues. There is no dust here. No dust on my soul.

I am also thinking of Mr. Assai. How sad I was to see him go. How much I care about him still. I wonder if this is what love feels like, but I do not know. What do I know about love? I am learning about it. I am learning that two people can be from different sides of the world, speak different languages, look different from one another, but still, there can be love. In a deep, deep place. I can say that I already love my mother. I loved her before I met her. It is a true and binding love.

Mama, she has me call her *Mama*, is climbing into the boat. I step from the dock and she helps me on board. I find a seat and straighten my sari. "Hold on tight," she says. "We don't have far to go."

My hair tangles in the wind. I will never get used to the glorious feeling of wind in my hair, of water beneath me or sunshine above me. I have found the most beautiful place on earth. Truly, I am a child of the gods if this is the land in which I was born. I do not remember it. It is all foreign to me, but every so often, I have a feeling of destiny as I am walking down the lane, looking at a tree, washing my hands in the creek.

We are happy here. Mama has made a wonderful room for me and we are both learning how to batik. She is as amazed at my skill as am I, though I see her work and I know my skill came from her. I am holding the Book of the Gods, which contains my mother's drawings and words. It is my most prized possession. It saved me when I was a child and allowed me to work beneath an umbrella, allowed me to use my mind and soul to create instead of crushing gravel, a mindless, thankless job. It is no wonder Buba is unhappy. He will always be a crusher. He has no skill, barely a soul.

"Here we are, Sunila. You see that? That piece of land that juts out with the grass and that lovely huge old oak tree? This is where he would point when we were children and say he was going to build a house."

Mama is quiet, remembering. Her eyes dance and glisten as she stares at the tree. "He never did build a house here, did he, but that's okay. He's in a better place." She looks at me and says knowingly, "Vesey's in heaven right now. If anyone is, it's him." She opens the container and closes her eyes. Her mouth moves. When she opens her eyes, she stands to see which way the wind is blowing. A breeze has picked up and the marsh grass is leaning. With a flick of her wrist, the white ash spills into the air and is lifted up over the grass, over the water, and I watch it travel far away out beyond this creek, Molasses Creek. A tear falls down my cheek for a love lost, for this man I never knew, for this woman whom I love so dearly, for Amaa and Mr. Assai. Let it all flow out to the river to be sanctified. Let it all flow. It is our destiny.

Ally

I feel strangely better after letting go of Vesey's ashes. I imagine he'll become part of this Lowcountry pluff mud and oysters and grass and fish we buy down on Shem Creek. He is given back to the earth he loved. In a crazy way, it all makes sense.

I wish he could have met her.

My daughter is the most beautiful creature I have ever seen. She is unlike any person in America. She is humble and has no idea of her beauty. She is kind. She always thinks of others and goes out of her way to make my life easier. She is talented beyond belief. When I found out she worked practically as a slave in a quarry her whole life, I nearly died all over again. How criminal can some people be? How real that there is evil in this world. Yet how real that there is good in this world too. I see it everywhere now, in every conversation I have with Sunila, in every memory I have of Vesey and Daddy, even in that sweet little Graison having a child at such an early age, I see good. And I have another chance to do good. I have a daughter again and I am here for her. I feel as if I have purpose. Real purpose. Imagine.

Vesey's ashes are washed away and I have fulfilled my debt to him, though it will never be enough. I will always strive to be the mother I should be because of how I was loved by Vesey, by Daddy, and by Mama. I am better because of them.

And I'm easing into everything with Sunila. I know all this, all of me, even, can be overwhelming, and the last thing I want to do is to make the girl more homesick than she really is.

I tell her Vesey's in heaven now as we watch the white settle and turn back in the boat for home. We are quiet for a few minutes, strangely no tears on my part, just as Vesey had wanted, and then she opens her sweet little mouth and says, "How do you know that he is in heaven now? He has reached enlightenment? Might he come back in another life in a better caste?"

"Oh, honey, we don't have the caste system here. Everyone in America is afforded the same rights."

I say this and I know it is a lie. This is not the time to lie.

"I take that back, Sunila. I want you to know the real America. It is a lovely place with lovely people who have a history behind them that is sometimes hard to shake. There are different races here, one big melting pot, and I think in many ways we are melting quite nicely—but some still choose to see our differences and use them against one another, between race, between class, rich and poor."

"Your friend, he was poor?"

"Not poor at all. He was rich in life. He was rich in integrity and character and family and friends. He was rich in intelligence and heart and humility. He wasn't poor at all." We are quiet awhile with the breeze blowing past us and the oyster bed safely out of reach. Then Sunila asks, "And my father. Was my father a rich man?"

She has not yet asked of her father. My heart stops. I think of Robert. I don't even know where he is now, if he's even alive. I imagine he's still a playboy or an aging pilot with growing girth and thinning hair. I haven't a clue. I don't really know what to tell her about her father. The poor thing has been through so much, having to figure out who she is now, where she fits in the world. Not to mention her memories of that awful man who stole her. It's a lot to handle. More for her than for me.

So I consider something.

My father once told me a lie. He told me that people could write notes from heaven to people here on earth so I would see it was a real place, not something he imagined. It was a lie. I know that now. And I wasn't very happy about it for a good long while. But now that I have Constance—*Sunila*—in my life, now that I know what it's like to hold your child's precious heart and mind and understanding in your very hands, I know Daddy did it because he loved me more than anything in the whole wide world. And you know what? I'm glad he did it. Understanding that sacrifice means the world to me now, as backward as that may seem. My daddy loved me enough to know I would be taken care of after he was gone. He worked so hard putting those notes up on the ceiling . . . worked so hard to continue the lie. And goodness, how I love him for it.

So when my daughter asks me if her father was rich, I hesitate for only a second before I begin my own white lie.

"Your father was very rich in all those things, Sunila. It's probably where you get it from." She smiles and puts her head down. "And honey, there's something I haven't told you yet. Something I think you should know, especially if you're trying to figure out who you are in this world. You see that house right there? Your father lived right there. Your father and I were the closest friends two people could be on opposite sides of the river. His name was Vesey Washington, and you were born out of love, child. I fell in love with your father the very first time I laid eyes on him. See there?" I take the sketchbook from her and flip to a page with nothing but Vesey on it. "See how handsome he was? And kind, and thoughtful? And you know, he would have been happy you were here with me today to give him back to the earth."

Sunila dabs at her eyes. "So the man in this book is my father? This man here?" She turns the page and shows me another drawing of Vesey when he was a boy.

"The very same. Isn't he adorable?"

She presses the book to her chest. "I have memorized every line in his face. Though he is not here, I feel that I know him." Sunila looks heartbroken.

"Don't be sad, sugar. I know you won't get to meet your daddy in this life, but I can tell you everything you want to know. And you know, your daddy left something just for you, something very special."

"For me?" Guilt pricks me, but seeing her face, it only lasts for a second.

"For you. Now, here we are." We hop up on the dock and I tell Sunila to wait right there for me. Then I head to Vesey's shed and rumble around in there. I come back with a gift in my hands.

"You told me about sitting under a rainbow-colored umbrella all those years and how it saved you from the sun. I know your father would want you to have this. This was his very own rainbow-colored umbrella he used to sit under out at his stand. You see, you've always had a connection with him. Isn't that something?"

Sunila takes the umbrella in her hands and runs her fingers along the colored stripes. "Your father was very interested in education and helping people to read. That's why he sat out there and labored hard."

Sunila's eyes light up. "I will learn to read. In English. I will speak well and I will learn to read."

"Yes, I have no doubts, honey." Then her eyes fall and a cloud comes over, casting a shadow over her face. "What is it? Don't you want the umbrella?"

"No. It is not that," says Sunila. "It is only . . . I am thinking of Amaa when I see this. It makes me very sad to think of her in the quarry crushing gravel. I know what she and Buba did was terrible, but I cannot help my feelings. Do not be angry."

"Angry?" I set the umbrella into the boat and take my child's face in my hands. "Sunila, my heart, you are my child.

I know how badly your . . . well, how she must be feeling now. She loved you. I believe that. Which is why I have something else to tell you."

"About my father?"

"No. Not about him." I pause for effect. "I have been in contact with Mr. Assai." At this, a light enters my daughter's eyes and she stands up straighter. I smile. I'm already learning my child.

"He would like to make another visit to come see us here. I wonder, is that okay? I told him that would be okay. I assumed anyway."

"Oh yes! Yes, I would like that very much."

"You like this fella, don't you." Sunila goes sheepish on me and her face turns beet-red. "That's what I thought," I say. Then she turns crestfallen.

"I do like Mr. Assai. Very much," says Sunila. "But . . . it is not possible. He is Vaisia, and I am outcaste."

"Oh, Sunila. You are in America now. You are not an outcast. You are my daughter. Please, honey, don't forget that." She is sullen, and I know I must lift her up. "Well, then, maybe you'd like to know something else about your Mr. Assai." I reach into my pocket. I've been carrying this around for a while now, waiting for the perfect time. "When you first came to see me, you brought me a wrapped package of the clothes you were wearing when you were . . . taken. You remember?"

Sunila nods.

"Here. I have a note I found in that package. It's from Mr. Assai." I hand it to her, but she looks at me, troubled. "Would you like me to tell you what it says?"

Sunila blinks and I know I cannot lie to her again. Not about this. It's too important. So I tell her exactly what it says, and as I let the words fall out of my mouth, I release myself from the hold they've had on me. I feel I'm on the verge of forgiveness, of letting go of what cannot be undone.

"It says that Mr. Assai cares very deeply for you, and he was very moved by knowing you. He says he understands how much you still worry about . . . your mother in Nepal. The woman who raised you." I swallow hard and try to appear at peace. "And so, Sunila, honey, look at me."

I take her hand in mine and squeeze it as I'm telling her this, partly for her but partly for me too. "Your friend, Mr. Assai, has been back to the quarry where you grew up, and he's paid the debt that your parents owe. All of it. Even for your running away."

Sunila goes weak in her knees and she falters. I hold her up. "Did you hear me, honey? Did you understand what I said?"

Yes," says Sunila, fresh tears pooling. "It means"—she looks up at me with sudden urgent understanding—"it means we are all free. All of us."

"It does indeed," I say to her, a wave of relief coming over me. "We are all blissfully free."

I used to dream about being right here, in this place, but for very different reasons. Standing here on Vesey's side of the river, the two of us watch as a white heron flies down straight from the sun and perches on the clothesline cross just feet from us. The bird isn't scared of us, rather addresses us, seems to know us. Ah. The bird. The clothesline cross. That's it, isn't it? My dream about the elephant and the bird? It's happening. Right now. *You're the elephant, old girl.* And the bird . . . I suppose the bird was Vesey all along, wasn't it? *I hear you, Vesey. I really do. I know you had your faith, and I'm grateful you've pointed me in a new direction. I have crossed over in my thinking, I have—but I'm not where you were. Not yet. I still have questions. Why would God allow such suffering? I wonder if I'll ever have my answers. You can send them to me anytime you like.*

Sunila and I watch the bird, breathless, and then just as quickly as it catches our eye, it opens its broad wings and flaps. It gains air and we watch its legs trailing behind and brilliant whiteness glowing in the sun. It soars over to my side of the river and seems to skim the stone statues in my garden. It was her all along, wasn't it? My fascination with the statues was just a deep maternal connection to a stone carver half a world away.

I look back at the cross with the reds and pinks and purples of the sunset fanning out behind the trees. It's still here, that cross, unmoved and constant, after all these years, the one thing that's stable even after Mama and Daddy and Vesey are gone. It's still here, and looking at it now, I am excited for another day. Once upon a time that was an impossibility for me.

I smile to myself and wrap my arms around my daughter, my own flesh and blood, and as the breeze picks up and blends us together, I know without a doubt, we've finally crossed the river.

Epilogue

Kathmandu, Nepal
Ally

OUR JET IS LANDING. WE'VE FINALLY COME BACK TO THE
scene of the crime. Sunila grabs my hand, and I squeeze. I pull it
up to my heart and close my eyes. I kiss her knuckles. I have my
child. We are together again. *Don't be afraid. Be strong for her.*

Look at her. A year in the States has definitely changed her
some. She has taken to wearing blue jeans and slacks. Her skin is
lighter and smoother, thanks to modern sunscreens and lotions.
Her hair is smooth and pulled back into a ponytail. Her skin and
body are slightly plumper, as they should be. She is my daughter, after all, and a daughter of the South. Her favorite food is not
my macaroni with oodles of cheese or anything else I cook, for
that matter. Her favorite food is the fresh fruit and vegetables she
gathers from Vesey's garden. Yes, it's still growing, long after he's
gone. He built something that lasts and continues to thrive.

"I love you, honey," I say to my daughter. "Look how far we've come, huh? We left, what, three days ago, took a plane to Chicago and another to Abu Dhabi, spent the night, and now finally, we're here. How do you feel? Other than completely exhausted."

Neither of us speaks for a moment as the wheels make contact with the runway and we feel the heavy rumble of the asphalt below. For a brief second I remember the story of a plane that overran this runway in May 1972, right before I came to Nepal. We won't overrun today. Everything will be just fine. We can't travel all the way back here to face our demons and start anew, only to have our jet crash, now can we?

The jet comes to a jerking halt and then . . . we are still. I take a deep breath.

Sunila looks out the window beside me. She seems to be taking in each brick of Tribhuvan International Airport, the mountains, this Kathmandu Valley that once swallowed her up.

"You want to know how it feels," she says. "It is hard for words."

"I know," I say. "It's hard for me too."

"I am changed," says Sunila. "I am . . . *who I am* now, not who I was forced to be. Do you understand?"

"Yes, honey. More than you know."

"In America, when I stand on my father's corner and sell his newspapers," says Sunila, "I make more money one Saturday than one whole year carving stone in Nepal. People smile and they are kind to me. And under his umbrella, I think my father speaks to me. He tells me to educate so I can teach others."

A tear drips down slowly to my lips. I cannot look at Sunila, but instead watch out the window as a cart comes around to gather our luggage.

"It is my dream, coming here," she says. "I think, if one Dalit

293

woman can be free, this school is my destiny. You understand? My life is okay."

I do understand. Over the next two months, we're going to be working with an NGO to establish a school for Dalit women and children in Kathmandu. It's exciting. It's terrifying. But it's what we need to do to make sense of it all. I've seen the light in my daughter's eyes over the last several months as she's saved her money and poured her soul into planning this school. I am so proud of her.

And yes, maybe if we help one woman, this will all have been worth it. But I don't feel that way yet. I am not as evolved or forgiving as my daughter, though I hope to feel that way one day. My path is still long and winding.

The flight attendants open the door to the aircraft, and we gather our things and shuffle out. When we enter Immigration, Sunila slows. "Don't be afraid," I whisper. "You are an American citizen now. You are not untouchable. You hear me? You are not untouchable." I squeeze her hand until I can no longer feel my fingers. We hand the man in the window our passports and he eyes us, almost bored. "Americans?"

"Yes," I say.

Sunila swallows heavily. She puts her hand behind my back, and I can almost hear her protest. *No,* she wants to say. *No, I am not an American but a Nepali citizen. I always will be.* She doesn't speak up, but my heart continues to race. The man stamps our passports and tells us to have a good stay. We move solemnly to Customs downstairs and, without much to declare, step into Arrivals.

My daughter freezes and drops her bag. We are expecting to see him, so I don't know why she seems so shocked, but when

I look in Mr. Assai's face and then into hers, I know. Sunila has found that love I always dreamed of. And twice as lucky, it looks as if it is returned to her.

It strikes me in this moment that these two may never have met if I had never come here, if my daughter had never been taken from me, if she'd not had the courage to break free. Is it possible that True Love would go to such great lengths to bring these two people together? My gut instinct is to wrap my arms around Sunila and flee from this place, back to our lazy spot on Molasses Creek—but if there's one thing I've learned in life, it's this: we must hold lightly to those we love most. They are gifts but for a short while, and we are privileged for the time we spend together.

My daughter is frozen, as if turned to stone.

I move forward, hands outstretched. "Mr. Assai?" I say. He nods. He doesn't look quite as I remembered. He's lighter-skinned and missing more of his hair. Still handsome in an interesting way. Maybe it's just the way he looks at her.

"Ms. Green," he says. "It is so good to see you again." He reaches forward and hugs me.

"Thank you," I whisper into his ear. "Thank you for so much." I am crying now. I did not expect to melt this way over him, but I have. He is all that is good with the world. And he has my daughter's heart. We pull apart and he turns his attention back to Sunila, whose hands are clasped in front of her. She is delicate as a flower, and I long with all I have in me to pull out my sketch-book and etch this memory permanently on paper, but it is not the right time. Instead, I must soak in every detail in my mind.

Mr. Assai steps forward to her, hands at his sides. He moves slowly, then comes close, nary two feet away. He is quiet. There are no words between them, but Sunila stares up into his brown eyes, returning his gaze. Mr. Assai smiles warmly, a boyish grin. Sunila does the same and then blushes. Yes. This is her true love.

My heart stirs and I think of Vesey Washington. I imagine him smiling down on us now, watching all of this, and I am warmed from the inside.

"Namaste," Mr. Assai says to my daughter.

"Namaste," she says, honoring the light in this man.

"I am very glad you came," he says in English.

"I, too, am very happy," says Sunila. "It is a long time."

Mr. Assai and Sunila do not embrace. Though she is an American, he understands she is Nepali at heart. He understands this possibly better than I do. He knows that she is still not accustomed to embraces from the opposite sex, and I can see it on his face—he will play this thing just right to win my daughter. I won't ever let on, she's already been won. She reaches out to him and touches his shoulder with a trembling hand.

Suddenly, fear grips me. I envision a wedding. What if she wants to stay here in Nepal? What if she never comes home?

No. I can't live my life in fear anymore. I won't do it. She deserves better. I deserve better.

Take care of her, I say to my white bird in the clouds. *She's all I've got.*

No, says a voice deep in my spirit, rumbling, almost audible. *You have so much more, and you always have. Now relax. You made it. The best is yet to come.*

Together, we exit the airport and then out to the streets of Kathmandu in Mr. Assai's small vehicle. I am struck once again by the incredible beauty of this place that captured me so many years ago, and for a fleeting instant, I remember the elephants that once haunted my dreams. They don't haunt me anymore.

"To the Garden of Dreams," I tell Mr. Assai. "Please. If you don't mind. We need to revisit it. And then to the café. The one where—"

"Are you sure you are ready?" asks Mr. Assai, turning his head from the wheel to look at me. He is concerned.

"We're as ready as we'll ever be," I say. "We've come here to face things head-on, Mr. Assai. We are two strong and capable women, and together, we can do this." I look at my daughter. "Can't wait to see the Shangri-La Hotel," I whisper.

"And taste dal bhat," says Sunila. Then she breaks into a wide grin. After a moment, she begins to giggle like a child. And I join her. I laugh and laugh until all my nerves and fears and ghosts have vanished, and we speed off together toward a glorious new day.

Acknowledgments

CERTAIN ELEMENTS OF THIS STORY WERE LOOSELY inspired by real instances or individuals. This book got its beginning in 2008 when my husband and I were in an Indianapolis airport on the way to a wedding. I bought a *Forbes* magazine that had a cover story about child labor. I remember one particular seven-year-old girl named Santosh in India who made cobble in a stone quarry for a living. I was struck by her. I hadn't known about current child labor or "debt bondage," how the problem is widespread and affects millions of children worldwide. Americans buy products made by children unknowingly all the time. Had I? I felt helpless. And then I thought: *What if this was an American child? Or my child, even? Would I be more horrified? Would it change my perspective enough to do something about it?* When I began thinking about a new book, I remembered that article and knew it was time to write.

As for the rainbow-colored umbrella, it's been on the corner of Johnnie Dodds Boulevard and Houston Northcutt Boulevard at the foot of the Ravenel Bridge for as long as I can remember. Beneath that umbrella stands a man named Hassie Holmes selling magazines and newspapers. He's the most visible figure as we've got here in Mount Pleasant. Nearly every day, one can see him riding his bicycle with a trailer on the back filled with everything he needs for his stand. He's there in front of the Hardee's when it's one hundred degrees outside. He's there in the rain. Although we've never spoken, I've always admired his tenacity and faithfulness to that corner and to the people of our town. My character, Vesey Washington, although inspired by that corner stand and that faithfulness, is completely fictitious and wholly born from my imagination. Any further resemblance to Mr. Holmes is completely coincidental, though I do encourage you to stop and buy a newspaper or magazine from him if you find yourself in Mount Pleasant anytime soon.

On November 28, 2010, while I was writing this book, I received this message from our beloved "Uncle Mel" Nathanson, my husband's uncle in Raleigh, North Carolina:

Nicole, I've asked Mel Jr. to send something like this, which is a recent note, to one of my boyhood friends. It's a short self-edited thought. If it appeals to you, please use it in one of your novels, my dear, should it be appropriate. Feel free to edit as appropriate.

Love to you and Brian, Uncle Mel

Your name is on a list of people special to me. Mel will send a note when things are over. I don't want any big deals when I'm gone. No on-and-on obituary, no pretentious ceremonies, and hopefully, no tears. I lived my life well, did lots of good things, learned a lot, had a number of dear friends (of which you are one), lots of amazing adventures, and few regrets. Sailor, private pilot, husband, father, farmer, instructor, field engineer, entrepreneur, and finally an old geezer waiting out my time. Managed to do just about everything I ever wanted. I hope things may work out for me to see my friends again. Nobody knows that part or where that spark of life winds up. I have asked my folks to scatter my ashes on the seashore as I have scattered those that left earlier. Do not grieve over what is natural. Celebrate my passing as a life lived successfully. I wanted you to have my words in event that things move faster than I would like. If not, that would be fine as well. Our lives were entwined, and for that I am grateful.

On December 12, 2010, two weeks later, I received this note again from his son, letting me know Uncle Mel had succumbed to mesothelioma, which he had been diagnosed with ten months earlier. To honor this amazing man, you will notice some similarities between his note and the sentiments in chapter 49.

I'd like to thank several people who have inspired me on my journey to write this book. To my editors, Amanda Bostic, Rachelle Gardner, and Becky Monds, thank you for your encouragement and enthusiasm for this story as well as your expertise in making the words sparkle. I appreciate so much the room you've given me to test the boundaries of storytelling. To everyone else on the fiction team at Thomas Nelson, thank you for your skill and prowess in packaging my work and getting it into readers' hands.

To Mary Edna Frasier, thank you for inviting me into your

studio years ago and allowing me to witness the magic and beauty of your batiks. You inspire me.

Now to some delightfully unexpected "soul mates" I've met along the way: To author Shellie Rushing Tomlinson, words can't explain what your friendship and prayers have meant to me in the writing of this book. Thank you for understanding me fully and supporting my efforts from all the way in Louisiana. To Ric Cochran, radio personality extraordinaire in Charleston, West Virginia, what can I say? For someone I've never even met in person, you've had quite an impact on my life as a writer and person. You inspire me to do bigger, better things, and I can't thank you enough for being such a gracious example of an honorable man. I am blessed to call you my friend.

To my family—my parents, in-laws, children, siblings, aunts, uncles, nieces, and nephew—you are a constant source of inspiration and the foundation on which I stand. I love you and thank God for you. To my mother, my reader, my dear friend, thank you for always lifting me up and urging me to keep going. And to my husband, Brian, you are so gracious and understanding of my need to write. Every day I know how blessed I am to have you in my life. I'm sure the people who enjoy my books thank you as well. You have my unending love and respect.

Now to my Father in heaven, thank you for the words, for the mountains you've moved, and for the prayer partners you've put in my path. I love this journey we're on together and can't wait to see where we go next.

Reading Group Guide

1. In the prologue, Ally admits, "Sometimes stepping back in time is the only way for a girl to move forward." Is this something you've experienced in your own life? Do you agree or disagree with the statement?

2. The themes of "coming home" and "escape" are threaded throughout *Beyond Molasses Creek*. Discuss each of these concepts with regards to Ally and Sunila.

3. Both Ally and Sunila long to be free in their own ways. How does this search for freedom affect their lives? What brought them to a "captive" state in search of freedom? Is all captivity imposed, or is it possible to keep oneself in captivity?

4. Education is important to Vesey and later to Sunila. Why? How can education be a world-changer?

5. *Beyond Molasses Creek* confronts diversity and prejudice in both the American South and in Nepal. Have you ever witnessed discrimination against a person because of their race, religion, or beliefs? What changes have you seen in your lifetime with regards to discrimination?

6. Ally is an artist and keeps a sketchbook to chronicle the world around her. Is it possible for one person's art to

become the lifeline to another? Do you think art is made for oneself or for those around us?

7. How does the setting of Molasses Creek and the South Carolina lowcountry in this book contribute to both the harming and the healing of those who live there?

8. Discuss the relationship of Ally and Vesey when they were children. How and why does it change as they get older? What outside influences affect that relationship? What about internal influences?

9. In many ways, *Beyond Molasses Creek* is the story of transformative Love and Loss. Whose love in this book has the ability to transform? Is Love or Loss the victor?

10. Ally spends many of her latter years traveling the world and collecting stone statues for her garden. Discuss the symbolism of this garden. Can people (or stones or something else) become gods in our lives?

11. Sunila's character explores the age-old concepts of genetics vs. rearing. How do her genetics play into her survival in contrast to her upbringing? Have you ever seen someone thrive because of some internal strength even in the midst of poor circumstances?

12. To which main character do you most relate—Vesey, Ally, or Sunila? By the end of the book, which secondary character became most dear to you? Ally's father (Doc Green), Margaret, Graison, or Mr. Assai?

13. Did the dream/theme of the elephants and the white bird fly right over your head, or do you see the symbolic importance to the book? Several characters in this book "cross over". Discuss.

14. Doc Green named his cat "Kat" or "Kathmandu". Why would he do this after what happened there? Do you ever keep painful reminders of your past close at hand?

15. Discuss the importance of lying and truth-telling in this novel. Ally catches her father telling a lie. Or does she?

AN EXCERPT FROM

The Inheritance of Beauty

Annie

It started when Miss Magnolia got this great big package in
the mail on the very same day Mister Joe moved in, just a few
doors down from her. At the time, I didn't put two and two
together, but I know better now. Something was different
about that very morning—the air was cool and crisp on an
August day, the birds were quiet, and the cat was prowling
some other corner of the house, not the first floor like it
usually did . . . waiting for some old folk to die.

Nobody died in Harmony House that day the man come
hightailing in the front door, carrying that package all in a
hurry. None of us aides had ever seen anything that big, so
we was all eyes, you know, wondering who it could be for. I
seen it said *Mrs. Magnolia Black Jacobs*, and I remember feeling
pride 'cause she was one of my own and being so surprised

'cause I never known she was a Black. In the two years I'd known her, she'd just been Mrs. Jacobs, Miss Magnolia, George's wife, to me. That package hinted she had a life before—before Harmony House, before age came and stole her away, before she ever married George Jacobs and had a family with him.

I walked with the package man back to room 101 and asked what was in it. "Don't know," he said. "Maybe some kind of painting?" It was a large, rectangular thing. The address was from New York City, but there weren't a sender's name.

I opened the door and found Mister George and Miss Magnolia still sleeping sound in their bed. It had been a rough go for them, 'specially the last six months, for Miss Magnolia losing her mind with each pin stroke, losing her independence, her ability to communicate. But for Mister George, I declare, it was even worse. For a while, his wife seemed to be forgetting everything and everybody. Even him, her husband of seventy-some years.

After the man helped me heft that package into the room, I leaned it up against the wall. I tiptoed on over to the bed, and Mister George stirred. "Goo-ood mornin', Mister George," I sang in my brightest, happiest voice, wanting to wake him with a Southern smile. He deserved some sweetness.

George

I open my eyes and see Miss Annie hovering over Maggie, her large frame blocking the sunlight, her face hard to wake up to. I've been spoiled by my lovely wife. "Good mornin'?

Sheesh, maybe for you—you got all your teeth." I reach over and fumble, trying to find my glass.

"Over to the right a little," says Annie. As I reach into the water, I realize what a stupid thing I just said. Miss Annie, the colored woman who takes care of my wife, has terrible teeth, all crooked and small and yellow, like little bits of corn left out in the field too long. And a face like a beat-up frying pan, but sweet like an angel. *Think, George, before you speak.* That part's never come easy for me, thinking. I pop my teeth in.

"Ah gee, I didn't mean . . . I'm sorry, Annie."

"For what? I ain't understood a thin' you said, what with your no-tooth self." She winks at me. "You sleep good?"

"Yeah, reckon. Fair to middlin'."

"Mornin', Miss Magnolia," Annie sings. "How we doin' today? Rise and shine. The Lawd done give us a new day together."

I turn over because I don't really know how my wife is going to react to being woken up. She doesn't know me anymore, and I'm pretty sure she doesn't know Annie either, and I just don't want to see a whole production right now. It's something that's hard to prepare for, and you never know when it might happen. Not too long ago when Maggie could still speak, Miss Annie was putting her to bed one night, and she turned and looked at me and said, "Where's he sleeping?"

"Right here, in the bed."

"With me?" said Maggie.

"Of course," said Annie.

"The hell he is."

My wife had never used a profane word in all her years,

but it's not what bothered me. I was a stranger now, just like everybody else.

Miss Annie knows enough to leave me alone every now and again. Occasionally she finds me lying on a bed of white towels in the bathtub, crusty tracks on my face from crying half the night. It's been hard. I won't lie.

I sit up slow and hang my legs off the bed, struggle to find my slippers. I rub the back of my head and my whiskers, my unshaven face. And I tell her about my dream, hoping to smooth over any unpleasantness on the other side of the bed.

"Miss Annie, last night I was young again. How 'bout that."

"That right?"

"Yes, ma'am. Old George. Dreamt I was sitting at this watering hole we used to have near the farm. I'd sit there as a boy, eight, nine, ten . . . with crickets or worms on my hook. I'd get bream on a good day, catfish any other. Sometimes we'd sell 'em at the store, Jacobs Mercantile. In this dream I had, there was somethin' on the line. It was a big somethin'. I was pullin', haulin' it in. The water was dark and I couldn't see, but I was pullin' and pullin' and pullin' and—"

"Well, what it was?"

I realize my hands are stretched out like I'm fishing, so I stop. I turn and watch Annie helping my wife sit up, the powder white of her hair like snow on her sweet little head. I miss touching that softness. I miss those shoulders, that body. I miss the woman who knew me. I miss my wife. But I'm not complaining. She's still here, see. That's more than some people can say.

About the Author

Author photo by Kristine Dittmer Photographers

NICOLE SEITZ WEAVES ENCHANTING TALES OF REDEMP-tion filled with unforgettable characters and a refreshing Southern voice. She lives near Charleston, South Carolina, with her husband and two children.